the Corpse Wore a Sombrero

A Sharp-Dressed Corpse Mystery

MJ O'Neill

---

1.   http://StreetlightGraphics.com

To Brynn - "Your Mom"

Chapter 1: Did Someone Order a Corpse?

When you lived in the hood, you assumed the door locks were only for show. Anyone motivated had the necessary skills to bypass your comfort and security without much effort. So when I heard the tumble of our locks in the middle of the night, I was startled awake. Then I remembered Mom was out late at a charity event. I breathed a sigh of relief, certain it was her, and rolled back over, bonking into Grand, my grandmother, with whom I shared a bed, and closed my eyes. The front door creaked open. Raspy grunting and manly groaning sounds entered the apartment.

Not Mom.

Burglar? Damn. Or something worse? Double damn. I could see the headlines in my mind. *Katherine Waters, Suspected Mob Daughter, and Hero Grandmother Found Dead in Apartment.*

I turned back to search for my phone and quickly realized it was in the living room with the assumed burglar. *Triple damn.* Visions of Grand yammering on about what a sucky, unprepared Girl Scout I was as we were simultaneously being chopped into tiny bits by whatever madman now occupied the living room danced in my head.

Six months ago, our rich-burbia St. Louis McMansion was seized by the Feds. We now lived in an apartment only slightly larger than a thimble. Unless the thief was schooled in antiques and relics that my Grand pilfered from our old house like Indiana Jones at a temple, they would most likely be highly disappointed in their impending score. That probably upped the odds of us being chopped to bits.

I rolled to where I could see Maybell's crate. Maybell was my three-year-old potbellied pig. She was wearing her night mask to help reduce stress and looked to still be fast asleep. If we were being robbed, the last thing we needed was Maybell squealing hello to our potential criminals.

"Grand," I whispered, nudging the tightly compressed ball lying next to me in bed.

"B Fourteen!" She rolled over, smacking me with her outstretched arm.

At barely five feet four and prone to curling into a ball like a cat, she was usually hardly noticeable in the bed, but she did talk in her sleep. Not a plus if you are being robbed in the middle of the night.

"Shh. Wake up." I shook her lightly.

"Don't you know it's bad for my chemical rebalancing to be woken up in the middle of the night? Someone better be dying," she groused in her sleep.

A loud thud sounded in the other room. The groaning grew louder.

"Shh," I said to Grand and put my finger to my lips like a crazed school librarian. "I think we're being robbed. If you wake Maybell, we might as well draw them a this-way-to-your-victims map and light it with neon arrows."

"Robbed? Are you still packing heat?" she asked.

During a recent run-in with the Russian mob, I'd halfway learned to shoot a gun. I was mostly still afraid of it.

"I don't think that's a good idea. I might shoot someone again," I said.

"Well, I wasn't thinking you'd be painting with it."

"I left it at DC's." DC was my best friend.

"It's not gonna help us much at DC's."

"He has a rat problem," I said. DC had a flair for creative problem-solving.

"Rats?" she squeaked, eyes wide.

"It could be a possum. Possums eat rats, though, so it could be both."

A crashing sound of glass breaking came from the other room, followed by a low-toned, nearly inaudible grumble.

"If they've broken my Tiffany, they're gonna wish they'd broken into Gotti's instead of this place."

I pitied the burglar who came between Grand and her Tiffany lamp.

"Let's get in the closet," I said.

"Because no half-wit burglar would think to search our shoebox of a closet for valuables. Think they'll shoot us on sight?"

"Okay, no closet, but we can't stay here, either. Maybe we can get a jump on them."

We were too exposed where we were. I pushed her out of bed and grabbed my Louis Vuitton umbrella for a weapon. On our current reduced-calorie macaroni diet, she'd lost a fair number of pounds recently. Her new height-weight combo comfortably allowed her to shop in the kids' section at Walmart, and since her run-in with the Russian Mafia, she'd found a new sense of fashion freedom. Tonight, she wore her glow-in-the-dark Ninja Turtle pajamas she'd recently picked up on clearance with an accompanying expression of the joy that "everything old was new again."

I threw a blanket over Maybell's crate in hopes of keeping her asleep and peeked around the doorframe, down the hall.

Grand was in front of me. At five feet ten, I towered over her. We looked like a two-headed monster peering out from the bedroom doorway.

The house was in a trendy part of town near the university. Grand's seventy-nine-year-old boyfriend, Claude, set us up with it after my dad's arrest on racketeering charges resulted in the seizure of our house and the freezing of all our assets. In all, it was nine hundred square feet of compact efficiency. The refrigerator and the pantry couldn't be opened at the same time. The bedrooms were both in the back, separated from the main living space by a long hallway. The kitchen was accessible from an opening in the hall, and it also opened to the main living space. There was no sneaking away with us in the back of the apartment and nowhere for us to hide if they headed to the bedrooms.

We peered down the hall. No sign of them, but I could still hear them.

"Did you grab your phone so we can call 911?" she asked.

"It's in my bag in the other room," I said.

"So much for the wired millennials."

"Just lie down," the raspy voice said in the other room.

Usually, I find myself cursing the paper-thin walls in our current hole-in-the-wall. Given that I could now partly hear our intruders, I was forced to reconsider the appeal of economical construction.

"I think I'm dying," groaned the other intruder.

"We have to get out of here before they come home," Raspy said.

We were all supposed to be with Mom at her charity benefit tonight, but Grand wasn't feeling up to going. Claude, who was in prison for the same incident with the Russian mob that brought my gun acquisition and Grand's new fashion, had refused to see her since the shooting, souring her usual crankiness. As a hot babe who'd have to fend off a bevy of admirers, she said she didn't think she had the energy to fly stag tonight.

Allegedly, Grand was in the early stages of Alzheimer's, prone to sudden outbursts of belligerent behavior. Under normal circumstances, it was difficult to decipher the disease from the cranky-old-lady behavior. Either way, she couldn't be trusted to be left alone, so I was Grand sitting.

I took momentary comfort in the fact that whoever was here had planned for us to be away tonight so as not to have to deal with trouble. That was quickly smashed by realizing that whoever was here somehow knew our schedule and now had us for unexpected company.

"They're gonna find us tomorrow hanging upside-down and bloody," Grand whispered.

"Shh." I clutched the Louis Vuitton umbrella. My heart pounded. I thought I could hear the intruders' rasping coming closer to the hallway entrance. I slightly raised the umbrella, readying to whap whoever came down the hall to us.

But he didn't come down the hall. Instead, it sounded like he turned toward the kitchen.

"Maybe it will stop if I stretch out," the other intruder's muffled voice said. He then let out a loud groan.

"Watch out for the rats in this dump," Raspy said. "Have you ever seen so much crap in such a small space?"

"They do have lovely antiques. You see their Queen Anne in the back?" Groaner asked, his groaning interrupting each syllable. "Why couldn't they live at street level? Lugging that damn thing up those stairs almost killed me."

"They've brought a torture device," Grand whispered.

"Maybe while they're distracted, I can sneak out and get my bag," I said. We were sitting ducks in the bedroom. We needed to get down the hallway. At least if we made it to the entrance of the hallway, we'd have a better shot at running to the door if they found us.

"Your jumbo pods would give you away at the first thud on the creaky floorboard."

I did have large feet, often causing angst when I coveted designer shoes that didn't come in my size. It also meant that anyone could hear me coming from down the block.

"I'll go. I'm like a ninja," she said.

"We both need to go. We're trapped here. I can wield the umbrella for backup."

I heard the cupboard door open in the kitchen. The sink turned on, and then I watched the large figure move back to the main living space. *Is he wearing a suit? What robber wears a suit to a break-in?* From the back, he looked formidable. His muscles slightly bulged through his nicely tailored, expensive suit. I'd peg it as Italian, but it was hard to tell at this distance.

"Drink this," Raspy said. A loud groan rumbled through the apartment. "Stop your damn bellyaching. You're gonna wake the neighbors with all that caterwauling."

That was our cue. We tiptoed down the hallway, and I shoved Grand across the kitchen opening at the end of the hall. The bigger opening at the end of the hall ran parallel to the breakfast bar, framing the space and opening into a room that could conservatively be likened to something out of that show Hoarders—not that I watch that.

Between the dark and the clutter, it was hard to find the intruders. Among the antiques were enough scrapbook supplies to stock Hobby Lobby. Not new-mother-chronicling-her-bundle-of-joy scrapbooks but congratulations-your-son's-in-the-slammer "incarci-books," preserving every related fact and news story of my dad's imprisonment. Moved by the spirit of Ms. Marple, Grand used the book to run down leads to free Dad. When Claude followed Dad to jail, Grand duplicated the process. Our small apartment did not have the required room for one more person to be sent to prison.

"If I hadn't had to lug that damn thing up here, none of this would have happened," Groaner groaned.

"We do what we gotta do. If I'd known you had a bad back, I'd-a gotten someone else to help. Honest."

I scanned the room for the attack-inducing object that Groaner had lugged into our apartment. Crouched down, I couldn't see anything. The dim kitchen lights and prolific piles of stuff obscured the view.

Whispering this close to them was not advised. Grand must have thought so, too, because she started making bad charades gestures. She did a motion for a phone at her ear.

It was over by the door somewhere. I waved my hand to gesture it was far away. She pointed to herself and then made two of her fingers look like a person walking.

I pointed down to the illuminated bug eyes of her Ninja Turtle pajamas. We couldn't risk the attention.

"Have you had issues like this before?" Raspy asked Groaner. "We have excellent health insurance. At your age, you should get a checkup."

Health insurance? Seriously? These guys had broken into our house for who knew why, and they were talking about health insurance, something Mom and I didn't actually have at the moment. Thank goodness for Medicare and piggy Medicaid covering Grand and Maybell. Groaner didn't answer Raspy but let out another wail.

"We gotta get out of here. Do I need to carry you?" Raspy asked.

"No, help me up." A sound like a dying animal came from the groaner. Two heads popped up from the piles near the door.

And then, with a loud slam of the door, they were gone. *What just happened?*

Grand and I stood up. The door slam had woken Maybell. Loud squealing and snorting came from the bedroom. I looked around. To the side of the door was a large white chest freezer.

"Why did they leave a freezer?" I asked.

"Freezer?" Grand asked and strained on her tiptoes to see over the piles into the room. "Maybe they brought us steaks."

"I doubt whatever's in there is steaks, Grand. Go get Maybell, and we'll see what they did leave."

Chapter 2: I'm Just a Girl Who Can't Say No

Grand disappeared down the hall, and I headed toward the freezer. I was stopped in my tracks when I heard a knock at the door.

"They've come back," Grand said, running back to me.

Maybell assumed attack mode, snorting, and waddled quickly to us. I petted her head, trying to decide what to do. I still had the umbrella. If we didn't answer, maybe they would go away.

"I know you're in there," Raspy said from behind the door.

"Are you going to shoot us?" Grand yelled back.

"I'm not gonna shoot no one," Raspy said. "I forgot to leave something."

In a pretend show of practiced beauty pageant confidence, I stood tall and slowly opened the door. He looked me up and down, and I was glad I'd done my beauty routine before bed. If I was going to get shot tonight, I wanted to go out in style.

The first thing I noticed about him was the gun pointed at us. The man must have clocked in at six feet plus. He was heavy, but he carried it well, as if his frame was built for girth. I'd guess he was in his fifties, and he had a dark comb-over with too much hair product. He had olive coloring and a big schnoz of a nose. On closer look, his suit was an impeccable Italian bespoke. Maybell sniffed his matching Italian loafers. I hadn't seen craftsmanship that good since I was last in Sicily.

"What's that?" Raspy asked, pointing at Maybell.

Maybell snorted up at him. She did not appreciate insults.

"That is a who, not a what. I thought you said you weren't going to shoot us," I said and pointed at his gun.

Maybell snorted in agreement. The man eyed her as if she might charge him at any moment. She was more likely to sit on his shoes. Maybell liked good leather.

"It's just a precaution. There any more of you?" he asked and peered over our heads into the apartment.

I scooted Maybell out of the way and gestured him inside.

"We have a whole protection force in the back room who just didn't bother to attack you when you were here earlier," Grand said and rolled her eyes. "Where's the groaner?"

"I got him down into the car. He threw out his back."

"Could be a slipped disk," I said and reached to pet Maybell.

He was waving the gun way too casually as he spoke, if you asked me.

"He should get it looked at. An average of two million Americans a year suffer a back injury, and five percent end up with chronic conditions." I have a panache for spouting interesting but mostly useless facts whenever I get nervous.

Raspy blinked at me for a moment and then said, "I thought you were a dead-people doctor."

I shrugged, my stomach tightening. I didn't want to know how he knew that. In addition to the apartment, Grand's little old boyfriend, Claude, had also helped hook me up with employment as an assistant at the county morgue. While the pay wasn't great, it came with an added bonus of being in a position that irritated both of my parents. They didn't believe a Harvard girl should be working in a morgue. With a degree in art history, a growing reputation of being a mob princess, and no other refined skills, I felt fortunate to have even been hired for that gig, glad we didn't have to live in some homeless shelter.

"I know things. Like that people with bad backs shouldn't be lugging a freezer into the middle of our house," I said.

"It's not like it's going to kill the ambiance," Raspy said and waved his arm to indicate all the stuff in the house.

"Depends on what's in it," I said.

"It ain't my place to tell you. It comes with this." Raspy reached into his pocket with his free hand and produced an envelope with my name, Katherine "Kat" Waters, on the front in beautiful calligraphy. He presented me with the envelope.

Maybell snorted loudly with disapproval.

Grand intercepted it. "That's beautiful calligraphy. People don't take the time to address invitations properly these days."

"It's for Ms. Waters," Raspy said, snatching it from Grand and handing it to me. Instantaneously, his demeanor transformed from street thug to English butler. "But thank you. I did the calligraphy myself. I'm taking a class. I apologize for having inconvenienced you this evening." He bowed. "I will be leaving you now."

"Wait, you can't leave that thing here," I said, pointing at the large chest. "Even if we did have somewhere to put it."

Maybell snorted her concurrence. The freezer was sitting where Maybell's nap pad usually went.

"Maybe it'll be useful. We can buy bulk in the meat department," Grand said. I knew it wasn't going to be that simple. Nothing in my life lately had been simple. When Italian-looking wise guys made a delivery, I could only imagine an extreme amount of complication was about to ensue. Nothing good was in that freezer.

"What's in it?" I asked.

"It's all explained in the envelope. You should read it before you open the chest. Again, I apologize for the circumstances. Thank you."

And with that, Raspy walked out the door.

"Maybe it's a whole cow, like on that butcher commercial," Grand said, heading for the freezer. "I can't remember the last time I had a steak."

"I wouldn't do that, if I were you, Grand," I said, opening the envelope.

Before I could read the contents, the door opened again, causing Grand, Maybell, and me to jump. I should have expected it. Mom had been due any moment. We were lucky she hadn't run into Raspy. That would have been a disaster worse than strange Italian men in suits breaking into our apartment.

"Why are you all still up?" Mom asked. "I thought you'd be in bed hours ago." She took off her earrings as she moved through the doorway. She patted Maybell's head. Maybell was always her favorite. She looked at Grand then at me then back at Grand and finally at the chest freezer.

"All right, what's going on?" she asked.

Almost anyone would look gorgeous in the black Vera Wang Mom wore, but she was a stunning, timeless beauty. No one would ever guess that she was flirting with sixty. Her skin didn't have a wrinkle, and the light flecks of gray that had recently appeared in her natural baby-thin, auburn hair only made it look fuller and her younger. The grace of her appearance generally matched her temperament—unless we were talking about the morgue or the mob. I feared we were about to have to discuss both.

"We had a burglar," Grand said. "Only, instead of stealing, they left steaks, and one of them almost croaked."

In as delicate a manner as I could, I explained what went down. She sat there, taking it all in, petting Maybell furiously and not responding until the whole story had been delivered.

"I see," she said, bending to take off both of her heels. "Now will you believe me, Katherine? These peculiar, lascivious events are never going to end until you quit that wretched job of yours."

"We don't know this happened because of my job," I said and moved to clean up the barstool mess.

Maybell came to sniff.

"Of course we do," Mom said, heading toward her bedroom to change. "The man... What was his name?"

"I must have missed it while he was waving his gun around," Grand answered and wiggled onto one of the barstools. Her feet dangled.

"Gun?" she asked with a high-pitched squeal. "And he knew you worked at a morgue? If this isn't connected to that unseemly disaster magnet, I'll buy your favorite flavor of ice cream next time."

"It could be related to *your* 'unseemly' job, you know," I said, making air quotes. My mother had recently taken a job with a defense contracting firm owned by Charles Montgomery, a person I considered my archnemesis.

I didn't actually have proof he was my archnemesis, but the first time I met him, he was hitting on my mom, knowing my dad was in jail, and in the close company of a man who I eventually ended up shooting to death. I figured both of those whammies were sufficient for hating the man.

"We've been through this. Charles Montgomery is an upstanding member of the community. At least I'm not wasting my Ivy League education working at a job only fit for the depraved!" she yelled from the hallway.

"Yeah, well, I'll believe Charles Montgomery is 'upstanding' when you start appreciating that my job at the morgue helps keep the roof over our heads. Things have changed, Mom."

And there it was, the heart of the ongoing tension between my mother and me. When Dad was first arrested, we were all in shock and denial, going through the motions. But it's been almost nine months now. Nine months and one murder investigation proving that Dad was somehow, at least tangentially, mixed up with one or more mafia families. Yet we all kept pretending we were in a limbo that would eventually end with Dad's freedom.

"That fundraiser was horrible. The venue was packed and didn't have any air conditioning. I smell like chicken. Open the letter so I can go take a shower," she said, and went into the bedroom. She returned to us wrapped in a towel.

The typed note was printed on beautiful light-blue grass paper.

Dear Ms. Waters,

I apologize in advance for the circumstances under which we are making acquaintance. I further offer my regrets for the contents of the chest now residing in your apartment. Unfortunately, neither of these occurrences can be avoided.

I have a mutually beneficial proposition to present to you. Please accept this invitation to dine with me at Charlie Guido's tomorrow at 11:30. I appreciate your discretion in coming alone. I assure you that your safety will be maintained.

In exchange for your time in hearing my proposal, I'm offering an incredible five-course authentic Italian meal prepared by my personal chef.

I look forward to our meeting.

Warm regards,

Saul Toucci

Saul Toucci, leading St. Louis businessman. Saul Toucci, head of one of St. Louis's leading mob families. I put the note back into the envelope, and we all headed for the chest, even Maybell.

"That ain't steaks," Grand said as we peered into the chest together.

Inside was a frozen dead body, his legs and arms bundled at odd angles to ensure all of him would fit, his private parts covered by a large sombrero.

"Unbelievable. Now what am I going to do?" I asked more to myself than anyone else.

Maybell snorted.

"Wish they'd left a brisket instead of the Mexican corpsicle," Grand said, peeking under the sombrero.

"You realize I get to buy butter pecan now instead of that chocolate monkey chunks you like. Rule ten," she said as we closed the lid. She turned and headed for the shower.

My mom managed her whole life according to a set of principles that had each been given a number and driven into my head repeatedly from the time I could understand language. Given my affliction of chronic indecisiveness, I often found them some amount of comfort.

I sat down next to Maybell, who nuzzled me. Rule ten—sometimes a choice isn't a choice.

Apparently, I'd be dining with one of St. Louis's most notorious mobsters tomorrow.

Chapter 3: Wedding Central

"What the hell happened to your hair?" Grand asked, staring at me as I stared at my closet.

"When I'm nervous, I don't sleep well. I tossed and turned, and it teased my hair." The night had been a sleepless one as I pondered my impending doom. I could feel the now-voluminous locks sticking straight out in places. I imagined I looked like Einstein.

"You had your damn knees in my back all night. I'd have been better off in the mobster torture chamber I kept dreaming about. Your hair looks like that's where you were anyway," she said.

With all our assets frozen, I can't afford my stylist anymore. My long honey-brown hair is too curly to be straight and too straight to be curly. Most days I put it in a ponytail and pray that the universe will put a stylist in my path to provide me a pity-do. At least once, my prayers had been answered, but then I ended up looking like Dolly Parton.

"What should I wear to the luncheon?" I asked.

"I think you should go for menacing. Do you own any leather?" Grand asked.

Clearly, I'd forgotten who I was asking.

"If you keep associating with these kinds of people, Katherine, everyone's going to get the wrong idea about your father," Mom added, poking her head through the door.

When they first arrested Dad on racketeering charges, I was sure it was all a big misunderstanding. He said so. My mom said so. The idea that Clarke Waters, a man who believed adding Apple stock to his portfolio was risky, belonged to the mob seemed preposterous.

Since then, I'd been given proof that my dad was somehow mixed up with organized crime.

Okay, it wasn't exactly proof. A facsimile that looked like missile launch codes had been found in a dead reporter's office with Mob Money written above them in big red letters. An exact duplicate of those secret codes appeared in Grand's scrapbook about Dad. She couldn't remember where she got them, most likely from Dad's office. Since shooting a man, I'd realized that people are often capable of more than outward appearances would suggest. At some point, I'd have to figure out the real story with my dad.

But that was a problem for a different day. What I needed most right now was fashion advice. *What does someone wear to meet the head of a Mafia family?*

I grabbed several outfit possibilities with matching shoes and headed to see Daryl Clayborne—or DC to his friends—the only person I trusted in a situation like this. DC had an epic fashion sense.

One of the few facets of St. Louis I usually preferred over my former Boston home was the climate. St. Louis was more prone to a full set of seasons, while Boston felt like part of the tundra, even in the hotter months. About two weeks of each St. Louis summer, though, the irrepressible heat made me question that assessment. As I stepped outside my apartment to head to the car, the heat enveloped me like a body wrap at the Red Door Spa. Given I currently didn't have three hundred bucks to drop on a spa treatment, rather than curse the sweat sliding down the small of my back, I considered it a discount pore opener and climbed into my beater Escort wagon.

I could always tell I was getting close to DC's place by the increasing number of EZ Pawns. It was a neighborhood where wrought-iron bars on the windows and doors were security, not a high-end design feature. The best option for security in DC's neighborhood was to pay one of the kids loitering at the corner twenty bucks to make sure your car was still there when you got back. Of course, these days, twenty bucks was a lot of money for me, and usu-ally I figured if anyone wanted to steal my beater Escort wagon, more power to them. Since the shooting with the mob, though, every time I went to DC's, a parking space magically opened up in front of the building, and my car was well attended in my absence.

I parked at the curb and headed into the beautiful rehabbed brownstone where DC lived. Immediately, my head was attacked by a balloon arch. A series of at least one hundred various cake toppers stood at attention on a console table next to the door, looking as if they were prepared to invade a Barbie colony. Color swatches littered every other available surface. Place settings covered the dining room table, surrounded by chairs that looked dressed for prom in various coverings. Napkins, invitations, and party favors were strewn as far as the eye could see.

Under normal circumstances DC's house was an eclectic mix of clutter. He's addicted to informercials and the home shopping net-work. His girlfriend, Kimi, is a hypochondriac with the means to purchase every fake cure for a plethora of fake illnesses she's sure she's dying of, and DC's momma frequently made up holidays for the sole purpose of giving her only son presents.

Today, though, the place looked as if it had been invaded by a wedding planner convention.

"Holy matrimony," I said, batting at the flower-shaped streamer chains hanging down and passing under several flower-draped arbors as I crossed the threshold.

DC turned around, holding several samples of invitations. At his heart, DC radiated drama queen, but the drawn expression of his face looked distraught, even for him.

"Oh, Kat, thank goodness you're here," he said, throwing his arms up in the air and running to me for an embrace. "They've gone mad." He wrapped his slender, dark arms around me.

DC was a beautiful, petite black man who prided himself on maintaining a badass street persona. Usually, he wore some combination of leather and studs. Today he'd dressed in one of his colorful tailored suits. That meant he'd been to his momma's.

"Do you see this?" he asked, holding up the invitations, opening his arms, and circling around.

"What's going on?" I asked, looking for a place I could set down my outfits.

"They're conspiring. It's a conspiracy like on one of those ambush reality TV shows." When DC was excited, which was frequently, he spoke very quickly. "You have to help me. We have to stop them, or I'm going to end up in a lifetime of servitude." His breathing had quickened, and tears came to his eyes.

"Servitude? Is someone trying to sell you?" I asked.

"No, it's worse. She wants to get married."

"Who? Kimi?"

"Yes, Kimi and Momma. They have it all planned."

"Kimi wants to marry Momma?" I knew better than to poke DC when he was already wound up, but this situation wasn't making any sense.

"No, no." He closed his eyes, put his hands out in front of him, curling his index finger to his thumb, and began to chant, "Hummus, hummus, hummus."

"What are you doing?" I asked.

"Dr. Maija says it's important for me to maintain my inner balance during stressful times," he replied, not opening his eyes.

"Who's Dr. Maija?"

"My new meditation counselor."

"Okay, I'm lost. You need to start at the beginning, and I need somewhere to put these down."

"Did you bring me new suits?" he asked, studying my garment bag. "Suits are always so comforting."

"I'll explain later. First," I said in a grunt as I stretched to hang the dresses on the top of the closet door, "you're going to tell me what the heck is going on here." I set the bag of shoes down next to them, grabbed DC's hand, and headed to the back of the apartment. Pushing aside bags of party favors, I pulled us both to the couch. "Talk."

Normally, DC keeps his Southern accent in check. He lived in what his momma calls "the North" for most of his life. But when he's telling a story, his Louisiana roots tend to present themselves like a gale-force wind.

"Well, it all started with the Illinois legislature," he said in a slow Southern drawl.

"We live in Missouri."

"True, but Illinois is only a short drive across the river. In case you are not following the Illinois congressional calendar as closely as someone in my position, Illinois has approved the sale of recreational marijuana." A big smile crossed his face, and he emphasized "recreational marijuana" as if he were a preacher at the pulpit, proselytizing.

This was not where I imagined this conversation was going to go. DC only worked in the morgue with me to pay his bills. His heart and skills belonged to his plants. By "position," he did not mean head of the Chamber of Commerce. DC was the current president of the St. Louis chapter of the National Organization for the Reform of Marijuana Laws. He was convinced that once Missouri legalized recreational marijuana, he would be able to patent his custom-made genetically modified lines and become bigger than Monsanto. He'd explained to me before that medical marijuana was so highly controlled, most licenses to grow only went to the big pharma producers. Recreational was where it was at for him, his ticket out of the morgue.

"Okay. That's good news for your future, I guess, but I don't understand how that lands you in the middle of a wedding planner conspiracy."

"Since Illinois is just over the border, I thought it would be a great idea to put into action my business plan for industry domination. Kimi and I were going to be partners. We put in an application for our business license and the background check for the marijuana license, which triggered a visit from Immigration and Naturalization Services. Don't you think not having a green card is something you should tell someone you're about to embark on a business venture with?"

"It would seem to be an important piece of information," I said.

"We needed advice, so naturally, we went to talk to Momma. You know what a head for business she has." DC's momma owns her own skin-care company, focusing on the needs of people of color.

"I don't know what I was thinking. The next time I get a big idea that involves Momma and my girlfriend, hit me." He put his head in his hands and took deep breaths. I couldn't help smiling big and patting his back. "Boom," he said looking back up. "Just like that I'm facing a life of servitude to prevent Kimi from being deported. Momma declared it the only option, and Kimi was thrilled. Apparently, this plan came with the bonus possibility of Momma getting real grandbabies instead of the fur ones I bring her now. She has a spreadsheet and a timeline. I'm doomed."

He had become distraught again. I handed him a tissue from the coffee table, which was hidden under wedding program samples. He took it, crossed his legs on the couch, closed his eyes, and placed his hands at his knees, finger to thumb. He began chanting again, "Hummus, hummus, hummus."

"Why are you chanting, 'Hummus'?"

He opened his eyes. "I like hummus. Plus, it has a rhythmic ring Dr. Maija says will help focus my inner voice."

"So, Kimi needs to get married to stay in the country?"

"I am not a marrying man, Kat. You cannot tie down the impeccable Daryl Clayborne. How are we going to get me out of this?"

Chapter 4: Wait. Did You Say We Were Dating?

DC sat on the couch with his head between his knees, alternating between breathing deeply and chanting, "Hummus." Occasionally, he lifted his head to speak to me.

"Before I could figure out how to tell them both no, Momma was dialing wedding planners and talking about wedding registries. We went to breakfast with her this morning, and by the time I'd returned, Kimi had hired a wedding planner, and our apartment had been turned into an Interracial Vogue wedding issue," he said.

"So, I'm guessing you're moving so quickly to stop her deportation?" I asked.

"That's the worst of it. On such short notice, there aren't many good venues fitting our station. They want me to get married in Iowa," he said with a wail. "I am not getting married in a corn field, wearing cowboy boots and saying yeehaw. You have to help me figure out how to get out of this!"

"Why don't you just tell Kimi no?" I asked.

"She'd end up back in Korea. We'd be done, finished. And now Momma's involved, which makes it even worse. I can't say no to Momma."

"Okay. I'll help you figure something out. But I need a trade."

"A trade?" he asked. His eyes grew big as he contemplated my request.

"Yes, through no effort of my own, I've managed to get myself mixed up with the mob again."

"Well, you are a mob princess," he said with a smile, returning to his usually jovial demeanor. DC loved to tease me about my mob ties, first with my dad and then with the Russians. "What did you do this time?"

"I didn't do anything! I was lying in my bed, babysitting Grand and minding my own business, when two mob thugs broke into my apartment and left a dead body in a chest freezer with a sombrero covering his johnson and an invitation to lunch from Saul Toucci."

"Woot woot!" he yelled, waving his fist over his head. "Ladies and gentlemen, our girl has hit the big time. Toucci's no small-time mobster. We're talking serious crime lord here. What are you going to do?"

"You don't get to say no to an invitation from Saul Toucci," I said to DC. "So I'm going to lunch. I need fashion advice. I don't know what to wear to dine with the head of the Italian mob."

"Sugar, you have come to the right place!" Looking giddy, he jumped off the couch and raced to the closet where my outfits were hung. He sighed as he fawned over my Donna Karans.

"Grand says I should look menacing and wear leather. But that didn't feel right."

"These are not those lowbrow, cutthroat Russians you're used to dealing with. The Italians are all about class and style. You were right to think upscale." He laid them all out side by side with their matching shoes. "This one," he said as he plucked the bold blue double-breasted linen suit. "The color says power suit, but the style says refinement."

I looked at the suit he chose and nodded. "I imagine he wants me to do something with that body. If I help you with this wedding mess, you have to help me with my body."

"Deal. I haven't had any place to wear my superhero outfit since the Russians, and I could use the distraction."

"Are you sure you don't want to get married? You're already starting a new business. Change can be good. Moving forward and all that."

"Says the woman in a semipermanent socialite stasis, waiting for her daddy to get sprung from the hoosegow so she can go back to her old life and drop me like a bad habit."

"I'm not in stasis. I'm being cautious about my future. That's all," I said. If I said it with enough force, maybe it would be true.

"Maybe. But if you're so accepting of your new reality, how come you're not taking that scholarship?"

After my work on the Russian case last time, it had been suggested that I had a talent in forensic investigation I should explore and enhance with a degree from the university. Burns had found me a program with a scholarship. The deadline for acceptance to the program was closing in on me, and I was happy to ignore the whole conversation until I absolutely couldn't. DC had found the brochure and the application in the car. Plus, I thought Dr. Jaffe, who had helped arrange it all, had said something to him. For all his drama, DC was a smart cookie. Moving forward with that program meant the end of my former life. No more Boston. No more museum work.

Ignoring the question, I said, "Besides, you know I'd never drop you. You're my favorite bad habit. We've hidden a body together. We're our own little mob, now, aren't we?"

He smiled widely. "Oh! We need a handshake or a secret sign," he said.

"Why do I think I'm going to regret this agreement?" I asked but couldn't help smiling back.

"Well, our agreement can't be any worse than lunch with a mobster," he said.

I wasn't sure which I should be dreading more. Before lunch, though, I had one more stop to make. If I was really going through with lunching with a mobster, I needed information.

I changed clothes at DC's and, wardrobe sorted out, headed to my next stop at the coffee bar for a meeting with Fletcher Reid. If anyone could give me the skinny on Saul Toucci, it would be Fletcher. He was a beat reporter at the city's paper.

Normal people cannot understand the anxiety a coffee bar brings to the decision impaired, such as me. Regular or decaf? Espresso or latte? Add a flavor? Maybe tea instead? And don't even get me started on milk options—cream, half and half, nonfat, oat, almond, soy, or two percent, foam, no foam, whip... It's exhausting. If only I liked plain black coffee. I arrived early and studied the menu, hoping to come to some choice before being embarrassed in front of Fletcher.

"I don't know what's sexier, Stretch, that dress or the Loretta Lynn hairdo," a soft baritone voice said into my ear.

"I'm not trying to look sexy," I said with a smile.

He'd taken to calling me by my nickname since I'd first tackled him to the ground, me naked, coming out of my shower.

"That's a bonus," he said but didn't move from my left shoulder.

"Sixty-five percent of coffee drinking occurs at breakfast," I said.

Smiling, he walked up to the counter. "Two nonfat hazelnut carmelattas."

"You ordered for me?" I didn't know if I should be relieved or offended.

"Seemed easier. If you don't like it, we'll order something else."

Fletcher Reid was a lanky, brilliantly blue-eyed specimen who belonged on the cover of *Surfer Weekly*. Even in winter, he seemed to have an exquisite California tan that contrasted with his perfectly mussed blond hair. At the peak of summer, he was a golden god. As usual, he was in the standard beat-reporter uniform of casual dress slacks, polo shirt, and well-worn comfortable loafers. The outfit always seemed to look classier on Fletcher than other reporters.

He got the drinks, and we looked for a table, but they were all taken. A giant, puffy purple couch had openings in the back. We both sank in a bit when we sat.

"First, this is an off-the-record conversation," I said, trying to balance crossing my legs in the purple pillow while not spilling my coffee all over myself.

"Of course. I wouldn't dream of our date being on the record," he said.

Date? "I'm merely asking a friendly acquaintance for some information."

"I like that you think we're friendly."

"If I see one word of this from you in print, I will hold a press conference alleging that you have a thing for old ladies and tried to molest Grand."

"Well, she is a hottie." He smiled and took the lid off his coffee.

"I'm not kidding."

Okay, maybe I was a little. And after everything with the Russians, I did trust Fletcher. A little. But my family could not afford any more mob-related publicity.

"All right. Effective blackmail. I'm impressed and sufficiently deterred," he said.

"So, what can you tell me about Saul Toucci?" I asked.

"Ah, the mob princess is moving up in the world." He crossed his legs effortlessly and turned toward me on the couch. "The thing you have to understand is that the mob is not one thing. Everyone says 'the mob' as if it's all one big happy family, but in reality, it's a pretty cutthroat, competitive business environment. Each family is a mini corporation."

"Okay. So what kind of CEO is Saul Toucci?" I asked.

"Saul 'the Gentleman' Toucci has garnered a reputation of being deadly nice. In his old age, he's become big on personal responsibility. He's only in criminal businesses that can be characterized by personal choices of corporate corruption, gambling, loan sharking, and the like. His organization stays away from things that prey on the vulnerable. No sex trafficking, for example. He stays out of drugs because it preys on addicts, although gambling seems to be more of a gray area for them. Over the last decade, he's shifted the business almost entirely to laundering. His organization acts as the banker to other mob families. Even when he has to flex his mob muscle, he has a reputation of taking care of the families of the men he offs."

"So if you're going to get taken out in a mob hit, you want it to be Toucci?"

"Exactly. Don't get me wrong. His organization is formidable, and he doesn't think twice about removing people he thinks have earned it. But he tries to fill the niche of a kinder, gentler mob organization."

I took a drink of the coffee, slightly cursing that after fifteen seconds of staring at a menu, Fletcher had nailed an order I couldn't have pulled off after half an hour, and tried to process the information.

"So, you haven't answered my question. How did you get mixed up with Saul?" he asked.

"It's complicated."

"Always is with you, Stretch." He blew over the top of the coffee.

"Let's just leave it at he invited me to lunch today, and I assumed it was an invitation I couldn't refuse."

"Good assumption. The suit was a good choice. Saul appreciates refinement." He put the lid back on his coffee and glanced up at me with an expression meant to disarm but that I had come to recognize as his attack face. "How's McPhee?"

Burns McPhee was the owner of McPhee Security. Because of the Russian fiasco, he had accidentally become my partner in crime. We were both currently trying to decide whether that partnership would extend into other areas. Fletcher and Burns shared both a healthy respect and a mutual annoyance for each other. It bordered on sibling rivalry, which made me a prize in their latest competitive squabble, a position I loudly objected to but had no qualms in using to my advantage.

"Why, I would think with Gillian's case behind you, that hatchet would at least be partially buried," I said.

Gillian was the reporter who was murdered investigating the prostitute serial killing case that Burns and I solved. She was also Burns's ex-girlfriend and Fletcher's best friend.

"The only thing that seems to get buried where McPhee is concerned is bodies."

"As eager as I am to discuss my becoming the latest tug-of-war item in your schoolyard brawl with Burns, I have to go if I'm going to be on time."

He stood up with ease and reached out to help me off the sinking sofa. "I think our second date went well," he said, holding on to my hand.

Our first supposed date was a dinner with Grand when he gave her the peacock lamp Wheezer broke.

"This wasn't a date," I said, pulling away.

"We met at a restaurant. I ordered and paid. We shared something personal. All checks in the date box. But that's okay. I understand that you're used to being more impressed. I'll plan something bigger for our next one." He opened the door for me.

"I'm not sure there's going to be a next date."

He pointed at his car in the parking lot. "Now that you've accepted that this was our second date, I'm sure you won't be able to resist seeing where we go from here."

He put me in my Escort and glided toward his own car, waving as he went.

Before pulling out, I took a minute to reflect on my morning. *Am I dating Fletcher Reid? Or Burns McPhee, for that matter?* Dating led to permanence. I'd only been unengaged from my Boston boyfriend for a few months and at one time had thought we'd pick things back up when my life was back to normal. When my mom and dad were safely ensconced back in their house. When Grand and her cute bow-tie-wearing boyfriend were back at assisted living. When I was back in Boston, at a museum.

The brochure for the forensics course sat on the seat next to me, and I contemplated DC's words. I couldn't imagine going back. Leaving my mom and Grand to go back to my boring job in Boston. I didn't use to think it was boring. I didn't use to know how to shoot a gun, autopsy a body, or have lunch with mobsters either.

But I was. In five minutes, I would be sitting across the table from one of the biggest mob figures in the city. I closed my eyes and mentally heard myself chanting, "Hummus, hummus, hummus."

Chapter 5: A Lunch to Die For

St. Louis was best known as the Gateway to the West, home to the Arch, the world series champion Cardinals, and Budweiser. To the local foodie scene, St. Louis was synonymous with Italian cuisine from the Hill, a quaint neighborhood where Yogi Berra and Joe Garagiola both grew up, and my current destination. Instead of pool tables, bars here all came with boccie courts.

Given the proximity to the lunch hour, I assumed parking would be impossible, and unfortunately, my insight proved accurate. I circled the restaurant twice with no luck. Panic grew at the realization that I was going to be late for failing to factor in lunchtime parking traffic. As I started past the restaurant a third time, a kid flagged me down. I stopped, eliciting frantic horn honking from the cars behind me. The kid, dressed in black pants and a red suit jacket and sporting slicked-back black hair, hurled expletives at them and motioned for them to go around me as he approached my driver's-side window. I didn't know what to think. He swirled his finger around, indicating he wanted me to roll down the window.

When our assets were frozen, I could no longer afford the payment on my hybrid. I missed my hybrid. Instead, I now owned a 1999 Ford Escort wagon purchased on the internet, sight unseen, on the advice of an article that certified it as one of the most reliable beater cars of all time. While it had mostly lived up to its reputation in the reliability department—with the minor exception that sometimes I had to talk nice to it to get it to start—none of the windows were functional. This was a plus when being solicited at red lights for money by street panderers but a definite bummer at drive-through windows. Or in times like this. I cracked the door open instead.

"Yes?" I asked.

"Ms. Waters? I'm Mr. Toucci's valet. I've been looking for you."

"You have?" I blinked at him in confusion.

"Yeah, lady. If you don't get a move on, you're going to be late, and that is not going to bode well for me." He whipped the door open and practically yanked me out of the car.

"Wait, I need my bag!"

Sliding into the driver's seat, he thrust my purse at me.

"Do I get a ticket or something?" I asked as he slammed the door and waved. I took that as a no.

A portly doorman waited at the entrance to the restaurant. For lunchtime at arguably the most popular restaurant in town, I expected there to be a big crowd. Instead, the place was empty. The deafening quiet was interrupted by an occasional clang of a pot or bark of a chef from the kitchen.

A brunette in a sleek black dress approached me. "Ms. Waters, welcome. I hope you found us okay. Please follow me."

I had been to this restaurant several times when my family still had means. The decor had a definite air of being Italian but not in a cheesy tourist kind of way. The floors were Venetian marble, the walls were covered with a combination of stunning hand-crafted cream plaster and lush golden silk drapes. Beautiful crystal chandlers that emitted the exact right amount of light hung from a ceiling that had been painted with a replica of the ceiling at the Sistine Chapel. Not a single detail had escaped thought.

In the movies, you always heard that mobsters didn't like to sit in the middle of a room, exposed. I expected to see Mr. Toucci in the rear or at the far side, his back to the wall. Instead, he sat precisely in the middle of the dining room, reading the paper. That showed you what the movies knew. At a distance, surrounding him, stood men in lovely Italian suits. I recognized Raspy off his right shoulder and Groaner off his left. As I approached, Mr. Toucci stood, Groaner pulling his chair back.

"Ms. Waters," he said in a husky voice with a slightly detectable New England accent. He moved toward me, took my outstretched hand, pulled me in close, and kissed me on both cheeks. "Thank you for joining me." He held my hand for a moment and outstretched our arms to survey me. "Young people these days usually have so little regard for proper decorum. You look lovely."

I did look lovely. I felt lovely, too, which was a bonus. There was nothing more empowering than the feel of a well-tailored garment, and I sure needed it today.

"S-So do you," I stammered out with a blush.

Mr. Toucci had the look of a distinguished businessman. He was tallish, at least my height, with chiseled features and bushy eyebrows. His receding hairline served to accentuate an already unusually long forehead. Despite its shift north, the salt-and-pepper hair parted on the side still appeared featherlight and full. He wore an impeccably tailored black suit jacket over a royal-blue silk dress shirt, giving the appearance of being color coordinated.

"Royal blue is such an empowering color," he added.

"It was against the law for the lower class to wear royal blue in the days of the monarchs. Lower classes mostly wore an off shade of blue, instead, made from a flower that had to be mixed with manure to bring out the color. It smelled so bad Queen Elizabeth forbade it to be made within a mile of the castle."

Great, I had now talked about manure with the head of the mob and all in one breath. He stared for a moment and then smiled widely.

"That gives new meaning to the phrase 'having the blues,' doesn't it?" He laughed at his own joke.

I forced a smile despite feeling horrified at myself.

"Please, sit," he said, letting go of my hand and motioning me to the other side of the table.

Without being asked, Groaner took away the newspaper Mr. Toucci had been reading. One of the other men quickly appeared next to me, pulling out my chair.

"But then again, you come from a refined background. Don't you, Ms. Waters? May I call you Katherine?"

"Yes, please, Mr. Toucci," I said, thrilled I had managed to make it into my seat without falling.

"Saul, please. I hope you don't think I was being presumptuous in my assumption that a fine-cooked meal might be appreciated, given your current circumstances. Even if it is with an old man."

"Not at all. I'm honored you've gone to the trouble, and I would never characterize a generous, distinguished gentleman such as you as an old man." There. Finally. Something that didn't make me sound like a dimwit.

"I think your reputation for manners and charm may have actually undersold you. It's a good thing I'm old, or I might have to give your boyfriends a run for their money," he said, tucking his napkin under his chin.

I felt the heat of a blush in my cheeks.

"February 13 is National Eat Italian Food Day." And I was back on track to the land of the dimwits.

I had great admiration for Italian food, not because it's delicious—that's a bonus—but because authentic Italian meals adhere to a strict structure that can be illustrated in a project plan with a task breakdown. Very few decisions needed to be made during an Italian meal, a good thing, because I didn't think I could have handled any more anxiety in the situation. As it was, I continued to spout ridiculous facts with each course.

The first course, or in proper Italian, as I was informed, the antipasto, arrived.

"I took the liberty of establishing the menu. If you find something not to your liking, please don't be demure about it. We can always alter it," he said.

That was a man I could come to like.

I responded by reciting that there were more than six hundred pasta shapes produced worldwide.

"My chef, Enrique, is outstanding. I don't know what I would do without him. When my doctor started harassing me about my cholesterol, Enrique managed to reinvent all my favorite dishes using healthier ingredients without compromising flavor."

I thought it was funny that a man who killed for a living worried about his cholesterol, but he was right. The food didn't just taste good. It assaulted the senses at every turn.

The *primo piatto*—first course—consisted of the best risotto I'd ever eaten. When I blurted that in the thirteenth century, the pope was responsible for setting pasta quality standards, we talked about his meeting with Pope Francis when they were both much younger.

For first secondo came a pecan-encrusted halibut followed by a lemon sorbet for palate cleansing and then a marvelous duck plate for second secondo. He shared stories of his personal life, speaking of his daughter, an author of children's books, who lived in New York, and his son and grandson, who had teamed up to live the Silicon Valley start-up dream. I recited statistics from a leading women's literary group about how female authors are published and reviewed at a statistically lower rate than men.

When I didn't think I could eat one more bite or say one more stupid thing, the dessert platter arrived. The server asked me to choose one. Realizing the difficulty this presented for me, Saul ordered the entire platter to be left.

Once the desserts were cleared and the espresso arrived, Saul's demeanor changed. He quieted, and the smile he'd worn through lunch vanished. Business time.

"I'm sure you're wondering, Katherine, why I've asked you here and why there is a chest freezer currently sitting in your apartment. You've been most gracious in allowing me to work my way up to it."

Until this moment, the whole thing had almost seemed normal. But there were ongoing reminders that I was dining with the head of a prominent organized crime family besides the nagging thought of the dead man in the freezer in my living room, like the bevy of guards surrounding us at the peak of the lunch rush while beautifully set tables sat empty.

"I can hardly complain. Between the delicious food and your captivating conversation, it's been a lovely experience," I managed to get out.

"Again with your charm and manners. Your parents should be very proud of you. But there's more to you than meets the eye. Isn't there, Katherine?"

I didn't know how to answer this abrupt change in conversation. I assumed he was referring to my recent shooting of a serial killer. If he thought I was now some gun for hire, he was going to be very disappointed.

"No disrespect intended," he said when I didn't respond. He took three raw sugar packets and emptied them into his espresso. "My one vice that I can't seem to kick. I like my coffee too sweet," he said, setting the empty packets on the table. They were quickly scooped up by a busboy who seemed to come out of nowhere.

"My therapist says that we can't shy away from who we are at our core. After sixty-eight years, a good chunk of that spent trying to be something I wasn't, I think it has merit. I don't know if it's two-hundred-fifty-dollars-an-hour merit but something to think about. The way I understand it, you killed a man who would have harmed someone you cared for. It was the best of two bad choices."

"I suppose that's true," I replied. I didn't like to think about the shooting, let alone talk about it. But I had made a somewhat-nervous peace with it on exactly those grounds.

"Not that the bastard didn't deserve it anyway. The Russians have no class. Preying on helpless women. They irritate me to no end," he said, vigorously stirring his espresso, as if it might have some effect on the Russians. "In my line of business, I often come across information that I hold on to because at some point it may be useful. In your case, I have come across such information."

In my master's class on negotiation, the professor had stressed over and over that the first person to put terms on the table in any negotiation was the one at a disadvantage. Now seemed like an ideal time to counter move before I ended up in a position of needing to say no to someone I couldn't possibly say no to. I took a big drink of water and looked him straight in the eye. "Mr. Toucci, who is the dead man in my living room, and why do you want me to care?"

Chapter 6: Check, Please

"*Mr. Toucci, who is the dead man in my living room, and why do you want me to care?*"

Bingo. He paused, my statement as unexpected as it was bold, doing its job in interrupting his thoughts. Leaning back in his chair, he took his napkin from under his chin and threw it on the table, letting the silence linger. I held my breath.

"It's my nephew, Nile." He picked up his espresso, tilted it, and stared into the too-sweet brew.

"I'm sorry for your loss. How did he die?" I asked.

"That's what I'm hoping you will find out for me." He put the mug down without having taken a drink.

"Where did he die?" Talking about his nephew seemed safer than jumping into a negotiation for whatever he wanted.

"I don't know. His body was dumped at a location certain to make it look like the Palmeros were involved."

I didn't know much about the Palmeros, but I did know they were a rival mob family. Some would say *the* rival.

"But you don't think they were?" I asked.

"I did at first. Let's just say I have been persuaded into reconsidering and looking closer to home." He pushed back his chair, folding his hands over his stomach.

"You think someone in your family may be involved?" I couldn't imagine how such disloyalty and treachery so close to home was playing well with Saul Toucci. I hadn't known him long, but clearly family was high up on his values scale.

"The Palmeros and I have agreed that we'd get a neutral third party to investigate," he said.

"That would be me?"

"We both agreed you'd be an excellent choice. We admired your courage and tactics in the handling of the Russians."

This wasn't adding up. Even if I could imagine the circumstances that had led to the Palmeros and the Touccis calling a truce while the facts of the death of a close family member were sorted out, I couldn't imagine either of them allowing an outsider into it.

"I don't mean to pry, Mr. Toucci, and please pardon my bluntness, but why would you turn to someone outside the family with such a delicate matter? Surely you have people who handle this kind of thing."

"That is an excellent question. See, I knew you would be perfect for this assignment. Despite having your doubts, you have stood by your father unwaveringly in his present circumstances. I admire that kind of loyalty. At this moment, I'm not sure everyone in my family shares that value. The Palmeros have their own concerns. It's not like we can go to the police, and what needs to happen requires a certain skill set that you are in a unique position to provide."

"Because of my job."

"I hear good things about your work, and I understand that you'll be attending school to further your education in your chosen specialty."

I wasn't going to let myself dwell too long on how he knew that. I hadn't even decided to enroll yet.

"We need someone who can help find out what really happened to my nephew. The Palmeros have been adamant that Nile wasn't killed on their premises. Someone with your skills could answer that definitively. Plus, I think I have something that will more than motivate you."

Ah, the terms. Not wanting to appear eager, I took my napkin from my lap and placed it on the table. I fiddled with my coffee cup and took a sip, waiting for him to continue, desperately trying to keep myself from yammering.

"As I said, in my business, information often comes my way. I propose a trade—a barter of sorts. In exchange for your working your magic to figure out who killed my nephew, I will provide you two key pieces of information, the first pertaining to your father's incarceration and the second regarding the death of Gillian Mathers."

My heart rate had been fast through the whole meal. The mention that he had information about my dad caused it to react as if I had ingested a handful of uppers and a Red Bull chaser.

"Gillian Mathers was murdered by the Russians to prevent her from exposing their business operations and to cover Victor Chentinko's involvement in the prostitute serial killings," I said, sitting ramrod straight in my chair, as if preparing for the final question round in a pageant. We had been sure of that. It was one of the few things Burns, Fletcher, and I all agreed was settled. There were a ton of other loose ends, but that was not one of them.

"I'm sure you have realized by now that appearances aren't always as they seem. I can assure you I have substantial proof to accompany the information I am prepared to share with you."

He was right. It was an offer I couldn't refuse, a fact I didn't think I had much chance of hiding. Whether he was lying or not was irrelevant.

"I'm not a detective, Mr. Toucci. Statistics show that the majority of cases not solved in the first forty-eight hours go unsolved forever."

"You are smart, gutsy, and adaptable. If I had any doubts about that, the way you handled Fergus last night belayed them."

He motioned with his hand to where Raspy stood. Groaner was next to him, sounding much better than he had the last time we'd met.

"I have no doubt that you will be successful. However, I can agree that as long as you put in a reasonable effort, I will hold up my end of the deal, even if you don't solve the case."

And with the offer presented, he folded his hands on the table and waited for what I was sure he knew would be an affirmative response.

While I didn't know how good I'd be at investigating another murder, I was certain I could pull off the try-hard part of the bargain. But to have any chance at actually solving the murder, unfortunately, I'd need help.

"If I was going to do this, and I'm not saying I am, I would need help from my team. I'd also need unrestricted access to your family."

"I assumed so. As I'm sure you can understand, discretion is of the utmost importance. No one can find out why I've hired you. That is a deal breaker. I've already prepared a cover story for you and arranged for you to dine with me and my family tomorrow night at my house."

"What kind of cover story?"

"They think you are Fergus's girlfriend," he said.

I nearly spewed coffee all over the table. I looked up to where Raspy... uh, Fergus stood off Saul's right shoulder. Fergus looked pale at the mention of it.

"May-December romances are very popular these days. Additionally, your actual boyfriend, Mr. McPhee, will be awarded a contract for helping with security at the house, and your friend Mr. Clayborne will be entertained as a consultant in a potential business expansion into the Illinois marijuana market. We can discuss anything else you might need later. I'll allow you to distribute the details to those needed as you see fit."

Apparently, he assumed there was nothing more to be said and, pushing back from the table, stood. "Fergus will provide you any additional details and help you with any arrangements you may need."

Still trying to process everything that had been said, I stood too.

"This has been a most enjoyable introduction. I look forward to working with you," he said and extended his hand.

"But I haven't agreed. What if I have additional conditions?" I asked, not extending my hand yet.

"Ms. Waters, I believe the offer you have in front of you is fair, but I understand you are in difficult circumstances. If you need additional compensation—"

"Mr. Toucci, this has been an enlightening and enjoyable lunch, and on that basis, I'd prefer to believe that your allusions to money were offered out of concern for my family and you didn't mean it as the insult it could have been interpreted as. My additional condition has nothing to do with our barter or money."

"Forgive me, Katherine," he said, bowing slightly. "And thank you for reminding me again why I am sure you were the perfect choice for this arrangement."

"We'll see if you still believe that after you've heard my condition. If I'm going to do this, you have to promise that if I am successful in identifying who killed your nephew, no harm will come to them. You will turn them over to the police."

I thought I heard a gasp from the crowd of Toucci and restaurant staff surrounding us, but it could have been my imagination. I had one murder on my conscience as it was. I didn't need another, regardless of whether the departed were bad people.

"Ms. Waters," Fergus said, stepping forward. With a slight raise of Saul's hand, Fergus stopped cold and fell silent.

Saul stared at me. I wondered if he knew I was holding my breath.

"You'd be willing to walk away from what I know about Gillian Mathers and your father to protect the life of a killer? A piece of trash?" he asked finally.

I closed my eyes, wanting them all to disappear, if only for a moment. What he knew about Gillian could give Burns and me the fresh start we both needed. What he knew about my dad could give me my life back. But at the price of someone else's life? Like it or not—and I really didn't like it—I knew that was too high a price. I was already responsible for one man's death. I didn't need to be seeing double every time I closed my eyes.

I blew out the breath I'd been holding. It was loud and filled the room. I opened my eyes back up. "Yes," I said, offering no explanation. I couldn't have articulated one right then even if I tried.

He was quiet for a moment, and the room felt like it was vibrating with the silence. Then he smiled at me. "In that case, I agree to your terms. I took the liberty of having Enrique prepare a couple of additional meals for you to take with you." He motioned to the kitchen. "The kitchen is boxing them up. If you'll excuse me..." He stepped to me and kissed me on both cheeks. "I have another appointment. I'll see you tomorrow for a family dinner."

And with that, he left, his entourage following, with the exception of Fergus, who I assumed was left to deal with me.

While I waited for the food to be boxed up, I excused myself for another trip to the bathroom. I'd consumed four cups of coffee and liters of water. Additionally, I needed some privacy to have a personal freak-out. When my stomach had settled enough, and I no longer feared hurling in the middle of the restaurant, I headed back to the main dining room.

On my way, the sounds of whispered yelling near the kitchen door caught my attention. Fergus stood with who I assumed was the cook, given the white apron and chef hat. He was a short, skinny man with a dark tan and matching dark features. I couldn't tell what they were saying. It was in Italian. Passionate Italian. The man flailed his arms as he strained to keep his voice low. I only knew Latin, but I recognized a couple of words that were similar in Italian and English.

Corpo and *documenti* as well as *libri masteri*, which I'd have to look up when I got home. It seemed as if Fergus was trying to calm him down.

The cook caught sight of me out of the corner of his eye, abruptly stopped talking, and headed back into the kitchen.

"I hope everything is okay," I said as Fergus approached.

"Yeah, it's all good," he said.

"I hope the extra food request hasn't upset the chef." I didn't actually think Fergus would tell me what he was really arguing with the chef about, but it was worth hinting that I knew he was.

"You know these creative types. They get in a snit over the slightest thing. It'll be fine. Now, should we prepare for tomorrow evening? Darling?"

Chapter 7: Holy Matrimony

Fergus and I spent a few minutes trying to sort out our relationship origin story while we waited for the food. We finally agreed to stick to something simple so that we could both remember it—we'd met at the grocery store in the frozen section.

"Look, if this thing is going to work, we need to adhere to some ground rules," I said to Fergus as we hauled my bags of food toward the main entrance of the restaurant.

Once outside, Fergus signaled to the valet, who ran away to get the car.

"First and foremost, no PDA."

"Look, doll, this ain't an ideal situation for me either. You're not exactly my type." He shifted the bags of food, setting one of them by the curb. "But the boss gets what the boss wants," he said, straightening and gripping the lapels of his suit jacket on both sides as if trying to hold himself in.

Not wanting to contemplate what Fergus's type really was, I asked, "How long have you been working for him?" I set my bags down as well and wondered where all the food was going to go. Saul's nephew might have to have linguine company in the freezer.

"Almost my whole life. He's been like a father to me."

The valet pulled up with my wagon, got out, and started loading the car.

"So, who do you think killed... him?" I asked, catching myself when I recognized that the valet was very tuned in to our conversation.

Fergus must have realized it too. He stopped talking and shifted his focus to ensuring the safe transport of my leftovers.

"Hey, knucklehead, buckle those in," he said to the valet, walking to the car. "She don't want linguine all over her back seat." Fergus quietly observed the loading, which went much faster under his appraisal.

When the last of the bags was secured, he sent the valet away and returned his attention to me. "You got to understand, Nile was not the person Saul thinks he was," he said.

"Did he have a lot of enemies in the family?" I asked.

"Let's just say Nile was not the most beloved Toucci family member."

"Maybe you killed him," I said as we started walking to the car.

"Trust me. If I'd killed him, there wouldn't be a body, and we wouldn't be going through this whole mess."

That, I believed.

"Police say the spouse is usually the best suspect. Did Nile have a wife?"

"That'd be the first place I'd start, if I were you. That woman is a psycho. I'll have some background put together for you on some of the key family members," he said, opening my door.

I got in.

"And wear a dress tomorrow. I like my broads classy." He shut the door and headed back to the restaurant.

I sat at the curb for a moment, trying to process the information overload. I couldn't decide what the more fantastic part of the last two hours was—the fact that someone knew something about my dad, that Gillian Mather's death might not have been what we thought, that I had a week's worth of delicious meals in my back seat, or that I had to solve the murder of a mobster. Regardless, all roads led back to DC.

First, I would need to talk him into coming to dinner the next day. Not only would he keep me from vomiting ludicrous—yet insightful—facts, but he would also have a unique insight into Toucci's family. With his current need to get out of wedding-planning drama, talking him into helping probably wouldn't be too difficult.

Convincing him he needed to help me sneak the body in my living room into the morgue for a clandestine autopsy might be a harder sell. Most of all, I would need his help in strategizing my impending uncomfortable conversation with Burns McPhee, without whom I was certain I had no hope of pulling off the impending murder investigation.

Not sure of DC's schedule, I called him on his cell phone.

"Oh, thank God," he said.

"Hi. Glad to talk to you too," I said.

"Are you done yukking it up with teamsters? You have to come over right now. They're insane. You have to save me," he said in a strained, screechy whisper.

"The Touccis are more Capone than Hoffa, but yes. I just finished. Who's insane? Kimi?"

"No, it's worse than Kimi and Momma. Just hurry!"

When I got to DC's, one of the kids from the corner was sitting on a lawn chair in the street in front of the building, reserving the parking spot. Lawn-chair parking reservation had become very popular in Boston, especially during the winter months, but it was usually carried out by hipsters with their Smart cars or Saabs. The more urban version seemed to be a new trend. As soon as he saw my car, he flew out of his lawn chair and motioned me in. He gave me a nod as I got out, but we didn't speak. I nodded back as he assumed a guard position over my wagon. I wasn't sure I wanted to know what was going on with that, and with DC in a panic, I didn't really have time to figure it out.

I heard yelling coming from DC's apartment before I arrived, but it wasn't coming from DC. A high-pitched woman's voice squealed in agony.

"You cannot possibly be serious!" she said as I entered, ducking under the newly installed balloon arbor.

"You bet your ass I can be," DC responded in an unfamiliar, calm voice. At first, I couldn't locate him among the debris of party central. On the far side of the room, I finally spied two dark, petite feet leaning against the wall like an umbrella. I followed them down until I connected with DC's face. He was in a headstand against the wall, aided by some contraption attached to his head that looked like a cross between a turban and a red mushroom. A perky woman holding a thin notebook with bunnies and flowers on the cover was bent at the waist to more easily turn her head upside down, perpendicular to DC. Her bleached-blond hair swooshed against the floor, exposing her brown roots. Next to her stood a very skinny man in a sweater-vest.

DC smiled widely when he saw me. "Praise Jesus!" He swung his feet down to the ground, causing Blondie to dive out of the way to avoid being hit by a flying foot. The mushroom hat followed him as he stood upright, towering above him and smashing into the ceiling.

"What on earth is on your head?" I asked.

Blondie and Sweater-vest, who had their backs to me, both jumped in surprise and turned, searching through wedding central to find who had asked the question. I was aligned with the balloon arch, making me hard to see.

"This is a trance-inducing support trilby, specifically designed to help increase the positive energy flowing to my cranium and open my clogged chakra." He spread his arms wide and pressed his middle fingers to his thumbs. "Dr. Maija says he doesn't usually sell them, but in my current condition, it would create a negative rise to his karma not to."

"And exactly how much does the good doctor get for a head ottoman?" I asked.

Blondie went back to scribbling in her bunny book, while Sweater-vest observed the conversation between DC and me, shifting his head back and forth as if he were at a Wimbledon tennis match.

"Now, don't be snarky. It will affect your complexion," DC said, walking past the two, toward me. "For a mere hundred fifty dollars, we could unclog all your chakras too. And trust me. You are one clogged-up mob princess."

"Mob?" That got Blondie's attention.

"Oh, yes," DC said, throwing his arms up in the air, his voice rising an octave in a fit of pretend drama as he approached me. "You have no idea the awful ordeal my maid of honor has been through."

In unison, Sweater Vest and I repeated, "Maid of honor?"

DC threw his arms around me, his magic brain mushroom squishing the side of my face as he pulled me in for a hug. "If you don't play along, that dead mobsicle can stay in your apartment forever," he whispered in my ear.

"Oh yes," I said as he released me from the hug. "I've dreamed of making this the perfect day for DC for months, but now, well..." I pretended to sob into my hand.

"Which is why her current situation is so tragic," he said, running a hand down my hair in pretend comfort. "I'm sorry, Kat. I know this is a difficult time, but allow me to introduce you to Freddy and Wilimmina, Momma and Kimi's wedding planners," he said, motioning as if he were revealing the game show prize on stage.

"It's Frederick," Sweater Vest said with a slight lisp and simultaneously pushed his wire frames back on his nose. "And what possible situation could be more important than the impending nuptials of your best friend, pray tell?" Freddy asked. He crossed his arms and aimed his thin, pointy nose toward the ceiling so he could peer at me under his lenses.

Blondie stopped writing in her bunny book and lifted her head to pay attention.

"Oh, you have no idea the terrible ordeal this poor dear has been through," DC said, taking both of my hands and staring into my eyes in fake sympathy. "First, her poor, sweet grandmother was diagnosed with a horrible, terminal disease, and then there's the police matter, the erroneous incarceration of her dear, upstanding father." He focused his gaze on the wedding twins, gauging the impact of his performance. I attempted to look stricken, slumping my posture and sighing at strategic moments in the speech. "And then!" He whipped one arm free and began flailing it. "Our brave Kat had to shoot a mobster to save her poor, afflicted, kidnapped granny."

He let my other hand go and, moving close to me, put his hand under my chin, lifting it to face the wedding twins. "Look at her. The poor child. She's clearly suffering from PTMD."

"PTMD?" Wilimmina squeaked.

"Post-traumatic mob disorder. She can't possibly plan my wedding in her condition," he said, letting my chin go.

"Oh no, I definitely could not," I said, sighing and lowering my head. "Creating all those happy family memories. Memories I may never have now," I said with a fake sniffle.

"Well, the wedding is supposed to be in a month," Frederick said.

"A month?" I asked, surprised.

"Yes. That way, Kimi and I can get her asylum application filed," DC replied.

"But my therapy!" I exclaimed. "How will I ever get better without your help?" I put the back of my hand to my forehead, pretending I might faint.

"Therapy?" DC asked.

"Yes, with Dr. Toucci," I said. "I was counting on you to go with me to my first appointment tomorrow and then help me with my on-going treatment these next weeks."

"Well, there you go," he said, motioning to the wedding twins. "We can't do this right now. Kat needs me. You wouldn't want me to start my new life with my forever someone under a dark cloud, knowing our happiness came at the expense of my months-long best friend, would you?"

"No, I guess not," Wilimmina said, putting the cap on her pen.

"Excellent! Then we're all in agreement. Now..." He skipped over to them, took one of each of their hands in his, and began pulling them across the room. "You'll let Momma and Kimi know about the slight delay in plans, and I'll get ready to be my excellent self for poor, dear Kat." Before they could say another word, he shoved them out the door and closed it on their agape mouths.

"Whew. Dodged a bullet," he said, leaning against the door. "You were terrific. I think I'm starting to rub off on you."

"That won't keep them at bay forever," I said.

"No, not with immigration breathing down Kimi's neck, but it will buy us some time to figure something out," he said, unstrapping the chakra declogger from his head and setting it down on top of the napkin samples. "What's this business about therapy with Dr. Touc-ci?" He moved past me, under the balloon arch, and headed toward the kitchen. He opened the fridge and took out a Coke, motioning an offer of one to me.

"No, I couldn't possibly ingest one more thing right now," I said. "It's lucky I've lost weight on the macaroni diet. Otherwise, I'd have popped a button after that meal."

"Oh, I bet it was fabulous."

"Well, you'll get to find out tomorrow night." I leaned against the counter for support of my larger-than-usual belly.

"What do you mean?" he asked.

"You've been invited to dinner with the Touccis under the auspices of discussing the expansion of their marijuana distribution into Illinois but really as a mole to spy on them."

He popped the top of the can and took a big drink, eyeing me with his dark-brown eyes over the top of the can.

"Since when am I a spy for the mob?"

"Since you just made me play the heroine in your little wedding-planner drama."

"True. Why does the mob need a spy?" He set the can down.

"Because Saul Toucci thinks someone in his family offed his nephew, Nile, the mobsicle in my living room."

We moved to the living room and plopped onto the couch while I explained the whole deal to him.

"Oh, sugar! What did Burns say when you told him about Gillian?"

"That's why I'm here. I thought you could go with me to tell him. Of course, I could undergo a magnificent recovery, and then you'd be too busy with wedding plans to help with Burns."

"What do you need my help for anyway? I thought you two were all kissy-kissy now."

"It's complicated. I feel like we're stuck in Gillian Mather's purgatory. We can't move forward, because whatever tie to his business she found seems to have gone *poof* into thin air. He won't say it, but I know he's stalled. He keeps showing up, getting me all hot and bothered. I don't think straight around him. And he's going to hit the roof when he finds out I had lunch with Saul Toucci. That's why you should tell him. He won't get mad at you." I put on my best pageant smile and batted my eyelashes at him in hopes of garnering some sympathy. Burns and DC went way back, and DC engendered a tolerance for his troublemaking ways I had not yet garnered.

He sighed and got up. "All right, I'll mob spy for you and tell your boyfriend the murder of his ex isn't quite as solved as he thought. But you'd better have PTMD for a damn long time!"

"Consider it practice for your blossoming acting career," I said.

"Funny. So, do you have any leads?" he asked.

"Well, Fergus, Saul's right hand, said I should focus on Nile's psycho wife. But when I was coming out of the bathroom after trying not to puke, I heard Fergus arguing with the Saul's chef. It was in Italian, but I recognized they were talking about a corpse."

"This is most excellent. I get to go to a murder-mystery dinner theater, and I don't even have to pay."

"With the minor drawback that one of these people may have actually killed someone, and they may not offer us the table centerpiece as a prize for figuring it out."

We headed down the stairs to get the extra food from my car to store in DC's oversized fridge before it spoiled. I nodded to the kid sitting on my car bumper as we exited DC's building. The kid hopped off and lurked a short distance away.

"What's with the pint-size watch dog?" DC asked.

"I don't know. They started appearing to ensure I had parking right after the freezer showed up."

"Well, you are a criminal celebrity now, between the shooting, the Touccis, and Grand and all."

After we loaded his fridge, we headed back outside.

"We are not taking your ghetto-mobile. Especially now that it smells like eggplant parmesan," he said as he pushed me past my car, toward his. DC drove the biggest Lincoln Town Car ever manufactured. If we ever crashed into water, I was sure it could double as a boat.

As I walked to the car, multiple versions of the bumper sticker Single to Mingle and Free Love greeted me.

"Really?" I asked, pointing.

"I'm all for the gays getting married. I just don't see why I should be roped into the event. When Kimi and Mama drop this ridiculous plan of theirs, I'll take them off but not one minute sooner."

Chapter 8: These Are No Clowns

Burns McPhee owned his own security company in addition to a stake in a nonprofit investment firm that built schools and roads in Afghanistan. The combined offices for the two ventures were in a trendy, modern building on the other side of the county from DC's house.

DC pulled the boat into the underground garage, and we headed up to the McPhee Security offices. McPhee Security was located in a posh neighborhood. The building and its interior reflected their tenant—sleek and masculine. Clean lines and dark woods and substantial metal accents gave it a slight industrial vibe.

Since I'd recently saved Burns's life, I'd become a minor celebrity with the McPhee staff. That made navigating the receptionist guarddog much easier than before the shooting.

"Oh, Ms. Waters, so nice to see you!" Amber said, jumping up from her receptionist perch, her blond ponytail protruding out of the top part of her head and bouncing with each word spoken. "And Mr. Clayborne. Yay." She grimaced when she saw DC with me. Amber and DC had not been on good terms since she'd used a new skincare line that DC had given her that he'd bought after watching one of his infomercials. It had turned her green.

Amber led us out the door, down a nondescript hallway, and through a series of unmarked, badge-controlled doors. I knew we were getting close when we crossed an aisle of cube land into darkness. Monitoring security feeds was apparently similar to watching porn, requiring darkness and screen wipes.

I heard people shouting before we arrived at the large viewing room that doubled as the shared office space for Neutron and Flynn. Amber heard it too.

"All righty, then. I think you can find your way from here. I'm going to go hunt up Burns for you." Not waiting for an answer, she turned around and headed back the way we had come, her blond ponytail shining like a bobbing beacon in the twilight as she marched.

DC and I simultaneously squeezed through the doorway from where the shouting emanated. Six monitors hung side by side high on the far wall, lighting up the dark space with various interior images of big-screen TVs, BarcaLoungers, and bad art, the trappings of suburban houses. Something seemed different about the space since I had last seen it, but I couldn't quite figure it out.

"It's not an actual sport!" Flynn said, crossing his arms in a huff.

As long as I'd known him, Flynn had always been Flynn, no last name. Like Cher or Madonna. Same attitude, less hair. His bulky muscles always seemed to bulge out of whatever black T-shirt he wore—and they were always black. He had a military buzz cut. A tattoo of a snake slithered down the length of his right arm, and what I had learned from Burns was, his special ops skull tattoo peeked out the sleeve on the other side. Burns had a matching one.

"I don't understand why you aren't being more open minded," Neutron responded curtly, accentuating each word, while staring at one of the feeds.

Every time I saw Neutron, I couldn't help but be reminded of the *Dexter's Laboratory* cartoon I watched growing up. Like Dexter, Neutron's head always seemed bigger than the rest of him, in part because of his big Coke-bottle glasses and bug eyes and in part because he was so scrawny everywhere else. I couldn't see what he was wearing, given he had his back to us, but it didn't look like the standard McPhee khakis and plain black T-shirt.

"I am not a circus clown!" Flynn yelled.

Burns had rescued Neutron from the psych ward where he'd been sentenced to after hacking the credit cards of the chief justice of the Supreme Court and sending him a lifetime supply of Viagra. A computer genius, he also had a souped-up computer lab down the hall that looked like something from the set of *Star Trek*. I didn't know why he chose to share space with Flynn. Or why Flynn allowed it, for that matter. The two of them bickered more than an old married couple.

"This is not a joke!" Neutron whipped around in his chair and stood up, grabbing his tablet computer from the table. He was wearing some sort of sports uniform and had paired it with baggy black jeans. He punched sharply at the tablet. A video appeared on the screen. It looked like an indoor soccer match. The men were all wearing uniform shirts similar to Neutron's. A whistle blew on screen. And then...

"Is that juggling?" DC asked before I could.

"Oh, great! This is all I need today. But maybe one of you can talk some sense into him," Flynn said, turning to DC and me.

That's when I realized what was different about the room. Space had been cleared in the back, replaced by racks of juggling pins and hula-hoop-looking circles on the floor. We watched as one of the jugglers smacked another player with his pins.

"That is not juggling," DC said.

"It's called combat juggling, and it is totally a sport. They have matches and referees and a league." He set the tablet down on the desk. "They're starting up in St. Louis."

"Combat juggling? Like a clown war?" DC interjected.

"Thank you," Flynn said.

I knew we were in trouble if Flynn was agreeing with DC.

That infuriated Neutron, and his big head became as red as a cherry. I'd never seen him angry before. "Do you see any wigs and noses? No," Neutron said. "It requires precision and physical endurance."

"It does look a bit... intense," I said as we all watched a man drop to the floor after being waylaid by a pin.

"We never go out anymore," Neutron said, as if his words explained everything.

"All this fuss"—DC pointed at Neutron—"is because you want to go watch this?"

"Seriously, is everyone associated here completely challenged?" Neutron asked.

It was an uncharacteristic snark. Neutron and DC got on well, and while I could always count on Burns or Flynn to say something sardonic, Neutron was usually the peppy one of the team.

"I'm wearing a shirt. I have pins." He gestured to the back.

"Is this one of those weird white-people things I won't understand?" DC asked, peering at the screen and then at me.

"You should be with me on this," Neutron said to DC. "The league is against testing and are big advocates of legalization. We're pursuing sponsorship." He took a flyer from the table and handed it to DC. Now that he was talking about the benefits of the league, some of the color had drained from his face.

"Really?" DC took the flyer.

"Okay. I understand that this is a bit of an unorthodox... sport," I said, choosing my words carefully so as not to inflame him again.

Flynn snorted in the background, and I gave him the evil eye.

"But why do you care if he plays? It can't be *that* dangerous."

"I don't know. That looks brutal if you ask me," DC said, pointing at a close-up of one of the players bleeding from his head.

"I signed us up together," Neutron said and, getting out of his seat, picked up another shirt. A very large shirt. And I finally understood.

"Ohhh," I said and smiled at Flynn.

"What does that mean?" Flynn asked, scowling at me.

"I'm tired of doing the same old things all the time. We're either here or at the gun range. Sure, he watches me play my video games, too, but I want us to do something more together." Neutron spit it all out in a single breath.

"I think it's a wonderful idea," I said. Judging by Flynn's demeanor, I was pretty sure he had no idea what Neutron had meant by his speech. I wasn't even sure if Neutron did.

DC eyed me, eyed Neutron, then eyed Flynn, and then a huge grin came over his face. "This is definitely a good thing."

"I know nothing about juggling!" Flynn raged again.

"Well, if that's the only issue, I'm sure Neutron could teach you," I said.

"Yeah, how hard could it be?" DC asked, picking up some of the pins and throwing them into the air. They hit the floor with a thud.

"Besides, we're about to be very busy. Having an outlet for the two of you will be good," I said.

At that proclamation, both Flynn and Neutron froze.

"What have you and the skirt gotten into now?" Flynn asked DC.

"Don't look at me," DC said. "She's the mob princess. I'm just the dashing sidekick." He stuck out his chin and stroked the side of his head.

"We haven't gotten into anything!" I said defensively. "Did you know juggling can burn up to two hundred eighty calories an hour?"

They all looked at me.

"What? Miss Indiana juggled for her talent," I said, rolling my eyes.

DC grinned and, turning to Neutron, said, "I believe my organization could be persuaded to sponsor your team, but in return, we do need some information on the Toucci family."

"Oh, for Christ's sake," Flynn said, turning in circles as if he could dodge the information just delivered.

"Sexy outfit," a sultry voice said from behind me.

The first time I'd met Burns, I could have sworn he was a lumberjack. At the time, his dark features and sloppy hair contrasted against his red flannel vest. Today he was in a suit.

"I wasn't trying," I said, thankful for the dark room because I could feel the flush in my cheeks.

"Bonus. Do you want to tell me why Amber says my mother is here and why Flynn looks like someone took away his gun?"

"It's complicated," I said.

"There's a shocker." He grinned.

"The Russians weren't bad enough. Now she's mixed up with the Touccis," Flynn interjected. "Collecting them like damn Monopoly pieces."

"Oh, I like Monopoly. I always have to be the top hat. It's debonair like me," DC said and brushed his hand across his dark fuzz.

I was thankful for the levity. Any time Burns was around, I felt like there was less oxygen in the room.

On the relationship front, Burns and I were in limbo. Dating would imply that we went places and did things. That didn't happen. Instead, we were in a situationship. He came over several times a week, bearing wine coolers for me and beer for him and Grand. They'd watch whatever soccer match was on the sports channel. One of her Grand Groupies had sent her Manchester United memorabilia as a support offering, and she'd become an obligated raving fan. When they couldn't find soccer, they'd watch baseball. I'd read or study for the forensics program. We'd chat during commercials. No public displays of affection were allowed in front of the old lady—although after the first beer, she was easier to manage—but I'd occasionally get felt up on the front porch when he was on his way out. That ritual was the sum total of our relationship. Situationship.

"What'd you do to get the attention of the Touccis?" Burns asked, a crease forming in his brow.

I had originally thought that this was going to be a difficult conversation. Looking at Burns's pensive expression, I'd revised that opinion.

Getting Burns on board with this was seeming impossible. Of course, I did have the ace in the hole with the information on Gillian, but I wasn't sure that wouldn't just add gasoline to an already-smoldering fire. The only conversation Burns hated having more than anything to do with me and the mob was anything to do with Gillian's murder.

My mind swirled. *If I can't get him to agree, what am I going to do?* I made a note to dig out Grand's *Private Investigation for Dummies.* If I did end up going it alone, I wondered whether Saul would still hold to the agreement. *And what does he really know about my dad and Gillian anyway?*

There was really only one way to find out. I had to make it good.

Chapter 9: Old Friends

"Why does it always have to be my fault? Something *I* did?" I asked.

"Oh, yeah, you're just an innocent trouble magnet. I forgot," Flynn said.

"I think her chakras are clogged. But she won't wear the trilby," DC added.

"I was just lying in my bed, minding my own business, when the Toucci mob broke into my apartment and dumped a dead body in a chest freezer."

"A body?" Burns ran a hand through his hair, his ritual reaction to my exasperation. "How do we give it back?"

"What do you mean?" I asked.

"Well, you sure as hell can't keep a dead mobster in your apartment," Burns said.

"It's his nephew. He wants me to solve the murder," I replied.

"Oh great. Here we go again. One solved crime, and she thinks she's goddamn Nancy Drew," Flynn said.

"What did he say when you told him no?" Burns asked.

"I'm guessing, based on her recent request for information on the Touccis, she did not tell him no, boss," Neutron said. He'd been at the computer while we argued. Pictures of various Toucci family members now covered all the screens.

"I'd assume that, too, but no one would be dumb enough to get mixed up with the Touccis," Burns said.

"Oh, so now I'm dumb!" I was almost to a full shout.

"Now, I'm sure Burns didn't mean it that way, sugar. We're all just worried for your safety," DC said. You knew you were in trouble when DC was the voice of reason in any situation.

"You mean *my* safety," Flynn said. "The damn woman's gonna get us all killed."

"Yeah, well, this 'damn woman'"—I made air quotes—"now has a lead on Gillian's death!" I hadn't meant to explode like that. But once I'd said it, the rest wouldn't stop. "Toucci's trading the killer of his nephew for information on Gillian's murder. So would anyone else in this room like to now ask me about the return policy on dead mafia nephews or tell me how dumb I am?" I looked around at the silent, stunned faces. "I didn't think so!" I pushed past Burns, feeling the heat from his body, and moved out into the hallway. I needed air.

While the death of Burns's ex, Gillian, which had initially brought us together, was mostly settled—or we thought it had been—there were still open questions. This could give us some answers and potentially a way for me to get out of involving the international soccer commission as chaperones for our dates.

"That's not quite the subtle, smooth delivery I had planned," DC said, coming out behind me.

Burns stood quietly in the doorway, his hands in his pockets, rocking back slightly on his heels. Calculating. The one thing I'd learned about him in the last few months was that he was a model of efficiency. Every movement made, every word said was with the least amount of energy to exact the most amount of impact. His teams in both businesses were highly organized with an enviable military efficiency my OCD list-making side marveled at.

"Neutron, start a full workup on the Touccis. Flynn, I'll need sitreps on all their facilities," he said finally, spouting military speak for situation reports.

Flynn and Burns had been friends since grade school and had served together in Afghanistan. Much like Saul and Fergus, what Burns wanted, Burns got, no questions.

Burns took his hands out of his pockets, walked to me, and took one of mine in his. "DC, we'll be back in a few minutes. I think Bradley just got in the newest round of suit catalogs, if you want to go look. Flynn will take you." Bradley was Burns's office manager, who had a love-hate relationship with DC. The love part was their mutual fashionista sides, and the hate part was pretty much every other thing DC did.

"Oh, yummy!" DC said, like a little kid about to dive into a Christmas catalog.

Burns led me by the hand down a hallway to a nearby conference room. Before we were even all the way through the door, he had whipped me around and to him, pressed his lips to mine, and wrapped his arms around me to ensure I stayed close. The kiss was urgent and greedy, his tongue brushing against mine insistently and instantly consuming any temper I might have had left. When it seemed as though he'd taken enough to ease the sharpness of his need, he edged away, leaving a cold vacuum in his place.

"No more sexy dresses on work days," he said.

My head was spinning, and suddenly I felt like the volume of Italian food I'd consumed a few hours earlier might not have been such a good idea.

"I feel sick," I said.

"That's not the normal response I get when I kiss a woman."

"There is not much normal about us."

He picked up the phone and pushed a button. "Hi, Amber. I need water in the Stealth room." Without waiting for a response, he hung up then led me to a chair.

"Sit, breathe, and then start at the beginning."

When I was midway through the story, Amber brought the water and then quickly left. As I inhaled water and exhaled information, the throb in my temples began to subside, and the room seemed to steady.

When I was done, he sat quietly again, slightly slouched in the uncomfortable chair next to me.

"How do we know he really has information?" he asked finally.

"We don't. But you've hit a wall. We don't talk about it, which is its own kind of weirdness, but you haven't made any progress on Gillian's case in weeks. I can tell by the cranky way you open your beer. This could be a new start," I said then took another pull of the water bottle. "Besides, Saul Toucci is a classy mobster. He doesn't hit me as the bait-and-switch type."

"The Gentlemen."

"Exactly. Why don't you pick me up at the Touccis' after the dinner tomorrow? You can meet him then and decide for yourself. DC and I will have the first impressions by then. We can get a game plan, and then you can help me sneak the body into the morgue."

"It's not funny that sneaking into the morgue has become a specialized skill set for my team," he said, sitting up and running his hand through his hair.

"It's a little funny."

He smiled. "I am sorry that I will miss watching DC have dinner with the Toucci family."

"Speaking of which, I have work to get through before this shindig," I said and stood up. "And it will take me at least ten minutes to get DC away from Bradley's catalogs. I'll see you tomorrow night."

I bent down and brushed my lips lightly to his. He pulled me in for more, knocking me off balance. I grabbed the table edge to avoid falling into his lap.

"We have to find reasons for you to wear sexy dresses that don't involve dead bodies," he said when he released me.

"That's something we can agree on," I said, heading to the door.

"I heard you had a date with Fletcher Reid."

I stopped cold and turned around. Round two of the macho tug-of-war. "It wasn't a date. I needed some information."

"You met at a restaurant. He paid. That's a date. And if you need information, you should be coming here."

"What? Are you stalking me now? You should be careful. The last guy who did that is dead," I said, half smiling. "Besides, you and Fletcher run in different circles, meaning you have different information. And I didn't want to upset you if I didn't have to. I was only thinking of you." I smiled and walked out without waiting for a response. I would not be mentioning that I would be seeing Fletcher for another not-date before my dinner with the Touccis the next day.

I collected DC, and we headed back to his boat.

"The new spring line is fabulous. I hope my Illinois business takes off so I can afford some new purchases," he said.

"You have to put all your money toward the wedding," I said, smiling as we climbed in, and he started the engine.

Before he could respond to wedding humor, my phone rang. Unknown number. *Great.* I had a history of cell phone trouble with unknown numbers. My heart rate quickened instinctively.

"Hello," I forced out.

"Hello, Katherine," someone with a thick Russian accent said on the other end. "This is your friend Simon." There was only one Russian Simon that I knew. Simon "The Mole" Milovich, head of the Red Mafia and holder of secrets about why my dad was in prison.

"Hello, Simon," I responded.

"Simon? That rat bastard mobster?" DC asked.

"Shh," I said to DC, moving the phone out of earshot.

DC eased the car out of the garage and headed toward my apartment.

"I hope you are well. It's time for us to conclude our business," Simon said.

"I wasn't aware we had any," I replied.

"As I told you last time we spoke, Katherine, you and I are very connected. I trust your father is well? Oh, but he won't see you, will he?"

Simon was right. Since I'd accused my dad of being mixed up with the Russian mob and the serial killer murders, he'd refused to let me visit. Mostly, he disapproved of his Harvard-educated daughter working in a morgue. I hated that Simon knew anything about us.

"He's well, thank you," I lied.

"Is he asking about your dad?" DC asked as he stopped at a red light.

"I'm so glad to hear that, because I believe I have a trade that will reunite the two of you," Simon said.

"What do you mean?" I asked.

"As I told you last time, you possess something that I need. In exchange for it, I am prepared to set in motion your father's release."

"I don't believe you can do that."

"Uh-oh. That sounds like trouble," DC said, keeping one eye on me and the other on the traffic.

"Then you are not the studious girl I was led to believe you are. Surely you understand that my empire is vast and my resources, extensive."

It was the second time in a matter of hours I'd found myself negotiating a barter with the head of a mob family. I felt emboldened.

"What do you want, Simon? Or I'll assume all this posturing is just to hear yourself talk, like it was with Victor." Victor was the deranged stalker mobster Simon had employed and who'd killed all the prostitutes.

"There's no reason to be uncivilized, Katherine. I assure you Victor and I have very little in common on that front. All I need from you is for you to return to me the contents of the storage locker your grandmother rented."

"What are you talking about? Grand has not rented any storage locker."

"Oh my god!" DC said, almost rear-ending the person in front of us, jarring me as he slammed on the brakes. "I bet there's a dead body in that locker. Another mobster with another dead body."

"We don't know that," I said, holding the phone away so Simon couldn't hear us. "Besides, the way you're driving, we'll be dead before any mobster has a shot at us. Eyes on the road!" I turned back to the phone.

"Not that she remembers, anyway," Simon said. "But I assure you there is a storage locker that your grandmother has the key to that has contents that I need. When you've retrieved them, I'll release information that will result in having your father released."

"Why don't you just go steal what's in it?" I asked.

He was silent for a moment. "We tried that. There was a... mishap, and since then, the pinhead manager has added extra security, specifically around that unit. It seems silly to risk more of my men, and the potential of additional police involvement is unacceptable. Especially when I have you, the perfect alternative solution. I thought I'd tackle the problem the old-fashioned way and call on my dear friend Katherine. It shouldn't take you long to retrieve the items. I get what I want, and you get what you want. A win-win, as they say. I'll be in touch soon to talk about the details of the trade." The phone went dead.

How in the hell could we have a storage locker that the Russian mob wants, and no one in my family has said anything to me?

"I have to go home," I said to DC. "I need to go see Grand."

Chapter 10: Geared Up and Ready to Go

DC drove us back to his place so that I could get my car and deal with Grand and the locker while he figured out what he was going to wear to dinner with the Touccis the next day. When we arrived at his house, my car was gone. In its place was the kid guard in the lawn chair. He was playing with some electronic gizmo. My heart skipped a beat. It might have been a beater car, but it was all mine, and more importantly, with our current financial situation, it was paid for.

"Uh-oh. Maybe your mob-princess celebrity has worn off already," DC said as we both surveyed the empty space where my car should be. "Maybe they found a better spot for it or something. I'll go park while you sort it out, but you can borrow the boat if yours doesn't turn up."

"It freaking better turn up!"

I slammed the door when I got out, causing the kid in the lawn chair to jump. He was scrawny enough that I wondered if maybe someone had stolen my car out from underneath him.

"Hey, where's my car?" I asked with a bit of an attitude.

"Don't panic, little missy. You needed a bath. It was getting me all grime-afied. And then the damn thing wouldn't start, so it's at Devon's," he said, pointing down the road.

I thought better of correcting his choice of swear words when I saw the gun tucked in the back of his pants as he twisted to point at a mystery garage up the road.

"Lovely. Well, I'm not trying to seem ungrateful, but I have appointments to keep. What am I supposed to do?"

"No worries, little missy. I gotcha covered." He pointed in the other direction, where a large black Escalade was pulling down the street. The SUV stopped in front of me. Another kid, who didn't look old enough to drive, hopped out and came around the hood to us.

"This ain't no little thing like you're used to," he said, eyeing me intently. He held out the keys. When I reached for them, he pulled them back and leaned into my face. "Be very careful."

"When looked at as a percentage of vehicles on the road, the Escalade is the most frequently stolen," I said.

He stepped back, looking confused.

"I'll treat it like it was my own."

"I seen your own. That is not comforting," he replied, handing the keys to me.

"No reason to get all moody," the lawn chair guard said to the car owner, putting his arms around him and backing him away from me. "You'll have to forgive him. He's having a rough time right now."

"Well, DC has a meditation guru who can help unclog his chakras," I said, pointing at DC as he came up to us.

"What did she just say?" the driver asked.

"Sweet ride," DC said. "Now this is a vehicle fit for a mob princess."

"His friend has clogged chakras. I told them you could help," I said to DC, pointing at them.

"Really? You like hummus?" DC responded, looking at the man boy.

While they continued chatting, I sneaked away into the SUV. I felt like I was mounting a Clydesdale, the giant horses St. Louis was famous for, thanks to Budweiser. "All roads here lead to beer." The car was monstrous. I headed for home.

The first thing I noticed when I entered our hoarder's cave was that the furniture had been rearranged. The chest freezer had been moved to the back of the living room. The second thing that dawned on me was that Grand must have gone "shopping" at our old house. By shopping, I meant looting the crime scene of our confiscated former house. The freezer was surrounded by barstools I recognized. I didn't want to know how she'd managed to get them back in an Uber. The freezer sported a plastic Mexican tablecloth and a blender and had margarita glasses on top of it. The sombrero that had been covering the freezer guy's manly bits provided ambiance as it hung on the wall above the whole setup. Where the chest freezer had previously been sat the Queen Anne side table that doubled as a scrapbooking workstation. Grand hunched, intently working on Claude's incarcibook.

"Where's Mom?" I asked as I entered. The last thing I needed was Mom knowing about Grand and the Russians.

"She's working on something for Montgomery. Something about a luncheon for bomb buyers. I told her I'd be fine until you got here. I'm not a child, ya know."

Uh-oh. Grand was in snark mode. That meant bad news from Claude.

"He wouldn't see you today?" I asked.

"Same old," she said, slamming the book shut and getting up from the table. She was dressed in a bright-yellow crushed-velvet jogging suit with a matching Chiquita banana foam sun visor, her signature headgear.

"Well, I have something we can do that might cheer you up," I said, trying to look chipper instead of nervous.

"Yeah? Lose another dead body and want to get me kidnapped?"

Definitely snark mode. She only referred to the kidnapping when she was upset.

"Now, perk up. I thought we could stop by that storage locker you rented and take a look at what's in it. Maybe you have some extra antiques we could bring back."

"What storage locker? Do you think if I had stuff stashed in a storage locker, we'd be eating dinner off a second-hand dumpster dive that's missing a leg?" she asked, pointing at the table I'd picked up at one of the nearby consignment shops.

She didn't remember the locker. *What am I going to do now?* Maybe a different avenue would jog her memory.

"I got a call today from a friend of Daddy's," I said, heading over to the margarita bar and taking a seat. "He mentioned the storage facility, and I thought you might have the key."

"I think I'd remember if I rented a damn locker. Those storage places are nasty. The one time I went with Claude, I thought I'd have to shower for a week." She joined me at the bar.

"You went to a storage place with Claude?" I asked, pretending to drink. Grand liked to pretend smoke. I assumed pretend drinking was the point of the martini bar. At her former assisted-living home, she'd had happy hour every Friday at four, but we couldn't afford liquor any more than we could afford a spot in that cushy residents' home. I knew she missed the routine of it.

"A couple of weeks before Clarke's arrest. I stayed in the car to avoid getting rabies from some rogue rat." She picked up her glass, too, and raised it in a toast then took a big pretend drink.

I stared at her, assessing what to do next. The only way forward I could see was some version of the truth. "Grand," I said and set my glass down, folded my arms over, and leaned into her. "Do you remember that case at the morgue I was working on before you were kidnapped? The one with the missile-launch codes from Dad's book?"

"Yeah, what about it? Damned near got us both killed, but we solved the case." She pulled down on what she called her Sherlock hat and beamed pride.

"Maybe not quite," I said and tried to gauge her reaction. "We did solve the prostitute murders. But we didn't find what the missile-launch codes went to, and now I have another connected case that I really need them for."

"Hot damn! Another case." Grand had never sworn until Grandpa died. At that point she'd declared herself too old not to be salty. "Why didn't you say so to start with? I'm going to have to rework my schedule now. That gives us a double header of investigations with the body in the freezer. Good thing too. I was getting bored sitting around here."

There was never any conversation as to whether Grand would be helping with the investigation into Toucci's nephew. Mom and I both knew it was a lost cause to even attempt to keep her from helping me. Saul Toucci might not have realized it yet, but one of the key investigators on his nephew's murder wore foam sun visors and had a Sherlock Holmes spy kit in her purse.

"Dad's friend said they might be in the storage locker you visited. Do you remember where it might be?"

"It was in West County. I remember too many manicured lawns for it not to be. How many West County storage facilities could there be?"

"Are you kidding me? Rich people have tons of stuff they lock away. We should know."

"True, but I'll recognize it if I see it. Let's go drive around. I need to change first, though. I stand out too much in this sunny frock."

I contemplated the whole scenario while I waited for Grand. My recent encounters with the seedy underbelly of crime had taught me that coincidences like being contacted by two mob bosses who just happened to have information I might want didn't happen. Maybe whatever was in the mystery storage locker would have the clues I needed to get my dad out of prison. Maybe it had whatever was tied to Gillian Mather that Saul Toucci was dangling in front of me. Either one of those might mean I wouldn't have to end up in the middle of a potential mob-family war.

Before I could come to any conclusions, Grand reappeared, ready to go, wearing one of her old riding outfits—sleek beige riding pants, a white shirt, a black riding jacket, and knee-high boots. She headed toward the entry closet.

"What's with the getup?" I asked.

"We're hunting. I thought I'd dress the part," she said as she rummaged in the closet. Grand's purse was always color coordinated with her outfit. I was expecting to see something worthy of a fox hunt. Instead, she pulled out a large leather-studded backpack.

"What is that?" I asked.

"It's got all my crime-fighting tools in it," she said, hoisting it onto to her small frame. Even adjusted to its smallest size possible, it still hung on her petite body. "Mace, *PI for Dummies*, extra shells for the gun you gave away, Sherlock Holmes lockpick set for if I should ever again find my delicate wrists back in handcuffs, and coffee creamer in case of a repeat kidnapping by heathens."

Chapter 11: Lockers and Keys

We headed out of the apartment to the Escalade.

"Where the hell did you get this thing? It needs an elevator," Grand said, sizing up how she was going to get into it.

"It's complicated. Let's just say mine's in the shop," I answered and hoisted her up.

"This is a pimpmobile. I feel like a gangsta. I need shades and bling," she said as she played with all the gadgets on the dashboard. Soon the running lights were pulsing rainbow colors to the beat of '40s swing music from the satellite radio.

We started nearest the old house and drove by over fifteen possible locker locations, all to no avail. To me, each new one started to look like all the others.

"This isn't getting us anywhere. Maybe we should try again after you've had a chance to think about it," I said.

"Nonsense. At my age, I could die in my sleep, then where will you be with no way to solve my last big case? My fans won't hear of it. I need a drink. All this pimp cruising's making me thirsty."

"There's a gas station coming up. I can stop and get us a soda."

"No, I want a vanilla shake. Wait! That's it. The storage locker's by the White Castle next to the golf course." White Castles, home of the slider, were a St. Louis staple. "I made Claude get me a large vanilla to make up for having to go to the nasty storage place."

I punched the info into the fancy GPS in the Escalade and bingo. The Stor-Inn was located across from the golf course and right next to the White Castle. We whipped through the drive-thru to get Grand her shake and then pulled into the storage facility.

We arrived quickly, and I pulled the beast of a car into two parking spots. The office looked open, so we made a beeline for it. A little bell rang as we entered. The office walls were all a light gray. Filing cabinets lined most of the available space. A single poster on team motivation hung crookedly on the wall.

A man appeared from the back room but didn't immediately notice us. He was trying to shove more paper into one of the already-overfilled file cabinets, and I saw two white earbuds sticking out of his ears, explaining why he hadn't heard the bell.

"Holy cannoli!" he shouted when he spied us as he turned from the cabinet. Reflexively, he clutched the paper to his chest and took several exaggerated deep breaths. "You gave me a heart attack," he said, taking the ear buds out of his ears and walking around the counter. He wore a brown polyester suit with pants that were too short and a crooked speckled tie in peach. His head was long and narrow, his brown hair spiky, and he had a large round nose.

"He looks like that Muppet," Grand whispered.

I covered my laugh by clearing my throat.

"Hi, I'm hoping you can help us," I said.

The man took a minute to size us up. I wasn't sure if he saw dollar signs or easy marks, but a glint came to his eye. "And what size unit are you interested in?" he asked, setting the paper down and pulling a laminated card from under the counter. "I would suggest one of our more spacious, climate-controlled units." He pointed at a picture of one of the higher-priced lockers.

"Oh, we aren't renting. We seem to have misplaced our key to our unit."

The twinkle quickly left the man's eyes, and he shoved the laminated card back under the counter. We followed him as he walked silently to the computer.

"Name and unit number," he said in a demanding tone as he began pecking at the keys.

"Well, that's part of the problem," I said. "Grand here can't quite recall the unit number."

"Lovely," he said and pecked a bit harder at the keys. "Does she at least remember her name?"

"Listen, sonny, you won't be a vision of youthful innocence forever, so don't go getting snarky with the old folks," Grand said.

"Theodora Waters," I added before he could reply and gave him a smile.

"There's no one by that name with a storage unit here. Are you sure you're at the right facility? We do have several locations."

"Of course I'm sure, you nitwit. You've got the milkshakes," Grand replied, as if that cleared it all up.

"Maybe it's under her boyfriend's name," I said.

"She has a boyfriend?" He eyed Grand with more scrutiny.

"You're never too old for a little hot loving, sonny, not that you're scoring much with the babes in a suit like that."

"Claude Pedersky," I said.

The man stood still, blinking at me silently for a moment, before he clapped his hands together loudly. His entire demeanor transformed as a look of thrilled excitement came over him. "Oh my God! You're her! It's you, the badass mobster-killing grandma," he said and rushed around the counter to begin shaking Grand's hand. "I should have recognized you."

"It's the hat. Usually, I'm wearing my detective's visor when we're on a case."

"It's such an honor to meet you. I can't wait to tell the others."

"Others?" I asked.

"Oh yeah, the Pedersky locker is the most famous locker we've ever had. The place off Delmar once had a pro football player that got busted for a domestic, but a mobster murderer trumps them hands down. Everyone here's been following your case. We were so relieved when the coppers didn't arrest you too." His brow creased in concern as he studied Grand.

"Well, we need to get access to Claude's locker, if you could help us, please," I said, trying to bring us back to the matter at hand.

"Oh, I'm sorry. I can't do that," he said with a frown toward Grand. "Her name's not officially on the account. I could get in a lot of trouble."

"But you know us. You know they were together," I said.

"Sonny, don't you want to help free Claude and take down more of the mob?"

His eyes widened to the size of saucers, and he stood up straight. "There's something from the mob in there? That's why those guys tried to break in, isn't it? I tried to tell Marvin that. He just thought it was because of all the publicity. Do I need a gun?"

"Maybe," I replied before Grand could give anything more away. "We really aren't at liberty to say, with this new case still pending and all."

"You're on another case?" He shifted back and forth on his feet, mumbling to himself for a long time before he spoke again. "Look, I'd love to help, but the others would kill me if I gave this away before the viewing. I'd totally be toast." He wrung his hands.

"What do you mean?" I asked.

"Well, the account has fallen in arrears. It's going up for auction, and my boss is sure it'll bring in the big bucks. We might even get some out-of-state buyers instead of just the regulars."

"Auction?" I asked.

"Yeah, we have one practically every weekend. All the storage places do. There's big business in unpaid lockers."

"Don't you watch *Storage Wars*?" Grand asked.

"The Pedersky locker is scheduled for the weekend after next, and it's all the buzz on the internet," the man said.

"Can't I just pay the balance?" Not that I knew where I would get that kind of money, but I was sure we'd figure something out.

"Like I said, your grandmother isn't on the account. So you can't, or the whole auction business would just be turned on its head, people paying off other people's balances and then demanding access to the locker instead of letting them go to the highest bidder."

I took a deep breath. Grand was frantically sucking down her milkshake.

"Okay. When's this auction, and how does it work?" I asked

"Like I said, the auction's the weekend after next. But because of all the notoriety, we're having a viewing in a few days." He took a flyer from behind the counter.

In a flair of blood red, a swirly font announced the date and time of both the final sale and a viewing. Hot dogs and soda were free of charge.

"What's a viewing?" I asked.

"Usually no one gets to see what's in the locker until the day of the event. We cut the lock and open the unit, and then everyone has fifteen minutes to view the contents before the auction. But with this, the boss wanted to generate more interest, so he's opening it up a couple of days ahead of time."

"So anyone can pick through the stuff to see how much they want to spend?"

"Well, that's the catch. Not just anyone can get in. You have to be bonded for the auction. In other words, cashola up front to get a look, and even then, you can't go into the unit."

"What do you mean, 'you can't go into it'?" I asked.

"That's part of the fun. The buyers have to guess what's in the unit from viewing it from outside the door."

"Sounds like stupidity meant to swindle people," Grand said.

"Yeah." The man smiled happily, like he was agreeing what a great method it was for parting people with their cash.

"Lovely," I said.

We thanked the man for his time and took the number we would have to call to be made a part of the viewing list. I wasn't entirely sure what we were going to do, but I was quite convinced Simon the mobster was not going to appreciate everyone seeing his business.

Chapter 12: I Could Have Danced All Night

Before I tackled the Toucci dinner, I needed to armor up with as much information as I could get my hands on. That meant going on another not-date with Fletcher Reid.

The Fox Theater was one of St. Louis's leading historical sites. Commissioned by the movie mogul William Fox in 1927, the playhouse originally opened as a film emporium in 1929. I marveled at the beautifully loomed red-and-gold elephant carpet and the brightly restored blue-and-gold mural on the ceiling as I walked to my meeting.

An usher opened the door for me and pointed to a head of hair sticking up over one of the center seats ten rows from the stage. Several other people sat a few rows forward. A man in the group talked frantically with his hands while a petite woman with a severe bun scrambled to keep up with notes. The familiar songs from *My Fair Lady* floated through the theater.

"Hiya, beautiful. Glad you could make it," Fletcher said. He smiled that bright smile of his, his blue eyes lighting up in the stage lighting. I could have sworn they got bluer each time I saw him, but maybe that was the reflection from the brilliantly painted ceiling mural.

"I should be the one thanking you for doing this on such short notice," I said and sat down next to him.

He pulled himself upright and perused me. "Looking good, as usual. I wasn't expecting our next date quite this soon, so I did have to scramble a bit, but I think I worked it out," he said, waving his arms out over the performance in front of us.

"I didn't realize you worked the theater scene."

"I don't, but Betsy in Features owed me one for helping with a broken-down car. Plus, she likes your grandmother." He took out his phone and started pushing buttons.

"Doesn't everyone?" I asked with a grin. It was becoming very apparent that Grand had developed quite the following since the shooting.

"How's she doing?" he asked, the genuine concern in his voice coming through.

"Claude won't see her. She's trying to be a trouper about it, but I know it's affecting her."

"Sorry to hear that, Stretch. I know she's had a tough couple of years." His eyes met mine as he put his phone back.

I took a breath to keep from becoming overly emotional. Fletcher was right. Of all of us, Grand had been having the worst of times. First was the death of my grandfather then Dad's incarceration, which resulted in not only the imprisonment of her son for a crime he hadn't committed but also the loss of her house, her care home, and the majority of her possessions. We'd thought her meeting Claude was a good thing, until we all ended up mixed up with mobsters, Claude having murdered a serial killer in cold blood.

Before I could respond, a woman rolled a cart into the aisle.

"I didn't know we were on a flight," I said.

"Well, I know you have dinner with Toucci tonight, so I didn't want to overload you with food. But a date that includes a good show should at least have snacks," he said.

The cart was full of every movie-house food you could imagine—popcorn, soft pretzels, candy, and nachos. I took the popcorn and a soda. Fletcher grabbed a pretzel and thanked the cart woman.

Before he sat down, he took a thick set of papers from his back pocket. "These are for you."

The papers were a complete summary of every article ever written about the Touccis or their family businesses. I had told Fletcher over the phone that the result of my lunch was further involvement with the Touccis and that I needed more information. He said he wasn't surprised but insisted we meet in person to discuss it.

"I assume you'll get more from McPhee's profile than that, but it might come in handy," he said.

After setting my popcorn down, I scanned the pages. He was right. Burns had a more exhaustive dossier. The Toucci enterprise was more expansive than I had expected. But the information provided some of the missing bits, the "whys" behind the "whats."

I put the papers in my bag to read in detail before dinner and took up my popcorn. The stage was full of people in beautifully clad outfits ready to rehearse a dance number at a party. Eliza Doolittle's formfitting, bejeweled dress was being adjusted at the hem while the orchestra warmed up, and the director ushered everyone to their places. The scene began as the orchestra played.

"So, are you going to tell me what's going on?" he asked, stealing some of my popcorn.

"Unofficially, off the record?" I asked and tried to scrunch my face into a stern glare.

"Of course."

"Until it's not," I said, eyeing him out of the corner of my eye. I did not need my involvement with the Touccis hitting the press. Still, as Fletcher was Gillian Mather's other best friend, I felt like he had as much right to know we might be able to get more information about what had happened as Burns and me.

"Consider my silence a gift for Grand. You have my word that not a hint of your Toucci involvement will hit my column." He made a sign over his heart.

"Okay, but you're not going to like it."

"If that's true, Burns must have hit the roof." He laughed at that and grabbed more popcorn.

I took a deep breath, considering how much information I could give him. "Saul Toucci is offering to exchange something he has about Gillian's death and my dad's imprisonment for a favor."

I felt his body tense next to me and heard his intake of air. He did not exhale right away but held on to it, as though the air could shield him.

After a minute, he slowly exhaled. "What kind of favor?"

"A partially illegal one that requires my expertise but nothing that would compromise me directly or you would morally object to."

He steepled his fingers in front of his face, his elbows resting on both armrests. I watched Eliza dance about her bedroom, being changed from her beautiful ball gown into bed clothes as she and her handmaids sang about how she could have danced all night.

"He wants you to look at a body," Fletcher said.

"Well, I suppose you're not an investigative reporter for nothing. But seriously, Fletcher, this could upend the whole thing for us. This is the one shot we have to get whatever he thinks is important information about Gillian. If you go blabbing this in the paper, we all get nothing. I didn't know Gillian, but I've learned enough about her through this whole mess to know that she knew when a story wasn't ready to tell. This one isn't."

We sat silently for a long time, watching the rehearsal. I didn't think the not-date was going the way he had hoped.

"Okay," he said finally and turned to me. "Without getting into details, what's the gist of your assignment?"

"I feel like I've already told you too much."

"The Toucci empire is massive and complicated. I can't give you the right information support if I don't have a target area," he said.

I considered that while I sucked down my pop. He was right. I was going to have to tell him something if he was going to be able to provide me the information I needed. I considered my words carefully.

"Let's just say Saul isn't sure he can trust those closest to him right now. He wants me to help identify whether someone in his family may have double-crossed him while simultaneously fanning a mob war with the Palmeros."

"Jesus." He blew out another breath and ran his hand through his floppy blond mop. "The Palmeros?"

"The body even came with its own sombrero."

"The Palmeros are serious business, Kat. Not that Toucci isn't, but I get the feeling he would consider harming you almost rude at this point. The Mexicans are knee-deep with the cartels and would have no problem taking off that pretty little head of yours."

"Saul won't let that happen," I said confidently.

"You trust him." He said it as firmly as I had, a statement, not a question.

"It's weird, but I do. I think this incident has really struck him hard, at his heart. He hopes he's wrong, that it's not someone in his family selling him out, but that would mean he's on the eve of a full-scale mob war with a notoriously brutal opponent. He seems... weary."

I slurped down the rest of my pop a little too loudly, causing the show's director to glare back at me. "So, what's not in your summary or Burns's dossier that I need to know to help Saul Toucci sort out whether or not there's a rat in his familia?" I finally asked, putting down the empty cup and picking back up the popcorn.

He didn't turn to look at me, but seeming to have come to a decision, he leaned back in his seat and crossed his long, gangly legs, stretching them out into the aisle. "The most important thing for you to know about Saul Toucci is that none of his kids are directly involved in the business. His daughter's an author in New York. His son has taken the Silicon Valley start-up world by storm. They had a third child, but the boy was killed in a boating accident. Really shook the whole family. They have a single granddaughter who is more interested in plants than mob power or family politics."

"Wow." I wasn't sure how to process all of that. Saul had told me some of it but not the full extent.

"Yeah. Saul is the oldest of three. He has a brother and a sister. They all have kids, and most do work for the business. But it's not just a nice story. All of that means only one thing will matter as you contemplate family dynamics." He looked over at me, touching my arm to get me to look him in the eyes. "Toucci doesn't have an heir apparent to his empire, but there are a bunch of wannabes."

A position worth killing for, I thought. The concern on Fletcher's face told me he thought it too.

Chapter 13: Appetizers

Since I'd spent some time with Saul, I at least felt more prepared to choose appropriate attire for the evening's event. I changed into a sleek black Donna Karan, which was perfect for daytime business but easily accessorized for a nighttime dinner party. Despite the circumstances, I had to admit it was a joy to be slipping into another of my old friends.

By the time I'd finished attempting to do something appropriate with my hair, a truly futile task, the senior Care-a-van had picked Grand up for bingo. I took the alone time to review everything Burns, Fletcher, and Fergus had provided me on the Toucci family. I knew Burns would have a suspect board set up for us to go through after dinner, but I wanted to be able to put faces with bios before anyone realized I was scoping them out.

Not wanting to be late, I gingerly climbed back up into the pimpmobile, which was quite the feat in my suit and heels, and headed to Ladue, a small city in St. Louis County.

When you were poor, like we were, you lumped everyone into the category of people with money and people without. At that juncture, we were clearly people without. However, when you had any means, categorization was much more complicated. There were tiers of rich. In fact, before my dad's imprisonment, we would never have considered ourselves rich. We were "comfortably upper-middle class." We certainly weren't old money. Of course, on days when I had to stuff toilet paper from the morgue into my purse because we couldn't afford two-ply on my salary, I was made painfully aware of what a crock that sentiment was. We had been rich.

But we were still not Saul Toucci, Ladue rich. Ladue was the wealthiest city in all of Missouri and one of the top richest cities in the country. Anyone with any power lived in Ladue, from heads of corporations such as Anheuser-Busch, Emerson Electric, and Pillsbury to Senator John Danforth and NFL player Otis Brown. It was the home of old money and new mansions.

The GPS had me turn into an opening blocked by an overly large iron gate. The impeccable detailed workmanship of the wrought iron was highlighted by the intricately carved life-size reproduction of the Pieta, Mary cradling the dead body of Christ, sculpted into the middle of the gate. Above the sculpture was the ornately fashioned metal word "*Figurato*," meaning a place of refuge or sanctuary.

Thankful that the windows in the Escalade actually worked, unlike those in my Escort, I rolled mine down and tried to decipher which button to push on the fancy security system protruding out of the post in the driveway. Before I could, the blank security screen came alive, and Fergus's face appeared in the monitor.

"Nice wheels, sweetheart," he said in his raspy voice over the speaker.

"It's a long story."

"Follow the drive all the way to the house. Someone will meet you and take you into the study. I have a few things to take care of before dinner."

The monitor went blank again, and the large iron gates began to swing open, cutting Mary and Jesus in half. The long, meandering blacktop driveway was surrounded on both sides with blooming oak trees. It reminded me of that scene in the movie *The Sound of Music* when the baron is driving up the drive to his home with the countess from their trip abroad. I kept half expecting to see blond children dressed in curtain remnants swinging from the upper branches.

The driveway ended in a large circle that curved in front of an elegant Colonial with large columns supporting a portico. I parked the Escalade in the circle and, getting out, left the keys, assuming the staff would move it if necessary.

The estate was massive. Neighbors couldn't be seen in any direction. The grounds were surrounded by a beautiful forest. At the center of the circle drive was a large fountain. The sound of the whooshing water helped to calm my nerves. I took a big gulp and headed for the front door.

Before making it up the last of a few steps to the large double front door, the right side opened. A small woman in a light-gray dress covered by a white apron stood waiting. Her dyed-red hair was in a tight bun that seemed to pull at the wrinkles on her weathered face.

"Miss Katerine?" the woman asked, dropping the *H* in my name and dawning a bright smile that made her whole appearance seem lighter. She opened her arms to welcome me, took one of my arms in both of hers, and kissed me on both cheeks.

"I am not normally so forward, but I am so excited to meet someone so important to Fergus. Come, come," she said and pulled me into the house.

As I was being tugged into the house, I noticed movement behind the curtains in the area over the garage. I was being watched. Maybe whoever it was had been watching the night Nile was killed.

The inside of the Toucci manor was as grand as the outside led one to believe it would be. The foyer sported gorgeous Italian marble. As I was escorted down a hallway, I passed a Louis XV entry cassone commode, a gilt baroque Lombardo mirror, and a Lombardy settee. The art history major in me was in antiquity heaven.

"I am very sure Fergus will be quite glad to see you. He has been speaking of your visit all afternoon," the maid said. She was a short woman with white Chuck Taylors and a large gap between her front two teeth.

I wasn't quite sure what to think of the comments about Fergus. Besides the quick five-minute conversation he and I had had outside the restaurant, I'd had zero time to contemplate the situation of being Fergus's supposed girlfriend. I wondered what impact the development would have on my already increasingly complicated romantic life. I also wondered if Fergus and I would be able to pull the charade off. The maid seemed very excited about my arrival.

"Well, Fergus always speaks so highly of all his coworkers. I look forward to getting to know you all a bit better, Ms...?"

"Oh, forgive me. I am Georgia."

Before I could respond to Georgia, I could hear DC's voice bellowing into the hallway. Entering the large gathering room, I immediately spied DC standing in the middle of the room, a black silk cape billowing behind him—not a cape like the one that belonged to his superhero outfit but one more fitting a count. He completed the outfit with a crushed velvet burgundy suit with black lapels and a matching black bow tie. I was sure to get the story of his chosen ensemble before too long. Surrounding DC were two women, one clearly of Italian or Mediterranean heritage and one clearly not.

"Katherine!" DC practically ran to me once he noticed me standing in the doorway.

Before he could pull me in, I turned to Georgia, taking her hands in mine. "So nice meeting you. I hope we can chat more next time." I kissed her on both cheeks.

One of the women in the room gasped loudly enough that both Georgia and I could hear, causing Georgia to blush and run from the room. Any investigator worth their salt knew it was the help who knew all of a family's dirty secrets. Regardless of the etiquette or family propriety, I needed to stake a claim early. Besides, I wasn't quite sure where Fergus stood in the hierarchy of things. He was clearly help, but neither Saul nor Fergus had shown any qualms about him attending a family dinner, as if it were a frequent occasion.

Steeling my features, I turned to face the lion's den.

"It's very gauche to fraternize with the help. Although I suppose we should expect it, given who you are dating," said a severe-looking woman in a black Bruno Cuccinelli culotte suit. I recognized her from her photo immediately as Saul's sister in-law, Francesca Toucci, Nile's mother. Salt-and-pepper hair peeked from beneath a black pillbox hat with a short lace veil concealing a bun. The small lump of it pushed up on the top of the hat.

"Francesca, your claws are showing. Behave," said the softer-looking woman next to her. She wore a black Armani pinstripe with shiny black jewel-spiked Girotti heels. I could feel my skin turn a bit greener with shoe envy. A soft gray-blond bob framed her face. Tiny wrinkle lines flowed around her eyes and mouth. She was Saul's sister. "I'm Marion Walker, and you must be Fergus's girlfriend, Katherine, yes?" The file on Marion had been much thinner than the rest of the Touccis. I knew her husband, the father of her children, Lucia and Marcus, had been killed in Vietnam and that she ran her own business, an antique shop. But that was the extent of what I had. Neither Fergus nor Burns had pointed to her as a threat.

"Of course this is Katherine," DC said, pulling me into the room. "My very best friend, who I can't thank enough for connecting me to this grand opportunity. We are all going to be one big happy family! Well, maybe not *family* family..."

"We've been through this countless times, Marcus. The price-earnings analysis doesn't support your conclusion." A slender woman in an exquisitely tailored gray suit stomped confidently through the door, blew past me, and made a beeline for the drink counter. Her long brown hair brushed over her shoulders.

"You keep telling yourself that, Lucia. I'm tired of hearing about all this eco crap," Marcus said.

"There's nothing in the family charter that says we can't worry about the environment as well," Lucia retorted in a tone meant for a small child.

I made a note to ask Neutron to see if he could figure out what business issue they were arguing about.

"Must your offspring always argue like adolescents in front of company?" Francesca asked Marion, waving her glass in the direction of me and DC.

"Lucia, Marcus, please," Marion replied.

"Oh, company!" Lucia said and turned from her drink prep, wine glass in hand, toward me and DC. "You must be Fergus's girl-friend." Her eyes swept over me almost seductively, as though I were a Chippendale at bachelor auction. *What is that about?* Her eyes moved back up and froze on my face. "You are not what I expected at all."

"Only 8.5 percent of all US marriages are in the May-December category," I stated and then tried to smile.

"Definitely not what I expected," she said and then turned back to her brother. "Don't think that we're finished with this conversation, Marcus. Uncle Saul does not need your dissension."

"Whatever," he said with an exaggerated New England accent that I couldn't quite place. Marcus looked fresh off the Jersey shore—spiked black hair, bulging pectorals protruding under a silky white T-shirt covered by a butterscotch leather jacket, an earring in one ear, and a gold chain around his neck. The accent was part Boston, part Jersey maybe but hard to pin down.

"Don't mind them," he said, crossing over to me with an out-stretched hand. "I'm Marcus. Nobody told me Fergus bagged a hot-tie."

I took his hand to shake it. I wasn't sure whether I should feel flattered or horrified.

"Marcus!" Marion and Lucia screamed at the same time.

"What? I'm sure Fergus would be thrilled to know we all think he has good taste," he said before kissing my hand lightly.

"Hands off the merchandise, you perv," Fergus said, entering the room and crossing to me before I blurted out something else inappropriate. "Hiya, sweet cheeks." He put his arm around my waist and kissed my temple.

"Well, she is definitely a fine-looking woman, Fergie. Can I call you Fergie?" DC asked. His rescue attempt would have been cute if it hadn't had the effect of causing Fergus to shoot him a death glare.

A clatter in the far corner of the room drew everyone's attention. What appeared to be a young boy was clambering down a tall ladder to retrieve something. I stomped on DCs foot before he could gasp as we both realized the boy was actually Neutron, complete with McPhee Security uniform shirt.

"Sorry," he muttered before scrambling for the tool he had dropped and climbing back up the ladder.

"Uncle's upgrading security again?" Marcus asked.

I looked around at everyone processing Neutron's presence. None of the people were viewing it casually. I could see everyone tense slightly, even Francesca, who was the best at hiding emotions.

"It appears that way," Francesca answered.

"Can't blame him, I suppose," Lucia said then took a sip of her wine. "After all the recent unpleasantness."

Francesca scoffed loudly. "Leave it to a Walker to describe the death of my dear son as 'unpleasantness.' I know you're thrilled that he's gone, as that increases your standing with Saul, but you could at least show a little couth." Francesca turned on her heel and stormed toward the bar servant before anyone could respond.

Marion sighed, and Lucia looked genuinely horrified.

"I didn't mean it that way, Auntie," she yelled across the room to Francesca's back.

Francesca waved a dismissive hand above her head without turning around.

I started to ask a question, probing about said unpleasantness, when Fergus cut me off. "I came to let everyone know it was time for dinner," Fergus announced and pushed me gently toward the door to the dining room.

Chapter 14: Main Course

The room was beautifully appointed in a baroque motif. Golds, creams, and blues filled the ornate space, from the chairs to the wall panels adorned with raised and gilded scrolls and flourishes. Curved legs and wooden inlays added warmth and flow. Cream accents on the walls and fabrics softened the look. All of it sparkled under the glimmer of a massive, gorgeous crystal chandelier.

Saul was already seated at the head of the table when we arrived. He chatted to a young woman in a bright flowered dress two seats down from him. An antique wooden high chair stood at the far corner. I made a point to remember to ask Marion about the piece later, assuming it was one of hers. I followed Fergus down the long table to two open seats. DC was sitting next to the woman Saul chatted with.

A petite woman dressed in a black lace Ralph Lauren jumpsuit entered the room, seeming to ignore everyone present. A toddler with curly sandy-brown hair struggled in her arms. She walked toward the high chair and began securing the child into it. "If I'm going to be forced to sit through this farce, I don't understand why we couldn't have it earlier and more in line with Camila's schedule," the woman said to Saul without even a greeting.

Saul ignored her in favor of cooing at the smiling child. When her task of buckling in her child was complete, she turned to face me, and I recognized Nile's widow, Joni.

Before we could be introduced, Francesca arrived, kissed her grandchild, and slid into the seat next to Saul.

Marion, Lucia, and Marcus filed in next and took places at the other end of the table.

"Hello, Joni," Marion greeted her.

"We're not going to pretend to be civil for the sake of the company, are we?" Joni asked.

"Yes, I should have realized that basic civility was beyond you, even given the circumstances," Marion said.

Behind them, a tall, slim boy sauntered into the room with a camera so glued to his face that I almost missed his wire-rimmed glasses.

"Jackson, you know the rules," Francesca admonished him. "No filming in the dining room."

The boy sighed loudly as he lowered the camera to his side. "That's a stupid rule," he said.

"Jackson." Francesca's voice went up an octave.

"Fine. It's an *insipid* rule," Jackson restated, apparently aware of the source of the reprimand and headed toward the empty seat between Francesca and Joni.

"Katherine, Mr. Clayborne, I don't believe you've met the rest of my family," Saul said and proceeded to make introductions to the newcomers.

"It's a pleasure to meet all of you," I said. "Thank you for inviting me into your home."

"The harlot says, as if we had a choice," Joni said barely audibly, because she said it half into her water glass. She was the only one at the table not drinking wine.

"I don't think you're in any position to be throwing out accusations," Marion said before I could reply.

"Katherine and Mr. Clayborne would not be here if Fergus and I were not confident of their loyalties," Saul said. His words had been chosen carefully, and he looked at each of his family groups to ensure they understood the intended meaning—DC and I were to be trusted.

"So we're all going to embrace this insane delusion, pretend this makes sense, and welcome the gold-digging bimbo and co with open arms?" Joni asked, pointing at me and DC. She obviously wasn't buying my relationship with Fergus, but I couldn't tell if it was something specific about me or general skepticism. I wondered how she knew we were faking it and if she had guessed what we were actually doing there.

"Ha," Marion said. "Those are some choices words for you to be flinging about."

I was going to ask Marion what she meant but was instead cut off again by Fergus. "Have a seat, doll. You're going to love the appetizer." Fergus shoved a large bite of brie brochette into my mouth before I could get a word out.

"I can assure you Katherine and DC are not after Fergus's money," Saul said.

I tried to control my surprise over the admission that Fergus had money and silently wondered how much the mob paid. He did say they had good health insurance when Wheezer was passing out in my apartment.

"Aw, of course not," DC said. "Fergie and Kat and have been like lovesick puppies since they met in the frozen-food section. Isn't that right?"

I watched the whole room almost collectively choke on their drinks.

Joni looked irritated by the whole thing, while Lucia aimed a smirk at us. Marcus leered, and Francesca fussed with her granddaughter, largely ignoring the whole conversation. It was only Marion who seemed to be incensed beyond what the situation called for. I didn't think she and Fergus were particularly close.

"Well, I think it's lovely that Fergus has found love after all these years," Elise, Saul's granddaughter in the soft-pink flowered dress, said. All eyes turned toward her in surprise. "No one should have to be so lonely just because of the career they've chosen or the family they were born into."

Before DC could add to our love narrative, Fergus called for more food and drink. The conversation turned lighter after that, but it seemed every time DC or I tried to ask a question or offer a comment during the conversation, Fergus interrupted. I understood that he was playing the possessive boyfriend, but his behavior was starting to make it look more like I had daddy issues than a boyfriend.

I thought I'd be able to wrangle the situation back when the main course arrived, but when he began to feed me bites of the meal from his own plate anytime I ventured into a conversation, I almost choked on the chicken.

"Can I film you?" Jackson asked, pointing his camera at Fergus and me. "Not that I'm into romances, but you never know what you might capture."

Fergus coughed loudly, sputtering on his wine. I took that as an opportunity to get a word out.

"Do you film often?" I asked.

"Little moron's never without that thing," Marcus cut in, simultaneously stuffing a large bite of picada into his mouth.

"Marcus," Marion cautioned him.

"What? It's true," Marcus shoved off his mother's warning.

"Well, I have to," Jackson answered, turning back to me. "I'm filming a documentary on Uncle Saul. Everyone knows the best documentaries have spontaneous footage."

Silverware clinked on several plates. Clearly the topic of Jackson's documentary was a sore point. I'd have to remember to ask Saul or Fergus about it later. Maybe Jackson had inadvertently filmed something important.

Fergus took Jackson's commentary as an opportunity to change the subject. "Elise, you may be interested to know that Mr. Clayborne has developed several of his own strains of medicinal marijuana," he said.

"Really? How fascinating. What breeding methods are you using?" she asked.

The question elicited an audible groan from several members of the family. DC was thrilled, however, and launched into an intense explanation of recurrent backcrossing and trait fixing.

Sometimes I forgot how talented DC was when it came to plants. As he threw out technical terms about crossbreeding and pollination strains, I was reminded that underneath all that purple velvet, a botany genius existed. Elise was enthralled.

Before the two could go further, Marcus chimed in, "So, you're really going to do it then, Uncle?"

I wasn't sure what "it" was, but the question seemed to capture the attention of everyone at the table, including Fergus. He paused in his feeding me. The room hushed, waiting for Saul's response.

Saul glanced at DC and me before he put down his wine glass and turned his attention to his nephew. "You know how I feel about the illicit drug trade, Marcus. My mind will not be dissuaded from that."

"But now's the best time. With the coppers all confused about which products are legal and which aren't, the cartels are making a killing. Government taxation is driving the price up for everyone."

"The Toucci family has never been involved with the cartels, and we never will be." He paused and looked at each member of the family as if wanting to drive the point home. No one responded, and he picked up his wine glass. "The emerging legal marijuana market, however, is another matter. But I will not entertain any further discussion on getting into the drug trade."

"Gang violence is actually down 12.5 percent in areas where marijuana has been legalized," Lucia said. She was a woman after my own heart.

Marcus slammed his napkin down on the table, clearly not as impressed as I was. "Yeah, 'cause decreasing gang violence is part of the family charter."

"I hear that the Palmeros have shifted almost their entire operation to the marijuana trade," Francesca said.

Strangely, it was DC who raised an eyebrow at that statement. I wondered how Francesca even knew such a thing.

"The Palmeros had best watch their backs," Joni said from across the table then took a large drink from her glass. She'd been quiet for most of the meal, tending to Camila and throwing out the occasional insult.

"Hear! Hear!" Marcus toasted.

"Marcus, we don't know that it was the Palmeros who killed Nile," Lucia said quietly and almost shyly, eyeing me and DC as if she realized it wasn't exactly appropriate dinner conversation, but she didn't want to miss an opportunity to poke at her brother about it.

"Alejandro Palmero came to Uncle Saul personally." She furrowed her brow.

That was new information. I knew that Saul had struck a deal with the Palmeros, but I hadn't realized it was directly with Alejandro Palmero. From everything I had read, Palmero was not an easy man.

Despite everything I'd been given on the Toucci family, I also still didn't know who had found the body or where it had been discovered. Clearly Fergus wasn't going to let me get those questions out. Not that family dinner was the proper place to ask them, but still, it could be my chance.

"They beat him to death. And then ran over him. You saw the body. How much more proof do you need that they did it than the sombrero over his—" Marcus said louder, frustration apparent in his voice.

"I've told you that I am taking the necessary steps with the Palmeros to properly investigate Nile's murder," Saul cut in. "I know this is a difficult time for all of us, but it is not a time to be rash."

"Rash is convening a family dinner when a killer could be among us," Marion said and eyed Joni.

"Oh, you'd just love to pin this on me, wouldn't you, Marion? Cover up your own shortcomings while putting those mutant morons of yours above my claim," Joni said and pointed at Marcus and Lucia. She threw her napkin on the table and stood abruptly.

I made a note to ask Burns and team what shortcomings Joni knew about that Marion might be covering up.

"Well, if the shoe fits, Joni," Lucia chimed in surprisingly.

Even Marcus sat a little taller, leaning in toward his mother in a protective stance.

"I won't continue to sit through this farce," Joni said to Saul. Without another word to Marion or anyone else, she grabbed Camila from the high chair and stormed back out of the room.

"As much as it pains me to say, Saul, I have to agree with Joni. This dinner seems premature," Marion said. "Katherine, it was lovely meeting you, and I hope we can do it again soon under less trying circumstances. Come, children. We should go."

I looked up to see Jackson following her with his camera.

"Jackson!" Francesca admonished him.

Before Saul or I could say anything, Fergus cut in again. "How about dessert, doll?"

Chapter 15: Fruit Salad and Stranger Danger

I left the Toucci residence not long after the blowup with Joni and Marion. My stomach was overfull from the bananas Foster that Fergus had force-fed me to keep me from talking to Francesca. Before heading to see Burns for the debrief on dinner, I stopped at the bingo hall and picked up Grand.

She rode in unusual silence. I studied her, wondering if something had gone wrong at bingo. *Or is it something with her health that she doesn't want to tell me?* After my grandfather's death, she had spiraled lower than I ever thought I could see her. It went on for over a year. The doctors said it was the early stages of Alzheimer's, but it felt more like the wound from a broken heart. She wandered out into traffic, screaming, one night. That was when we made the decision to put her in the assisted-living home.

Then she met Claude. He was nothing like my grandfather but exactly what she needed. Where Grandfather had been boisterous, Claude was quiet. Claude's actions did his talking. The dead mobster he'd shot point-blank seemingly with no motive could attest to that. So could his constantly bringing her flowers, taking her "shopping" at our old house, and making sure we had both a roof over our heads and a way to sustain it with my job at the morgue. He and Grand connected with a rightness about them that made me feel a tad jealous. I couldn't get lucky in love once. Grand had managed to find it twice. Perhaps it was a testament to the old that they understood that hearts could hold more than one love.

Still, she wasn't young anymore, and with Dad and Claude both in the clink, Mom and I both worried.

"Bad night with the cards?" I asked.

"I've been thinking," she said, taking out her fake cigarette, and gave it a puff. Fake cigs meant serious conversation.

"Okay." I watched her looking out the window.

"Maybe we should give the body back and pass on this case."

That was unexpected. She'd been hopped-up to get investigating the dead body almost since the freezer hit the ground in our apartment. I should have known something was up, though. She hadn't put back on her detective visor when she came out of the bingo hall. She'd brought a purple one that matched her flowered dress, but it must still be in her bag.

"Any particular reason?" I asked, giving her the side-eye as I cut across traffic.

She didn't turn to me but talked to the passing scenery instead. "Morrie Sutton has a new grandkid with a head the shape of a squished watermelon. Brought pictures and ate up a whole round of bingo time showing 'em off to that gaggle of cooing old biddies."

"What does Morrie Sutton's fruit-ninja grandkid have to do with our freezersicle?"

"We're never going to get our own fruit basket with you working for the mob. None of us is getting younger."

Babies. This is about my having babies. I should have known the recent mob business would only slow down the marriage-and-kids nagging for so long. "Do I need to remind you that I'm no longer engaged and that even if I were, given our current conditions, we're not exactly in a position to add on anything, let alone a fruit basket?"

"Well, I can't say I'm disappointed that you've cut it off with that dweeb, but you've got a couple of hunks on the hook now. Surely one of 'em can produce some prime fruit stock."

"Grand, I'm a long way from popping a pineapple with anyone. Even if I were... involved... with one of the hotties, the situation with Dad is too dangerous to even contemplate fruit salad. I know Dad and now Claude landing in prison has been a shock. But at some point, we have to start admitting that maybe there's more going on here than Dad's told us."

She took a long drag on the fake cigarette. "I know. Waters women don't live in denial. Even your mother has come around."

At that, I sighed. It was true. My never-had-a-paying-job-a-day-in-her-life socialite mother was running the events business for a multimillion-dollar conglomerate. "True. Even if she is working for a twat, at the rate we're banking money now, we'll be able to move out of that rat-trap postage-stamp apartment soon." I rolled that around in my head. Finding a new place meant accepting we might never be moving back into our old house. *But moving forward is good, right?*

"Don't either of you go getting ideas. I'm not going back to Shady Pines, not with all that's going on with Claude and Clarke. They'll both rot in there if we leave it up to them."

I giggled at that.

"I think it's something to do with this locker business," she added, pulling out her detective visor.

"Well, there's only one option to wrangle that clue."

"The Rambo hottie," she said with a smile and turned on some swing music on the radio.

I was thankful for the reprieve from the baby talk. We rode in silence for the rest of the trip, but I noticed she had dug out her visor and put it on.

I pulled into the lot at McPhee Security. If that was going to become the regular thing it seemed to be turning into, I needed my own key card. As it was, I sat at the security gate, waiting for someone to let me in.

"Oh, Ms. Waters, you must be here to see Burn," the man said. He had an armful of papers and looked frazzled. He was good-looking, in a polished, private-school kind of way. Where Burns was ruggedly handsome, the man at the gate was on the pretty-boy side—slick.

"I'm sorry. Who are you?" I asked.

Grand looked like she might whip out the pistol any moment.

"Oh, where are my manners?" He reached a hand out. "Gregory Hardt. I'm Burns's business partner in Ingensys."

Ingensys was the investment arm of the McPhee business. It worked public-private partnerships and government projects in Afghanistan to build schools and infrastructure. Burns had a huge soft spot for the work it did. We didn't talk much about it, mob and security business always taking up so much of our time, but Ingensys wasn't about money for Burns. It was personal.

"You gonna stand there and make moon eyes at my granddaughter, or you are going to be useful and take us to see the lumberjack? I need a Coke after all the action at the bingo," Grand said.

"You must be Kat's grandmother I've been reading so much about." The man's stare took on more scrutiny as he took in Grand.

"That's her, and I'm Gunslinging Bonnie's granddaughter." I smiled at him and waited for him to show us the way. But he didn't. He kept staring at us, looking from me to Grand, as if he were waiting for us to say something more. "I'm sorry. Do you know where we can find Burns?" I asked finally.

"Of course, of course. Follow me." We followed Gregory through several key-carded doors to the large conference room.

"Greg, I wasn't expecting you to be in tonight. Did you need something?" Burns asked, eyeing him intensely.

"No, no, just needed to pick up some files on the Hutton investment. You're working late," he said, glancing at the war room.

"Yeah, a contact of Kat's might have a lead on Gillian's case."

"A lead? I thought that was all settled." Greg's posture stiffened. He moved his head, trying to get a look at what we had up in the room.

After a moment, Greg finally got the hint that Burns wasn't going to respond to the question. "Well, if there's anything I can do to help, you know I'm here for you." His voice went soft, and he looked toward the ground. "Gillian was my friend too."

"Thanks, Greg," Burns said and waited for him to leave. He watched Greg go for longer than expected before turning back around. "Okay, what do we have?" he asked.

Chapter 16: Debrief

"All the cameras are set up and recording at Toucci's, everywhere but his office, per your request," Neutron began.

"I almost ruined my purple velvet when you came spilling down from the rafters," DC said and patted his jacket.

"Sorry. We didn't have time to warn you," Neutron said.

"I trust your meeting with him went well, then?" I asked.

Burns had originally planned to meet Saul after dinner, but a request for a new security installation came in first thing that morning. Burns took it as an opportunity to scope things out before DC and I went in.

"Mr. Toucci is quite persuasive." Burns smirked. "And is very fond of you."

"Oh, great, more fan mobsters," Flynn said.

"It's better than the alternative," Grand replied, and Flynn looked appropriately chastised.

"Well, dinner was something else," DC said. "I'm so full I have a food baby. Men do not look good with food babies."

Burns grinned. "Did we learn anything helpful?"

"Fergus was right. That Joni sure is a piece of work," I said.

"Nile's wife? Neutron, what do we know?" Burns asked and turned toward the screens.

A picture of Joni, Nile, and Camila came on the mega screen at the end of the conference room.

"Joni Baldelli comes from a working-class family," Neutron said. "Mother's a beautician, father worked at the shipyards until a heart attack a few years back. Most notable is that the not-so-happy-couple was in the middle of a nasty divorce. There was a prenup. Joni gets a lot more with Nile dead than she did with him alive and divorced." Court documents flew across the screen.

"According to Fletcher's information, Joni was having an affair with the kid's professor," I said.

Burns frowned at the mention of Fletcher.

"They weren't being shy about it, either, it seems," Neutron said. He put up footage of Joni and a man in various locations, looking cozy.

"I don't know whether that's gutsy or dumb," Flynn said.

"At least they do things together," Neutron said. Apparently, Flynn had still not agreed to join Neutron for combat juggling. Things were unusually frosty between them because of it. Flynn kept trying to push Neutron past it, but he had dug in.

"Professor? I thought the kid was only three," Flynn said, ignoring the comment.

I was happy not to have to discuss my source.

"Rich people," DC said.

"She won't be for long, it looks like," Burns said, nodding to the court records.

"I can't see Saul letting that baby go without. Everyone at dinner seemed to know it too," I said. "Joni could be a problem for another reason, though. She pressed on my relationship with Fergus quite a bit, not really buying our love-story cover. DC was a good distraction from things, but we'll have to keep an eye out."

"That Marion could help you," DC said. "She is not a fan of her niece-in-law."

Neutron cleared the screen and put back up the Toucci family tree, zeroing in on a picture of Marion.

"It seems like Marion here has her own money issues to be worrying about," Neutron said.

"What do you mean?" I asked.

A picture of a cute little shop in the West End materialized next to several bank records. "Marion's antique business is in trouble. Back in the seventies, when she first started it, it did pretty well. But she hasn't moved online, and other stores in the area have taken business. It looks like a lot of her regular customers have been dying off too."

"That's creepy," Grand said with a shudder.

"All that's led to a cash-flow problem. The business received a large cash influx from an unknown source a few months ago, but it's still bleeding money."

"Hm. Money's always a good motivator," Burns said.

"You're telling us. Living the dream, sonny," Grand said.

"Keep digging, Neutron. See if you can find out where the money came from."

"How are the kids being supported?" I asked, pointing at the picture of Marcus and Lucia underneath Marion's in the tree.

"All on the family payroll," Neutron said.

"Word from our chop-shop friends is that there's a huge power struggle between Saul's niece and nephews, and Nile was in the thick of it," Flynn said.

"My money's on the chick," DC said. "Even if she couldn't bludgeon her moron brother over the head with more statistics than I think even Kat knows, Saul is not down with Marcus wanting to climb into bed with the cartels."

"What about the rest of them?" Burns asked.

"Francesca's a snob but clearly mourning the loss of her son. The granddaughter's harmless," I said.

"Oh, I don't know about that," DC replied. "It's your harmless princess types we gotta watch out for. We were talking cross-breeding strategies at dinner. She was practically glued to my side in the conversation. She definitely knows her stuff, but the first mention of the

Palmeros had her going as stiff as a board. I thought she was going to hyperventilate right there."

"How do we know the Palmeros aren't actually behind this?" Flynn asked.

"Maybe they are. The man was sporting a nice, stiff sombrero," Grand added.

"We don't, really," Burns said. "We only have Saul's hunch."

"And the fact that Alejandro Palmero risked coming to Saul directly in hopes of stopping a mob war," I said. "Plus, if it's the Palmeros, what's the motive? They don't run on the same business turf, from what I know."

"Okay. Next steps?" Burns asked.

"I need to get that body out of my living room and into autopsy," I said.

"Yeah, there's a sale on beef at the Piggly Wiggly this week. I don't want to miss it, and we don't have the room with the corpsicle in there," Grand said.

"Someone needs to start digging on the Palmero side too," Flynn added.

"Saul said Fergus was arranging that part and a look at where the body was found," Burns said.

"I'll circle back with Elise and see if I can figure out what's got her all twitchy about them," DC said. "She's asked for a tour of my greenhouse."

"And Fergus knows more than he's said so far. I'm sure of it. I think my 'boyfriend' and I need a chat."

With everyone having an assignment, the meeting broke up.

I'd asked DC to keep Grand busy for a bit while I talked to Burns about my other problem. I corralled him away from Flynn and Neutron with a gentle nudge. "We need to talk," I said.

Chapter 17: Simon Says

“We need to talk,” I said.

He took a bottle of water and drank, eyeing me. “Most people dating take those words to mean relationship trouble. With you, I’m pretty sure there’s a crime involved.”

“Will being right make you more agreeable to helping me?” I asked, trying to look flirty.

“On a scale of one to ten, how much am I not going to like this?”

I wrung my hands and tried to avoid eye contact. “Like, a twelve.”

“Spill.”

“I got a call from Simon.”

“Simon? Simon Says, Simon Cowell, Simon and Garfunkel?” he asked, his face blank of all emotion.

“Ha-ha. You’re very funny,” I said.

“Of course I am, because you cannot possibly be in touch with Simon ‘The Mole’ Milovich, head of one of the most brutal Russian mob families.” *So much for emotionless.*

“He said he’d be in touch, and he has been.”

Burns ran a hand through his hair and down his face before he shoved both hands into his pockets. “What does he want?”

“Access.” I explained the situation with the storage locker.

He looked at Grand and then back at me. “Does it strike you as coincidental that you suddenly have men coming out of the woodwork to offer you information about your dad?”

“It’s a thought, but honestly, I’m not sure whether it’s my dad or Claude I should be more worried about right now.”

"You don't think this Toucci thing is enough on our plates?" he asked with genuine concern.

"Do you think I want anything to do with any of this? But, Burns, this is Grand we're talking about. She's been through enough and is still navigating this Claude mess. The Russians aren't going away quietly, but at least Simon seems saner than Victor was."

He sighed loudly and ran his hand through his hair again.

"Besides, I don't think you should be fronting the Russian operation."

"What do you mean?" he asked, his brow tightening.

"I'm sure Simon's keeping tabs enough to know that you're not out of my life, but there's no need to advertise how connected we are, especially with you running in Toucci circles now. I think we need a third party."

"You cannot possibly be considering putting DC in charge of something like this."

"Definitely not. Between avoiding getting married and staking his claim in the Illinois pot market, he's busy." I mentally ran through all my connections, considering who we might be able to use. "No, we need someone who isn't involved in the Toucci situation but can quickly assess information and knows some of the players. Someone maybe with a gambling problem." I smiled as it came to me and waited for Burns to catch up.

"Gambling?" He thought about it for a minute. "A certain med student who owes us a favor," he said, catching up.

Jeffery Jaffe was a pompous, egotistical, overworked med school intern with a gambling problem. He was often loaned out by attendings worried about diagnostic outcomes to help with autopsies. He had also been a key player in helping to take down the Russians and was someone I had become begrudging friends with.

"I think Dr. Jaffe would be thrilled to get that debt off the books."

"All right. You need his help with the autopsy anyway," Burns said.

That was true. While I had come a long way, I didn't feel qualified to take on a full autopsy on my own.

He blew out a loud breath. That was it.

"Thanks for not making this a big thing," I said. I looked up at him with a soft smile.

He wrapped his arms around me and gave a light squeeze then kissed the top of my head and looked over my shoulder. "Let's try to keep your grandmother out of business with the mob for a change," he said.

I squeezed him back, letting the relief of knowing that someone else would be watching out for her and that someone else understood my worry and cared to spread through me. I let him go to look at where she stood chatting with Neutron about their online gaming.

Burns and I watched them for a bit. I could tell he was contemplating things. The vein in his temple always pulsed a bit, and his lips were tighter at the corners.

Before I could ask about his thoughts, he shouted across the room, "And, Neutron, upgrade the security for this room. No one but us gets in or out."

I had a bad feeling he wasn't just being cautious.

AS I DROVE HOME THAT night, my head was spinning with everything I had learned. *How are we ever going to sort this out?* They all seemed perfectly nice. Well, okay, maybe not all of them. But it was hard to believe that I had just had dinner with a murderer. I couldn't imagine how Saul must be feeling, thinking he was living or working with someone who had killed a family member.

From everything I had learned about Nile, I thought maybe he wasn't the best nephew. But still, he was family. And no matter what family did, they were still family.

My phone buzzed, and I looked down at the caller ID. *Anonymous. Damn.* Nothing good ever came from an anonymous call.

"Hello?"

"I see you are running in interesting circles these days, Katherine." I'd know that Russian-accented voice anywhere. *Simon.* His ears must have been itching.

"I feel honored that you're keeping such a close eye on me," I said, trying to suppress my shiver at his creepiness.

"I do like to ensure that my investments are well secured."

I took a deep breath to steady myself. I always felt off balance when I was dealing with the Russians. Chentinko had been unhinged and crazy. Everything I had learned about Simon told me he was smart, cruel, and lethal. That made for a huge knot in my stomach for having to give him bad news.

"I'm sorry to tell you that we won't be able to access the storage locker as easily as we had both hoped. But I have a plan." I told him all about the auction and the viewing.

"I must say, Katherine, that it is less than ideal to have others accessing what is mine."

"Our other option would be to steal what you need, but you made the locker people so skittish with your last attempt that they have more security than Fort Knox now."

He sighed and was quiet for a minute. I held my breath. I did not need more issues with the Russians thrown into the middle of the Toucci mess.

"Yes, I suppose if we want to avoid drawing further attention from the authorities, your way is the best alternative."

And exhale. He bought it! "Exactly. Now, how will I know what I'm looking for once we get access to the locker?"

"Don't you worry about that. You focus on getting a viewing inside the locker and winning that auction. I will take it from there. It's almost as if your father's life depends on it."

The line went dead.

Chapter 18: You Need a Tan

The next day dawned bright with sunshine and the promise of no longer having a dead body frozen in my living room. I did a shift at the morgue during the day, making sure everything was ready for that night. Jaffe was lined up, and DC had helped make sure there was space where we could store Nile without anyone becoming suspicious. We just needed to wait for the morgue to clear out.

Well, that, and we had to figure out transport. The first problem we needed to tackle was how to get the frozen body out of our apartment without looking suspicious. Well, actually the first problem was how to get the ice block Nile had turned into out of the chest freezer, preferably without damaging it or ruining any potential evidence. Not that I held out a lot of hope for forensics. That body had been who knew where, doing who knew what. For all we knew, poor Nile had taken a joy ride as an audition for *Weekend at Bernie's II*.

We were already walking a fine line. If we kept the body too cold, too frozen, when we thawed it, instead of the moisture in it turning back to water, it would sublimate and evaporate. Poor Nile would look like a hollowed-out mummy. If we kept the temp too high, we might as well announce to the neighbors we were stashing a body. The scent of dead meat would lead a trail straight to us.

I could hear loud snorting coming from down the hall. We had locked Maybell in her pen. I feared that seeing what could possibly happen to her had she ended up in the wrong hands would be traumatic. Maybell did not need visions of ending up a frozen ham hock haunting her.

"If I have to bend much farther in there, I'm gonna get frostbite on my boobs," Grand said.

We had considered unplugging the freezer and letting Nile thaw naturally, but there was no telling how long his body had been sitting out before he ended up in the freezer. Anything that sped up the rate of decomposition would end with calls to our landlord over the corpse-rotting smell. We needed to fend that off as long as possible.

"What are we even going to do with it once we get it out of here?" Grand asked.

"I thought we could roll it up in the rug and take it down the fire escape."

"You seriously want to put that thing in a three-hundred-year-old antique?" she asked.

"Well, not when you say it that way." I tugged on the corpse a couple more times, but it was obvious that thing wasn't moving. "We need help." I pulled out my cell phone and dialed.

"What's up, sweet cheeks?" Fergus answered.

"I take it you can't talk," I said. He only called me that in front of Touccis.

"I'm glad you had such a good time at dinner. I can't wait for you to come for tennis," he replied.

"Oh, I have a great tennis skirt, but that's not why I'm calling. Your buddy Nile's too frozen for us to lift him, and unplugging him will make him smell. Not to mention the only thing we have to wrap him in costs more than Grand's total current retirement fund, so you need to provide supplies and muscle. Like a good boyfriend," I added.

"I'll be right over to help you move around that furniture," he said, and we hung up.

We closed the lid and had some fake margaritas while we waited for Fergus to show.

About twenty minutes later, there was a loud knock. I opened the door to find Fergus surrounded by a man and two women. They were wearing dark-blue coveralls and carrying satchels.

"Who are they?" I asked.

"That's no way to greet your boyfriend when he comes with help," Fergus answered. He pushed his way into the apartment.

His crew followed.

"You'll have to forgive me for not having a better grasp of the protocol I'm supposed to follow while actively committing a felony."

"Funny," he said and opened the chest freezer.

The crew began unpacking their bags.

Fergus was looking around somewhat frantically.

I gave him a look.

"Where's the killer bacon? I'm wearing the leather today, and I'd rather they not get covered in pink fur again," he said.

"She's in the back, in her pen. All this unseemly business isn't good for her anxiety," I said.

"You still packing heat?" Grand asked him.

"Why? You want to borrow it?" Fergus asked.

"Don't encourage her," I said.

The crew unrolled a large piece of black plastic.

"Do I even want to know why you have cleaning crew on speed dial?"

"Given your recent history, I would assume that you are not wholly unfamiliar with some of the peculiarities of our enterprise."

"Wholly Soprano," Grand said. "I'm never getting my own squished watermelon baby with the men you keep bringing home."

I choked on my fake margarita. Fergus's eyes grew wide as he became paler.

Before either of us could answer, the bald guy from the crew came up to me. "Where can I plug in?" he asked. He held the end of an extension cord that had a power strip plugged into it. On the power strip were four hair dryers.

I helped them get power. The apartment instantly became engulfed in the whirring noise of machinery.

"This is going to take forever," I said.

"You got any better ideas? It's not like we thaw out a lot of dead bodies in our business. Usually, it's the other way around," Fergus said.

I thought for a moment and then grabbed my cell phone and dialed.

"Malik!" I squealed into the phone.

I hadn't spoken to him since before Dad's arrest. Malik was the owner of the Tan Emporium. He also owed me big-time for helping him make franchise of the year through my referrals. All the Kappas frequented the emporium.

I made the arrangements for us to visit with our unorthodox client and hung up. "He's expecting us in twenty. We can unload in the back of the strip mall. He has a garage bay where he brings in new tanning beds. Said the place is mostly empty this time of day."

"Isn't tanning bad for the skin?" Grand asked.

"Well, we'll have to be careful not to dry him out, but a little browning around the edges won't hurt."

"Whatever you say, doll," Fergus responded.

Once Nile was thawed enough that he could bend some, they lifted him out of the freezer and onto the plastic. The four of them rolled him up and taped him closed, then they lifted him and headed for the fire escape.

"I'll ride with you," I said to Fergus.

Grand was going to visit a friend at her old home that evening, so she was covered. That would give me time to sort out things with Fergus as a captive audience. I needed to know what had been up with his behavior at dinner.

Once we were in the car, he looked me over before pulling out. I contemplated how to play things. I needed to know what he was hiding.

Chapter 19: Doctor's Appointment

"So," I said. "Are you going to tell me what was up with the Neanderthal act at dinner?" I started.

"What? I thought we did well. They all seemed to buy that you were my gal," Fergus said.

"Uh-huh. And the fact that you kept me from asking practically any questions that could help the investigation?"

"You gotta understand. It's my job to protect the family. First, last, and always."

"Protect them from me? Saul hired me."

"Yeah, well, there's a lot of that going around lately," he said but winced, like he regretted it.

I thought for a moment. "Who else has Saul hired that you're worried about?"

He sat still. I watched his eyes scanning, unsure what he was looking for or if it was just a nervous habit.

"He's been seeing other security men on the side. He thinks I don't know about it, but I know he hired some guys a while back, and he uses them on occasion when he doesn't want anyone knowing where he's going."

"Including you," I said.

He didn't answer but concentrated on his driving. I thought maybe we were done with the conversation.

Several turns later, though, he said, "Saul don't always know what's best for himself. Sometimes things are more complicated than they appear."

"So I should put you back on my suspect list?"

"I already told you. If it were me who done it, there wouldn't be no body."

"But you know who did it?"

"What I know is that people shouldn't go looking for answers to questions they really don't want the answers to. Family is everything to Saul."

"And Saul's everything to you."

Before he could say anything else, he turned into the back alley of the Tan Emporium. The van was already parked, and the crew had opened the back doors.

A man in a muscle tee and jeans stood next to it. He had weirdly curly salt-and-pepper hair, like a Cruella De Vil afro. His beard and mustache were dark. He wore shades, but underneath them I knew would be brilliant blue eyes moving over the scene at a hundred miles an hour.

"Katherine!" he shouted when he saw me, and we hugged. "Look at you, dear. When was the last time you cleansed?"

"I know, Malik. It's been some difficult months. But I'm hopeful for a return to normal soon."

"You are welcome here anytime. I would not be here without you."

"Thanks so much for helping with my... special friend."

"I read the papers, Katherine. I don't think I want to know where your friend is from."

"I'm quite sure you don't."

"I left booth five open for you. It's for my most discreet customers. You should be able to slip your... friend... in and out without being noticed."

The crew helped me get Nile into the tanning booth. We set him on low for only a short time. Once I was confident he was thawed enough that we'd be able to autopsy him, we loaded him back into the van.

Fergus drove us to the hospital.

I decided to pick up the conversation where we had left off. We needed to come to an understanding if I was going to make any progress with the Toucci clan. "So, you're just going to keep me from doing my job through this whole thing?" I asked.

"Ain't no one keeping you from nothing. Look, I'm helping you with the popsicle, aren't I?"

"I heard you arguing with the cook, you know."

His knuckles turned white around the steering wheel. "Enrique don't got anything to do with this."

I didn't know why I'd told him that. I didn't really think Fergus was a threat to me, but I also knew he was hiding things. I hadn't figured out how to get him to open up yet.

"Look, Fergus. I don't want to cause trouble for the Toucci family. And I don't want to cause trouble for you. I understand that you have loyalties. But so do I. If we're going to get through this thing, we have to find a way we can both meet our goals."

He grunted in reply but looked to be mulling over my words as he turned into the hospital driveway. The St. Louis County morgue was in the basement of the county hospital. Thanks to our last project, the morgue had recently undergone a makeover. No more drab carpet and puke-green walls. Instead, the space was a stylish mix of modern industrial. The makeover had come complete with a coffee bar and a security-system upgrade courtesy of McPhee Security. It came in handy when one needed access to the facility without being noticed.

We were arriving late enough in the day that most everyone was gone—everyone but Marshal Mathers. Marshal was the guy everyone picked on not because of how he looked, which wasn't great, but because he was himself. "Slimy" worked as an adjective to describe all aspects of Marshal, from looks to personality. He met us at the door.

"Babe. So pleasant to see you."

"It's not likewise, Marshal, and stop calling me babe."

"I'm hurt, Katherine. You and Uncle Marshal are partners now, remember. Where's your nod to solidarity?"

A lifetime ago, I had agreed to be Marshal's bowling partner. I had not yet recovered from the experience.

"He's your uncle?" Fergus asked. His face contorted into a bewildered scowl.

"No. Marshal thinks he's cute instead of a douchey pervert."

"Should I be worried that you're sneaking bodies into the morgue now, Kat?" Marshal asked as the cleaning crew moved past us, carrying the corpse.

I followed them, directing them to the autopsy room.

"If you ever want you and me to see another bowling ball together, Marshal, you'll keep everyone away from here tonight," I said as we entered the room.

"Babe, would I let you down?"

In the room waiting for us was Dr. Jaffe. "Are you ever on time?" he asked.

"Hello to you too," Fergus said. He seemed offended on my behalf.

"What's with the goon squad?" Dr. Jaffe asked, sizing up everyone who had entered the room with me. He looked twice at Fergus. "Although given the task, I guess I shouldn't be surprised."

"You sure about this?" Fergus asked before I could respond.

"I assure you, Fergus, that both Nile and I are in good hands." Ignoring their posturing, I pulled my hair into a pony and put on my mint-green hair cap. It matched my pumps. I didn't need to look up to know Dr. Jaffe would be rolling his eyes. I searched my bag for my matching shoe booties.

Dr. Jaffe already had on scrubs and a mask. He gloved up while the crew unrolled Nile.

"Was the body found with those goggles on?" Dr. Jaffe asked.

"Oh. No! They were left over from the tanning bed. I didn't want to damage his eyes."

Dr. Jaffe looked at me. I thought he expected me to say more, but before I could, Fergus moved into my space. I wondered if he was expecting some room-leaving affection, given how he looked at me.

"You do remember we're not actually dating," I said.

He laughed at that. "Believe me. That is something impossible for me to forget." Then he glared at Dr. Jaffe. "All right, doll, you've got it from here. Call us when you're finished, and we'll come pick him up." With that, Fergus left.

"I thought you were done with the mob," Dr. Jaffe said.

"Hello to you, too, Jeffery. How are your meetings going?" As part of Dr. Jaffe's punishment for his involvement with the body-snatching mess, he'd been sentenced to Gamblers Anonymous meetings. When we were alone, I used his name, but in front of others, his professional title.

"So we're going to be bitchy tonight, then?" he asked.

"You started it," I said, suddenly feeling twelve. "I'm sorry. These last few days have all been a bit much. I thought I was done with the mob too. Thanks for helping."

We began setting out the equipment we would need for the procedure.

"As though I had much choice." He loaded his instrument tray the way he liked it.

"Now who's showing their claws," I said.

"Pardon me if I'm feeling a little annoyed at our sudden close familial associations. I understand your mother is now working for my godfather."

Charles Montgomery was Dr. Jaffe's godfather. We were both convinced that he was also somehow mixed up with the Russians. Although we couldn't prove it.

"Well, as much as I hate her being near your godfather, I do appreciate that she's contributing. We're not as close to landing in the homeless shelter as we were before he took her on."

"You could solve that problem on your own, you know."

While Burns had been the one to give me the brochure on the forensics program, it was Jeffery who had told him he thought I'd be a great fit. He'd also connect me with a scholarship that would pay for the whole thing, courtesy of his family connections and an endowment from Teradyne Defense, of course. Not that I was opposed to using connections to get where I wanted. I just wasn't sure yet if that was what I wanted.

"I haven't said no," I said.

"But you haven't said yes, either."

"And that brings us back to my involvement with the mob. The Italians promised that if I helped them, they'd give me information that could free my dad. And they know something about your godfather." They hadn't said that, but I had a hunch, and I didn't think I was wrong.

He frowned at me. "I keep wondering if this nightmare is ever going to end for either of us." He sighed. "At least the Italians aren't likely to slit our throats in our sleep," he said.

We completed the setup of all the equipment and started with the external examination. That was largely my job and something that I kind of had a knack for.

"OK. Let's get this over with," he said. "Are you going to do the staring thing?"

The part of my job I liked the most was helping the deceased tell their stories. They all had one. Boring people did not end up on an autopsy table. Dr. Jaffe had previously found my need to connect with the victims annoying. Since our bonding session courtesy of the Russians, he had been more tolerant.

I started looking Nile over.

"This guy looks like he's been through the wringer," he said as we both examined Nile. It was the first time I'd been able to get a good look at him since he landed in my living room. He was a mess. He was covered in dirt and grime. His face was littered with bruises and pooling blood. His torso had tire tracks over it, and his rib cage looked crushed in. And there was a giant gaping hole in his abdomen.

"Nile Toucci, thirty-five," I said into my recorder. Not that I knew who would transcribe our off-the-books autopsy notes.

"I see we've moved up from prostitutes to mobster nephews, eh," Dr. Jaffe said.

"The body was supposedly found at a Palmero restaurant."

"Jesus, Kat, you certainly go big," he said as he picked up his scalpel. "Let's see what story Nile here can tell us."

We worked together for several hours to try to reconstruct Nile's last moments. By then, Dr. Jaffe and I had done enough autopsies that we moved well together. Like in a dance, I could anticipate his next move.

"That's it, then," I said.

"No doubt about it," he replied. "Nile Toucci was not beaten to death, and he certainly wasn't run over, at least not while he was alive. He died from a broken neck sustained in a fall, but if that hadn't done it, he would have bled out from whatever caused that hole in his stomach."

We'd found paint flecks and what looked like metal bits in the hole. We'd have to wait for the forensics to come back on them, but Nile had hit or been hit with something substantial, metal, and pointy.

"So, the question is, who hit him or pushed him and from where? And why do they want to cover it up?"

Chapter 20: Taco-Saki

"We're going to be late!" I yelled to Grand from the breakfast bar. Mom sat next to me, drinking her coffee and waiting. Maybell was under my feet. Mom had agreed to Maybell-sit so that we could go to the crime scene with Fergus and the McPhee team.

"I've never been to a crime scene before when I wasn't kidnapped. I don't know what to wear!" Grand yelled back from the bathroom.

She had already changed twice. I'd gone with a black-and-white polka-dot jumper that I could dress up or down. Paired with tennis shoes, it'd be stylish for crawling around a crime scene, but then I could swap to pumps and add jewelry for our update meeting later with Saul.

Since discovering that she fit into the Garanimals line at the Walmart, Grand had been expanding her fashion sense. Her abduction had also affected her. Before, she'd pick something ultra-elegant but difficult to move in. Now, she stuck to things that provided easy mobility and could be worn with comfortable shoes in case she needed to run.

"I can't believe you've agreed to this," Mom said.

"At least the body isn't in our living room anymore," I answered.

"And you're roping your grandmother into the middle of this mess."

"If there's any roping happening, I'm sure it's the other way around." I went to the kitchen to feed Maybell. She snorted happily behind me.

"It's bad enough you work at that place. Now you're taking side jobs."

My work at the morgue was an ongoing point of disagreement. Mom didn't approve of my working there. I didn't approve of us being homeless. I was thankful that Claude had been able to get me the job. And I was actually pretty good at it.

"I might go back to school," I said.

"Oh?" She perked up at this news. "A master's degree?" She loved to brag about her Harvard grad.

"In forensics," I said.

"Forensics! Absolutely not. This is all going to be over soon, Katherine, and then you'll be able to go back to Boston and back to the museum."

"Even if things with Dad get sorted out, I'm not going back to Boston." That was the first time I had admitted that. I didn't know what was going to happen with my dad or anything else, but staying home felt right. Having said it out loud, I knew it without any doubt.

She didn't respond. Instead, she stared at me and took another drink of her coffee, waiting for me to elaborate.

"I like it here. I have a job I'm good at and friends and a maybe boyfriend, and Grand's not getting any younger."

"I didn't realize it was serious between you and that young man."

"Because of course that's what you'd zero in on."

"Well, what would you have me focus on, Katherine? That you're throwing your life away because of this mess, that we've lost everything we've worked our whole lives for, or maybe that your father may end up spending the rest of his life in prison?"

"I'm sorry, Mom. I know this hasn't been easy for you."

At that declaration, she looked like a deflated balloon. She sighed loudly and put her coffee down then moved from the bar stool and into the kitchen, where we would be facing.

We weren't often an affectionate family, so I stiffened at first when she put her arms around me.

"What if he never comes home?" she asked.

I exhaled the breath I'd been holding and put my arm around her.

"He will. I believe that he will."

We stood there, taking in the comfort for a moment, before she pulled away.

I held on to her hands and looked into her eyes. "But that doesn't mean everything's going to be the same. It can't be. We can't stay frozen," I said.

Before she could respond, Grand emerged. She wore a dark-blue T-shirt with a large whale tail on it that said Make Waves over a pair of black biker shorts. Her sun visor looked like the ocean, and she was wearing her matching blue-and-white Golden Goose super-star sneakers. She headed for the closet.

"Try not to get into any trouble," Mom said.

"We're the ones bringing the trouble," Grand replied, pulling out her detective backpack.

"Have a good day with Maybell," I said.

THE SPRAWLING GIANT green octopus that topped the Taco-Saki could be seen from a block away. The restaurant had been voted best sushi restaurant two years running—Mexican sushi. It was Palmero territory. The building itself was bright purple. At noon on a Tuesday, the joint was packed. Several pickup trucks lined the sides of the lot, full of construction workers hoping to get picked up as temps for the day. The professional crowd from nearby Clayton zipped in and out of the curbside-pickup parking.

We pulled into the parking lot and looked for a place to park the Escalade. I spied a McPhee security SUV and pulled in next to it. The team was already out of the truck and sizing things up. Burns was on the far side. When we first pulled in, I hadn't noticed that Fergus was on the other side. They were chatting against the side of the car.

I looked them over before I got out of the car. It was going to be strange, having my fake boyfriend and my maybe boyfriend in the same place. I thought about my next un-date already scheduled with Fletcher Reid and sighed. *When did my life become so complicated?*

"Your stud muffin looks hot in camo," Grand said.

He did too. He had camo on the bottom and a tight black McPhee security T-shirt on top. The black matched the color of his hair.

Grand slid out of the Escalade and headed for Neutron. Since the incident with the Russians, they'd become pals. He was teaching her how to play video games. They were apparently working a virtual farm co-op together.

"Look, sonny, if we're going to take over the lead, we need to increase our milk and cheese production," she said.

I left them to their world agri-domination conspiring and headed for Burns and Fergus.

"Doll, you're looking good," Fergus said and slid an arm around me.

I assumed that meant we were being watched. He only did the fake-boyfriend thing when he thought we were on display.

Burns, however, did not seem amused. He squeezed his coffee cup tighter and stared at me. "Your show, *doll*. How do you want to work it?"

"Where's Flynn?" I asked.

"Inside. He thinks if he buys Neutron lunch, it will help get him out of trouble. I think he secretly wanted some of the kamikaze rolls," Burns replied.

I smiled. Under the right circumstances, lunch would have been a good start for Flynn, but it would likely not have the effect he was hoping for.

"Okay, Fergus," I said, turning my attention back to the matter at hand, "what do you know?"

"Not much. I got a call early the morning Nile was found."

"How'd they get your number? How'd they know to call you?" I asked.

"Why'd they call you?" Burns put in.

"Do you know the other security firms in town?" Fergus asked Burns.

He nodded.

"Of course you do. It's your business."

Neutron and Grand walked up to us at that point.

"If you needed to get ahold of one of them, you'd put your boy wonder here on tracking down the right person. I could get to the head of any of the families in the city if I needed to."

"It's like the red nuke phone in the White House," Grand said.

"Exactly. We don't want no war on accident," Fergus said. "The caller was adamant that something bad had happened, but he didn't want no war."

"So who was the caller?" I asked.

"Come on. I'll introduce you."

Chapter 21: Puddin

We followed Fergus across the parking lot and into the restaurant. On the far wall was a sleek black granite countertop. Galvanized-steel Order Here and Pick Up Here signs hung from the ceiling, flanked by octopus piñatas. Purple pleather chairs surrounded sleek gray tables lined with sarape place mats. Mariachi music played over the speakers. The silverware area held both forks and chopsticks. The sriracha stood next to the soy bottle.

A large mural covered the back wall. I didn't recognize the place. On second glance, I wondered if it were a real place at all. It looked like a mix of somewhere off the Japanese coast and Mexico City. I noted the row of sombreros on pegs above it. One was missing. I touched Burns's arm and pointed up at the empty space. He nodded.

I waved at Flynn in line. Fergus didn't stop at the counter but instead went around it. We followed him into the kitchen. He steered us back to a tiny office. Papers were stacked all over the desk. The piles were so high they blocked the window. Over the top of one, I saw a head bob up when Fergus appeared in the doorway.

"This is Kat Waters and her team," Fergus said to the man.

He was as short as Grand and had dark hair and tanned skin. He wore a Hawaiian shirt, cargo shorts, and long, dark knee-high socks. The man nodded at us with a serious expression, as if that information meant something. I caught a twinkle in Burns's eye. He was amused at being referred to as "my team."

"This is Puddin. He owns the Taco-Saki. He's the one who called."

"Your parents named you Puddin, or is that your crime name?" Grand asked.

The man smiled at her. "My daughter is a big fan," he said to her. "She wore her 'Stand with Grand' T-shirt today and hopes to meet you, Mrs. Waters," he said.

I thought Grand actually blushed.

"They call me Puddin because I like dessert." He smiled a big, toothy grin. His front upper tooth was gold.

"Mr. Puddin, can you tell us what happened that morning?" I asked.

"Octopus has to soak for a long time, or it gets stringy when you cook it. We are in very early to prep for the day. My opening manager called me at five a.m. There was a dead body on our patio."

"Where did your manager find it?" Burns asked.

Puddin pushed past us and into the kitchen. "Come on. I'll show you." He walked out of the kitchen, back around the counter, and through a side door. The door led to an outdoor patio seating area. "No one saw him right away because we don't usually come out here until closer to open. He was sitting at one of the tables here." He pointed at a table at the back of the patio.

"Think I'll skip the dine-in option and get my sushi to go," Grand said.

"From a distance, you couldn't tell he was dead. He was just sitting there. Of course, he was naked, so..."

Burns and I both looked around. A small barricade separated the outdoor space from the parking lot. I hadn't even seen the patio when we first pulled in. But if you knew it was there, getting a body into the seating was no problem.

"Neutron, take some shots of the table for me," I said. I examined the table and chair. There was no visible blood, but it had most likely, I hoped, been well cleaned since then.

"Mr. Puddin, where did the sombrero come from?" I asked.

"He was naked. It gave everyone the willies to have to look at his willie," he said with a shrug. Well, that was one mystery solved.

"How did you know to call Fergus?" Burns asked.

Puddin looked at Fergus intently but didn't answer. It was like he was waiting for permission to respond. Fergus nodded at him.

"I didn't call him right away. My first call was to Juan Carlos Palmero."

"Juan Carlos is Alejandro Palmero's son and right-hand man. If there had been a hit ordered, Juan Carlos would know about it," Fergus said.

"He had no idea why Nile Toucci's dead body was in my dining room," Puddin said.

"I don't suppose you've taken a look at the security footage?" Burns asked.

I looked around but didn't see any cameras.

"We don't have any video to offer," Puddin said.

Neutron snorted at that. "This a haunt for one of the most ruthless organized crime families in the city. I counted no fewer than four cameras on the way, and there are two with shots of this patio, and that's before I even start to look for cameras nearby that might have a vantage point."

"So you don't want to show us the footage," I said. "That's not exactly helping the case, here, Mr. Puddin."

"How'd you know it was Nile Toucci?" Burns asked.

Puddin exhaled at the welcome change of subject.

"Go on, Puddin. They're going to find out eventually," Fergus said.

"We'd had a run-in with him and his cousin earlier in the week. In fact, we have a run-in most every week. They come in all the time and try to stir up trouble," Puddin said.

"Do you know which cousin?" Burns asked.

"Smart mouth, dumb Italian guy. Always taunting the guys in the parking lot who are looking for work. Always giving my daughter a hard time."

As if on cue, a small Asian woman emerged from the patio door in a rush that caused her long dark hair to fly out behind her. When she saw us, her face lit up with a beaming smile.

She came to a stop at Grand. "You are the famous Grand Waters! May I have your autograph? Can I shake your hand? You must come see my kitchen and try my rolls. I made special Grand Slam sushi rolls for your visit."

"Eiko, your manners," Puddin said.

"Oh, sorry. I'm just so excited. My friends are never going to believe me. Can we take a selfie?"

"It's okay. I'm used to it. It's why I have security," Grand said, pointing at Burns.

He smiled.

We watched Grand and Eiko disappear back inside.

"You knew it was Nile Toucci, then?" I asked, getting us back on track.

"Yes."

"And you believed your boss when he said he didn't know how the body got here?"

"Look, if the Mexicans had been involved, they wouldn't have left the body in their own territory. And they sure as hell wouldn't have called us about it," Fergus said.

"Maybe they wanted to prove a point. Maybe it was a statement," I said.

"There are easier ways to make a statement than having Alejandro Palmero contact Mr. Toucci," Fergus said.

I looked at him curiously. He seemed adamant on that point. *If he wasn't involved with Nile's death, how is he so sure it wasn't the Palmeros?*

"Well, maybe it was an accident, heat of the moment, or someone accidentally killed him, and this is all just a big cover-up. I can't imagine the Touccis would be any less angry if that were true than if it were deliberate," I said.

We weren't going to solve anything there. I began looking around, peering up high. There didn't appear to be any kind of roof access there. Without access to a certain height, there was no way Nile died there.

"What are you looking for?" Fergus asked.

"Mr. Puddin, I don't suppose there's any roof access around here?" I asked.

"No," he said.

Before Fergus could get another question out, Grand ran through the door. "Come on. You have to see this." She grabbed my hand and pushed me through the small opening that separated the barrier from the parking lot. Over my shoulder, I saw Burns and Fergus trying to get through, but they wouldn't fit. Neutron managed to squeeze through, and I heard him behind me.

We walked quickly but quietly to the back of the building. As we came around the corner, Grand crouched, and Neutron and I followed. I was thankful the back of the building was littered with empty boxes from the morning's delivery. As we got closer to the dumpster, we saw two legs dangling over the edge of it. Someone was digging through the dumpster. The person popped up. Red hair flew back, revealing fair, freckled skin and thick olive-rimmed glasses. We all stared into the face of Elise Toucci, trying not to gasp.

"It's her, isn't it?" Grand asked. "The one on your hot stuff's murder board?"

"That's her," Neutron confirmed.

What in the devil is Elise Toucci doing skulking around a Palmero dumpster? A dumpster at the very place Nile's body was discarded?

I couldn't see what Elise was holding. She looked around to see if anyone had spied her. She smoothed down her flyaway hair and, feeling confident that she hadn't been seen, walked back to her car. While the three of us silently watched her drive away, Fergus, Burns, and Puddin appeared at the back door.

Chapter 22: Meet the Contestants

It was one of those days when I realized how entirely insane my life had become. We had just toured a crime scene in the territory of one mafia family. We were on our way to a meeting about a storage locker holding Russian mob secrets, and we would end our day in an update meeting with the head of the Italian mafia, hoping to arrange a meeting with the city's largest drug cartel. I would then be having an un-date with Fletcher to discuss information about said Mexican cartel.

While I held out hope I would be able to clear my dad of his legal trouble soon, I couldn't help realizing that I was becoming more embroiled every day with the very thing I was swearing my family wasn't involved with.

Grand and I loaded back into the Escalade. We needed to pick up DC before the update meeting with Saul and wouldn't have time after we met with Burns and Dr. Jaffe about the Russians, so he would be coming with us to meet them.

Fergus had seemed unnerved by the development of Elise Toucci showing up at the Palmeros'. He kept insisting that we couldn't tell Saul we had seen Elise. I understood he didn't want to damage Saul's opinion of his granddaughter, but we needed to know what her involvement was. It was too big of a coincidence for her to be at the site where the body was found.

"Are you going to tell him?" Grand asked as we drove toward DC's.

"I'm not sure. I get where Fergus is coming from. I don't want to upset Saul if I don't have to."

"Learning disappointing things about family is never easy," she said.

I knew we weren't talking about Saul and Elise anymore.

"No. But we don't know everything yet. Maybe there's more to her story. Maybe we should talk to her first."

"Maybe she won't be a stubborn ass and will actually talk to us," she said.

Claude was still refusing to see anyone. My dad had been denied visitors but wasn't saying anything either. The two people who could tell us the most about what was going on with our situation were currently not talking to us.

I pulled into DC's and found a place to park the monster truck. Grand and I headed up to DC's. From the hall, we could tell that the door was ajar, but the apartment was eerily quiet.

"You packing?" Grand asked. She must have felt the unease of the situation as well.

We slowed our approach. Since the Russian encounter, we were both more on alert.

"Grand, not every situation calls for a gun."

"Easy for you to say. You're not the one who's been kidnapped."

"DC?" I called out and pushed open the door farther. We moved into his apartment but were instantly at a standstill.

"Good lord, it's the Red Wedding massacre," Grand said.

Wedding Central looked like a hurricane had hit it. The army of cake toppers I had admired on my last visit had toppled and lay all over the floor. The table linens were strewn about. The balloon arch had halfway deflated.

I finally spied DC. He was upside down near a far wall. I bent in half and turned my head so that I could meet his eyes. "DC, what on earth happened?" I asked.

"Oh, Kat, thank god." He kicked down from the handstand he had been in. "She's gone." He let out a wailing sound and threw his arms around me. "I may never see her again." He sobbed. I patted his back in comfort and tried to get him to settle down so that I could understand what on earth had happened.

"Come on, sonny. You gotta breathe, or you're gonna combust," Grand said.

We cleared off some of the wedding debris and sat him down between us.

"Start at the beginning. What happened here?" I asked.

"INS came. They were going to take her away," he said.

"Well, you knew she was at risk," I said.

"I thought we'd have more time. And now she's gone!" He started wailing again.

"So immigration took her?" Grand asked.

"No, they were only here to make sure she was going to show up at her hearing. It's set for two weeks from now. But one of them was this really mean guy. You know the kind, a head too big for their body makes them have low blood flow? He kept talking about all the bad things they do to Asian women when they deport them. My beautiful Kimi was terrified. She's gonna need PTSD therapy now."

"So you defended her against him, and that's when they took her?" I asked, still confused.

"No, he scared her so badly she took off. She said unless I married her right now, today, she'd have to run. I don't know where she is." Two cats came out as DC wailed more. They ran around his legs and purred at each other. "Even Naomi and Morpheus are sad." He petted one of them.

"Look, we have to go see Burns now anyway. Let's see if Neutron can help find Kimi. We have our update meeting with Saul today. I'm sure they can help before we have to leave."

"You think he would?" DC asked.

"Of course he would," I said. Burns had a soft spot for DC. That was what had drawn Burns and me together in the first place. I knew he'd help if he could.

We all loaded back into the Escalade and headed toward McPhee Security offices.

Neutron was waiting for us at the elevator to take us up.

"Oh, thank god you're here!" DC said. He threw his arms around Neutron, who stood there, helpless, his eyes looking even buggier than usual behind his Coke-bottle lenses.

"Easy there, sonny. He can't help you if he passes out," Grand said.

"I'm sorry." DC choked back another sob. We didn't need him starting in again.

"What's going on?" Neutron asked.

We explained the problem as we rode up in the elevator. Neutron dropped Grand and me at the conference room then disappeared with DC toward his lair, where he could begin tracking Kimi's location.

Walking into the conference room, I noticed a whole new board with photos of people I didn't recognize. Burns and Dr. Jaffe were at the board, talking. Flynn sat in one of the seats, running the computer.

"Where's the wonder kid?" Flynn asked as Grand and I walked in, trying and failing to look casual about the question.

"He's helping DC with a personal problem," I said.

"That could take a while," Dr. Jaffe said. He grinned. As annoying as Dr. Jaffe found me, he tolerated DC fairly well.

"Got that right." Flynn snorted.

"How's the juggling lesson going?" I asked and smiled at him.

"We are not talking about it." He huffed.

I held in my giggle.

"Do we have new suspects?" I asked, pointing at the new board of pictures. I didn't recognize any of them.

"We've been tracking the movement of buy-ins for our little Russian project," Burns said.

"These"—Dr. Jaffe pointed at the board—"are all the current bidders who have paid the buy-in."

"The competition," Grand said.

"Anything to worry about?" I asked. I was surprised we were paying so much attention to the other bidders. "I wouldn't have thought we were that concerned. Simon's offered to pay whatever we need to obtain the locker."

"I wasn't worried until Neutron tracked this guy's money." Burns pointed at a photo of a gray-haired man in thick black shades. The name underneath was Larry Luce. "His buy-in money tracks to a familiar place." Burns put up a photo of Simon.

"So he's hedging his bets? Or does this Larry character have ties to the Russians?" I asked.

"We think he's hedging," Flynn said.

"Larry here is a professional," Dr. Jaffe added.

"A pro? You mean you can make a living off other people's crap?" Grand asked.

"Absolutely. Storage lockers are big business. You get the right locker, and it can be a gold mine," Dr. Jaffe said.

I should have known. It hadn't really taken much persuasion on my part to get him to join us. He'd expressed concern about the Russian ties, but the opportunity to get info about his godfather while simultaneously feeding his gambling addiction without really calling it that was too much to pass up. I supposed I should have felt guilty, but he had a look of joy on his face I didn't think I'd ever seen in the autopsy room.

"Maybe I've missed my calling," Grand said.

"So, what's his story?" I asked.

"Larry Luce is 'Loose for the Goose,'" Dr. Jaffe said. "He's known for taking big risks on lockers where the contents can't be well seen before the buy."

"His main competition is usually these two," Flynn said and pointed at a couple. The blond woman had a bright smile. The man next to her sported a shiny, bald black head and a sharp goatee. "Mandy and Jerome. The Consignment Couple. They own a resale shop on the south side of town and feed it almost exclusively with locker contents."

"Everyone's got a cool handle. I need a hip name if I'm gonna do this," Grand said.

We'd decided Grand would pose as Dr. Jaffe's grandmother.

"Dr. Jekyll and Mrs. Hyde?" Flynn asked.

"Watch it, pinhead," Grand said.

"I resent that," Dr. Jaffe added.

Burns glared at everyone, and we turned our attention back to the board.

"They're usually small time, so we're not sure where they got the money for the buy-in," Burns said.

"Neutron hasn't been able to trace it?" I asked.

"No. He's followed it through six offshore accounts already but has hit a dead end."

"That doesn't quite smell right for their background."

"Nope. Looks like this is going to be quite the auction."

"I shouldn't be surprised," I said. "Things with the Russians are always more complicated than they seem."

Chapter 23: A Nice Game of Chess

Burns, DC, Grand, and I piled into a McPhee Security SUV and headed for the Central West End and our update with Saul. The Central West End was nestled between Forest Park and St. Louis University. Not only was it home to the best fusion food, cute boutiques, and several tourist traps, but it also housed our current destination—the St. Louis Chess Club.

The chess club itself was impressive, with six thousand square feet of world-class chess-playing space. But what really put it on the map was how many world-ranked chess champions had come out of the club. International players from all over knew of the club. Grand was excited because it was adjacent to the chess-themed Kings Diner, home of great milkshakes and burgers. Burns was buying, following our update meeting with Saul.

Parking in the West End was never easy, but before Burns could turn to circle the block again, a familiar blond head popped out and stopped us, his arm lifted in a halt gesture. Lawn Chair Kid waved at the car in the spot at the curb, and it pulled out, freeing the spot for us.

"That's full service, right there," DC said.

We got out and were met with the familiar sight of not only Lawn Chair Kid but also my snarky car concierge, the one with the attitude and clogged chakras.

"Ray Ray," DC said and did the bro handshake, the half-hug-back-pat thing. "How are your chakras, man? Are you doing your meditation?"

"You know, I was a skeptic, but that hummus thing really works," Ray Ray said. His Afro bounced when he shook his head.

"Hummus is very good for your digestion," Grand said.

The men looked at her curiously.

"What are you doing here?" I asked.

"You need a pass," he said and held up a card. "They don't let just anyone barge into the club."

"You're a member?" I asked.

"Yes, I'm a member," he said, sounding offended.

"Ray Ray here's a rated player," Lawn Chair said.

"You shouldn't be so judgy. I don't think your affiliations limit your pageant potential."

"Oh, I didn't think that," I said. Which was true. "This looks a little too stodgy for you," I said, pointing at the stately brick building. "If you were going to take on the chess world, I'd imagine something more organic. Like speed playing in the park."

"That's where we started," Ray Ray said, his face less tight, some of the tension draining from him.

"We?" Burns asked, trying to figure out what was going on.

"My man Steven and I started hustling games in the park when we were ten," he said, pointing at the lawn chair kid.

"But you can't play international if you aren't ranked," Steven chimed in.

"You've played internationally? Have you been to Korea? Do they play chess in Korea?" DC asked.

Ray Ray thought for a moment while DC waited intently. "They only have one dude who's a grand master, and he was actually born in Russia, so it's kind of cheating. They play this weird game there called Janggi. I think we have a board inside." Ray Ray pointed at the door to the club.

"You can teach me? When I have to go live in Korea to see Kimi, I want to be able to impress her family."

Ray Ray and Steven led us into the building and down a set of stairs. A group of mostly boys was assembled in the hall, but I got a glimpse of a girl or two at the tables. The majority of the crowd was huddled around one particular table.

"This way," Ray Ray said and headed toward the crowd. "Crimson knows the most about Janggi."

When the group saw Ray Ray, they instantly parted and let us all through. A girl with bright-red hair sat across from a plain-looking boy in a button-up. The boy sucked on an inhaler.

"Come on, Cyclone. Give it up. Everyone watching knows your king's out of wind," the girl sitting at the table said.

He blew out a loud breath, and we watched him lay his king down on the board, and the crowd around us cheered.

The girl crossed her arms over her chest and looked smug. "Pay up," she said.

The boy stared at her for a minute. The crowd around them stilled, waiting to see if he would. Finally, he stood and dropped a thumb drive into the middle of the board. It landed with a loud thud, and the boy stormed away.

"Got him finally, eh, Crimson?" Steven asked.

Crimson smiled widely and picked up the thumb drive as she stood.

"We're now the eighth-ranked player in Twelfthnight," she said, looking at him with a grin.

She eyed all of us. Between Grand, DC, and Burns, I thought we must look like a strange group to the teenager.

"Is there some kind of administrative league audit happening?" Crimson asked.

"This here is my man DC," Ray Ray said.

"Oh, the hummus meda dude!" she squealed. "Your meditations are dope. My competition play is already up three points, and I just kicked the ass of one of the top-rated players here."

"See, Kat, the trilby is not to be mocked," DC said to me, but I thought he was blushing at the praise.

"DC here has a woman problem. He needs to know everything you know about Janggi."

Crimson's face brightened at that. She grabbed DC's hand and pulled him toward a board in the back of the room. Ray Ray nodded at us and followed them.

"Your meeting's being held on the second floor," Steven said and led us out of the room. He pointed at a large double door and then disappeared back down the stairs.

Before I'd even had a chance to take in the space we had entered, a hand came around my arm, and I was being dragged off to a side corridor. "My girlfriend and I need a word before we start," Fergus said.

Burns's face looked quizzical, like he didn't know whether he should be amused or jealous. I was neither.

"You can't tell him," Fergus said before I could admonish his lack of manners.

"Hello to you too," I said, pulling my arm from him. Since we had left Taco-Saki, he had been driving me crazy with his insistence that Saul not be told that we'd seen Elise driving away from the Palmeros'.

"And why not?" I asked.

"You don't know why she was there yet. Elise is one of the few in the family Saul's never doubted."

"Given where she was, maybe he should," Burns said. He had come up behind us.

Fergus opened the door, and we all entered the hall.

The upper hall was much like the room downstairs but polished. The wood finishes gleamed, and brass accents shone from all the clocks. The floor was a beautiful marble, and large windows let enough light in to put an extra shine on the whole space.

Saul sat at one of the tables. An old man sat across from him, hunched over the board. The man wore a fedora and a checkered shirt. Saul looked as impeccable as always in a dark-blue suit. He moved a piece, tapped a button on the timer, and looked up at us.

"Katherine." Seeing Grand and Burns, he added, "And friends. Lovely to see you all."

Both he and the man he had been playing stood. They shook hands. The man left.

Chapter 24: Grandmaster Grand

Saul walked over to Grand. It was odd to see the two of them next to each other. Saul was only slightly younger than Grand. In another life, they could have run in the same circles. "You must be Katherine's grandmother. I'm Saul Toucci," he said and took her hand in both of his.

"Theodora Waters," she replied.

"A true pleasure to meet you. I see where Katherine gets her grace."

"See there, buster," she said, turning to Burns, "that's manners. Maybe he can give you lessons once we crack this case."

Saul chuckled. Burns looked amused but didn't make an effort to defend his honor.

"I think your granddaughter knows well what she is about," Saul said.

"You have children," Grand said. "You know raising them to have common sense doesn't always keep them from bringing knuckleheads home."

"Burns isn't a knucklehead, Grand," I said while trying not to laugh.

"I'm touched by that stunning defense." Burns smirked.

Saul turned back to me and asked, "Do you play, Katherine?"

"Oh no, I can barely tell white from black. Grand's the one you want, if you're looking for a little competition."

"Truly?" he asked.

"Don't make me go all *Queen's Gambit* on you, sonny."

Saul seemed charmed by the moniker. "Well then, let us play while we discuss less pleasant things." He put out a hand and motioned Grand over to a new table.

They both sat. The board was already set up. Men magically appeared around us with more chairs. We all sat.

Grand made the first move.

"So, tell me what you have learned," Saul said.

"I can definitively tell you that your nephew died from injuries sustained from a fall from a great height."

Saul paused his movement over the pieces and sat back, staring at the board.

"I thought he had been beaten to death," Fergus said.

"That's why we do an autopsy."

"Surely, in your line of work, you all know that looks can be deceiving," Grand added and made her next move.

"The majority of the wounds on the body were administered postmortem," I said.

"So, like, someone beat him up afterward?" Fergus asked.

"And ran him over. Wanted to make sure he was good and dead," Grand said.

"Or wanted it to look like something it wasn't," Burns said. "Mr. Toucci, how much do you know about the goings-on in your family?"

"As your grandmother said, I'm aware that looks can be deceiving. Fergus, I find that I'm quite parched. Would you mind fetching me one of those delightful milkshakes from next door?"

Fergus paused for a moment. He clearly didn't want to be out of the room while we discussed the Toucci family, but it wasn't in his nature to deny Saul any request.

Before he could reply, Grand shouted, "Checkmate!" She jumped to her feet.

I wasn't sure whether she really had a checkmate so quickly or just wanted to make sure she didn't miss out on those milkshakes.

"I'll go with you. I have a tricky order."

So, milkshakes, then.

Saul's eyes twinkled.

"All right, boss," Fergus finally acquiesced.

We were all quiet until the two of them were out of the space.

"Fergus has found all this family business difficult," Saul said.

"You two are very close?" Burns asked.

We had never learned how Fergus and Saul hooked up.

"Fergus is like a son to me. The true son a mobster is expected to have. Tough, loyal, a bit of a chameleon. None of my own children were well suited to this life. But Fergus has always been my rock."

"He doesn't like this investigation. He's afraid of what we may find hurting you," I said.

"Yes. Fergus has been with the family longer than many of them have been alive. He hates when there is any strife."

"And right now, you have strife in spades," Burns said.

"You tell me," Saul said.

"Okay, did you know your sister was having financial troubles?" Burns said.

"Marion?" Saul asked, and Burns nodded. "She has always been very tight-lipped about her business dealings. You have to understand how difficult it was for her. The baby of the family. The only girl. My parents raised her in a bubble, hell-bent on protecting her and marrying her off to the right family. From the time she was able to string enough words together to argue about it, she's always been out to prove her independence."

"So she didn't come to you for help? Because we know she went to someone. Large amounts of money have been flowing into her accounts."

"No, it's not from me," Saul said. He furrowed his brow.

"The Palmeros told us that Nile and Marcus were often in their territory, causing trouble," I said. We needed to understand the connection with the Palmeros more. The story that Puddin and Fergus had spun seemed plausible, but I couldn't help but feel like we were missing something. "How do you know that this wasn't just a case of passions running too far? An accident in the wrong place?"

"As I told you before, Alejandro assures me that none of his people were involved," Saul said. "He doesn't want a war over this. If it had been an accident, I feel confident he would have been honest with me about it. I can't say that we wouldn't have been angry, but I wouldn't have let it get out of hand."

"Why's that?" Burns asked.

"It's a changing world, Mr. McPhee. You of all people know that my family is not the biggest threat in this city. The Palmeros wouldn't target us, and we both have other concerns."

"The Russians," I said. "That's why you're willing to use me. We have a common enemy."

"I respect you very much, Katherine, but yes, our common enemy does provide me with a certain amount of comfort."

"We'd like to talk to them. To Juan Carlos Palmero. There's a reason he decided to have Puddin call Fergus, and we need to know what it is. The timeline from the morning Nile was found just isn't adding up. They found the body at five a.m. Fergus didn't get a call until after ten."

"And they have tapes. Security footage of the Taco-Saki from the night Nile was killed, but they've refused to turn them over," Burns added.

"I'm not sure I would turn over tapes from a Toucci establishment to them either," Saul said. "It's just not done. This investigation is already pushing the envelope."

"Still, those tapes are the best way to reconstruct what Nile was doing at the Taco-Saki that night. If the Palmeros truly wanted to settle this for you, they would hand them over."

"Nile was last seen at the family dinner the night before at ten p.m.," Burns said.

"That's a lot of unaccounted-for time," I added.

"All right. I'll have Fergus arrange it," Saul replied.

"And we're going to need to speak to your family more directly. Joni in particular," Burns said.

Burns and I had agreed going in that if we could at all avoid it, we wouldn't tell Saul about Elise yet. At least not until we learned more about what was going on with her. We weren't telling Fergus that, but if we were going to get anywhere, we were going to need to pry into the family deeper than I had been able to at dinner.

"I believe we should continue to be discreet with dealing with my family. If they believe that I suspect things going on, I fear they will clam up, and we will get nowhere."

"Fergus and I are fine to continue as we have been. I've been invited to game night. I believe they all bought our story at dinner."

"Yes, I must commend you. That was quite a performance."

"I'm afraid with Fergus hovering, I didn't get as much as I'd hoped for."

"Well, Fergus was quite fond of Nile. Especially lately," Saul said.

"What?"

Burns and I both almost choked at that proclamation. Fergus had been very vocal to both of us about what a conniving backstabber he believed Nile to be.

"He had been trying to convince me that Nile was the best bet to take over the operation when I finally retire. I had my doubts, especially when things with Joni went so horribly wrong. A man who can't keep his home life happy shouldn't be running an empire. But

Fergus was adamant. I think Nile's death shook him. He's been withdrawn ever since."

With Fergus's continual pronouncements that if he were the one to off Nile, there wouldn't have been a body, I had dismissed him from our suspect list. I'd believed that he was sincerely trying to help the family. Something was not adding up.

I watched Fergus and Grand return, both holding a tray of milkshakes. Fergus and I needed to have a frank heart-to-heart.

Chapter 25: Sunday in the Park with Fletcher

I tried not to think about where I was going and drove partially on autopilot. Instead, I contemplated everything that had happened over the past few days. In some ways, I couldn't believe that I was in the middle of everything. The whole first round of craziness with the Russians had seemed surreal. Then came the Italians. And the Mexicans. And Dad's freedom on the line. Grand and Mom were both trying to adapt to our new set of circumstances.

I looked at the pamphlet for the forensics program staring at me on the passenger seat. We were all trying to adapt. So much seemed to be riding on the case. I honestly wasn't sure what would be better, solving it or not solving it. Knowing what we were facing would be better than the abyss of silence around my dad's situation. But I was pretty sure that I wasn't going to be thrilled with whatever information Saul had to offer on either of the cases. Still, I was trying to solve the case.

Solving it with a lot of help. I groaned at the thought of Burns and Fletcher and Grand with dreams of fruit-basket babies. That was a whole other mess to sort through. After the case.

I thought about what we knew about Nile's murder. Seeing Elise Toucci's legs dangling out of a dumpster at a Palmero restaurant certainly moved her up on the list of suspects. Marion was being blackmailed. Marcus and Lucia both seemed to have motive to want to get Nile out of the picture. Although neither of them seemed like the type.

But what really is the type? Would any of us have suspected Grand's boyfriend, sweet bow-tie-wearing Claude, would kill an unarmed man at point blank range? And what about me, for that matter? It hadn't been long since I had killed Dr. Hawthorne.

Because that was what we were willing to do for family.

After circling a couple of times, I finally found two spaces next to each other so I could park the monster truck. I felt bad, taking two spaces when parking was so congested, but I knew I'd feel worse if I accidentally rolled on top of someone's Tesla because of my inability to control the beast. As I walked through the park in search of Fletcher, I wondered if I would ever see my old wagon again.

Given my recent history with Forest Park, I wasn't exactly keen on meeting there. Lunch next to the spot where I had recently killed a man didn't seem conducive to good digestion. But Forest Park was one of the largest urban parks in the country, and Fletcher had suggested a location far from the scene of the crime.

A band played a gentle jazz tune that matched the warmth of the day and floated toward me. I followed the sound of the music toward the crowd and the band shell. Fletcher's floppy-haired head stuck up above the picnic goers as he searched the crowd. His lazy grin overtook him when he spotted me. He was dressed down from his usual beat-reporter suit, a salmon button-down over casual khaki shorts while those long, muscled legs screamed dangerous.

"Looking good, as always, Stretch," he said and kissed me on the cheek.

"Did you know W.C. Handy's recording of the famous 'St. Louis Blues' was based on his meeting an anguished widowed woman while homeless on the levee?" I thought I said that all in one breath.

"I guess that's why they call it the blues," he said with a smile. "Hope you're hungry." He pointed down at the orange, red, and white serape blanket covered in all the fixings for tacos and burritos.

"That's funny," I said. The premise for our latest encounter had been my retrieval of more information. He knew about the sombrero found with Nile, but I hadn't yet told him about the involvement of the Palmero family.

"Well, it's no Charlie Guido's, but I thought it would set the mood."

"Oh, if mobster ambiance is what you were going for, you should have brought sushi."

Fletcher cocked his head and looked me like I'd reveal the secret to the universe.

"Nile's body was found at the Taco-Saki."

"Ah, and the plot thickens," he said in a fake British accent.

We sat on the blanket, and he busied himself with fixing us plates. The soft jazz filtered down from the stage in the background. A gentle breeze blew. If I hadn't been there to ferret out info on the mob, it would have been a perfect date. I refused to think about Burns. Or watermelon fruit-basket babies and nosy old ladies.

"So, a potential heir to the Italian mafia empire turns up dead in their Mexican rival's backyard. How does that end up with you as the mediator?" he asked.

I noodled his concise summary of the situation, and he handed me a plate of tacos.

"The Palmeros swear they didn't do it. Alejandro Palmero himself came to Saul. He doesn't want a war with the Touccis. What I can't understand is why." I took a bite of taco. That was one of the puzzle pieces I couldn't quite fit yet that had been driving me bonkers. "I mean, I get why Saul would want to know the truth. What I don't get is why the Palmeros would go to such great lengths to ensure Saul knew it wasn't them. Why do they care?"

"You mean, why aren't they bragging that they took out one of the heirs apparent of the Italians?"

"Exactly. Even if they didn't do it, why not take the credit any-way? What do they have to lose?" I took another bite of my taco. "This is really good."

"Let me check some things. I didn't do mob until you... ya know. So I'm not as versed in the St. Louis organized crime scene as Gillian was." He frowned at the mention of his murdered friend. Burns got that same dark look whenever Gillian's name came up. I let myself feel some satisfaction that all the weird, dangerous work might give them both some peace.

"You know I appreciate anything you can give me."

"That's me, Mr. Helpful," he said, a smile replacing the scowl. "I'm here for you, Stretch," he said then took a bite of burrito.

I sat listening to the music, taking in the normalness of things. Everything with Fletcher was always so easy. Easy enough to forget about my dad being in prison and my trouble with the Russians. That I was investigating for the Italian mafia. A breeze blew, and the smell of tacos had me breathing in.

I felt Fletcher move closer. He put a hand on my arm. "But, Kat," he said, and I opened my eyes to look at him. "Whatever else I can find for you on the Palmeros, it won't change the only thing that matters. The Mexicans are a ruthless, brutal organization. You don't want to get on the wrong side of them."

Easy but not quite easy enough for me to forget that soon, too soon, I would be meeting with one of the most notorious crime boss-es in town.

Chapter 26: Swimming with the Shark

Juan Carlos "*El Tiburón*" Palmero was every Mexican drug lord *Narcos* and *Breaking Bad* had warned me about. Despite his five-foot-six stature, he commanded the room. His dark features—tan skin, dark hair, shadowy eyes—only made him seem more menacing. That and the large scar on his left cheek that ran from his ear to his chin. He had a small potbelly that hung slightly over his belt. His high-end designer cowboy boots were well-worn, not just for show. Juan Carlos didn't need to try to be showy.

I wished we'd had more time to gather information on the Palmeros before the meeting because I felt like we were going in blind. But as Flynn had pointed out, it probably wouldn't have helped too much. "Think mean and nasty," he kept saying any time I asked a question about them.

We were going in heavy. Even Neutron and I were carrying.

I'd convinced Grand that it would be a good day to visit Dr. Jaffee's grandmother at Autumn Springs. As amusing as it would have been to watch Grand smack down El Tiburón, I wasn't sure my heart could take it.

The event had taken endless rounds of negotiations to finalize—who, where, and what questions we could ask. Fergus, Burns, and Saul had decided that it would only inflame tensions for a Toucci representative to be present. They and the Palmeros did agree that Puddin from the Taco-Saki would be there. That helped me breathe a little more easily. I'd only met Puddin once, but I didn't think he would let anything get out of hand. He seemed genuinely amiable and good at handling people, something I thought the conversation was going to require as I watched Burns and Flynn load automatic weapons and holster boot knives in a practiced manner.

We had originally been told we'd be meeting at the Palmero estate, which was more like a compound. That was what had been negotiated. But the meeting had been switched at the last minute. I guessed that was to keep us off guard and off-balance. We had been prepared for the switch, though, despite not having a ton of information. The new location was actually better for us. The Palmero compound was an impenetrable fortress. Any trouble, and getting out would have been difficult.

St. Louis didn't have an especially large Hispanic population, but it did have a well-entrenched enclave in the south city. To find it, one had to walk down Jefferson Street until they ran into the large Cherokee statue on Cherokee Street, home to the first Wehrenberg movie theater ever and the proud location for every large Hispanic celebration worth noticing.

And it was apparently the current "office" location of the Palmero Cartel. We'd been ushered into an older cream brick building just down from the historic Casa Loma ballroom. A scrawny, goateed man wearing a dirty white tank top, baggy khaki shorts, and a large handgun prominent on his thin hips pushed through a puke-green door and into the waiting presence of El Tiburón himself.

There were no greetings, just staring all around. I bit my tongue to keep from blurting out anything ridiculous. I finally spied Puddin near the back of the room. He smiled and waved at me. I smiled back.

Without a word, only a nod from Juan Carlos, we were surround by several beefy men. Burns and Flynn both stiffened. Neutron inhaled. We'd known it would happen. It had been part of the negotiations. But Burns and team weren't going to be seen as weak wallflowers about it either. They'd all dressed in camo. Burns and Flynn cut an unmistakable figure of the all-American heroes they were, poised and ready. Taut muscles bulged. Their matching Special Forces skull tattoos peeked out from their T-shirts. After seeing them in suits so routinely, I often forgot how menacing they could look when necessary. There was no subtlety in their "Don't mess with us" military vibe.

Oddly, the Palmeros hadn't requested Flynn and Burns relinquish their weapons, which was a good thing and the first hurdle I thought could trip us up. There was no way Burns was going to let me anywhere near a drug cartel without some serious firepower, regardless of whether the meeting was arranged and supposedly friendly or not. Instead, the cartel searchers seemed more interested in ferreting out listening devices. They waved wands over us and patted us down.

"You should at least buy me dinner first," Flynn said. He smirked at the guy feeling him up, who actually blushed.

Burns and Neutron were next. The man patting down Neutron took several electronic devices off him and examined them.

"If I wanted to spy on you, you'd never know the device was there," Neutron said.

That garnered a raised eyebrow from Juan Carlos but no comment. He sniffed and nodded, and the man moved to me.

My research told me that cartel men were more apt to respect a high-class, well-adorned woman. Well, respect as much as their machismo-based, egotistical male hierarchy allowed without my first killing a man in front of them all. Nonetheless, never one to shy away from an opportunity to dress up, I wanted to play my part and had gone with a power suit—a Moschino single-breasted crepe jacket with sartorial details and cream trim layered over matching single-trim crepe flare-legged pants.

Still, when the man came close to pat me down, I tensed. Instead of thinking about what was happening, I focused on the spider on the man's shirt as he ran his hands over my suit jacket. His shirt was from Pure Blanco, the fashion line from The Queen of Cocaine. The black-widow-spider logo paid homage to her tendency to murder her exes. That there was such a thing as narco-fashion boggled my mind. That perhaps I should be considering alternative plans for my ex was a better thought.

That was until the man moved his hand under my breast. I tried not to show emotion, knowing I wanted to come off as cool and controlled to get the information that I needed. But it wasn't working.

"Did you know a male spider forces itself into the mouth of a red widow until she eats him?" I asked.

He stilled and looked at me. Before he could respond, Burns had the man on his knees with his arm wrenched behind his back.

"Apologize," Burns said.

The man looked at Juan Carlos. Instead of intervening, he smiled so widely I could see all his teeth, reminding me why his nickname was El Tiburón, the shark. His teeth all looked pointy, like they could rip open anything, including flesh. I noticed Puddin had moved to the front, close to Burns and the man. Soon, it was clear Juan Carlos would not be saying anything. Burns wrenched the man's arm a bit higher.

"I apologize for my forwardness," the man said finally in a thick accent, and Burns released him, throwing him to the floor.

I'd known this meeting was necessary, and we were missing some piece of the puzzle that my gut told me lay with the Palmeros. That didn't make the whole thing any less terrifying. Burns squeezed my waist in reassurance.

Juan Carlos snapped his fingers, and most of the men left the room, leaving us, himself, Puddin, and two very large bodyguards. That was when I finally noticed a younger man lurking in the background near the bookcase. In all the commotion, I hadn't seen him before, which was hard to believe because he was beautiful. He had feathery-light hair, perfect glowing skin, and a chiseled jaw. He was fit but not overly bulky with muscles and decked out in an exquisite

Barcelonan Massimo Dutti summer suit. He looked like he had just stepped out of a fashion magazine.

Burns followed my gaze and also caught sight of him then. "Who's the twink?" he asked.

Juan Carlos smiled widely at that but ignored the question. "Please, make yourselves comfortable," he said and gestured to the couch and chairs in the sitting area away from the desk he had been leaning against.

Burns and I sat on the couch with its back to the entryway. Flynn and Neutron lurked behind us, between the bodyguards and the door. Puddin and Juan Carlos sat in side-by-side armchairs, facing us. A midcentury coffee table sat between the couch and the chairs. Copies of *La Voz* and *El Mundo Latino* littered the top. In the middle sat a depression-glass bowl with fruit. Apples, oranges, and bananas looked inviting but out of place in the otherwise-dreary space.

The pretty man in the back was fidgety, shifting his weight and scuffing his shoes, but he didn't make a move to come closer. Burns was stiff against my side. He watched the pretty man. Juan Carlos watched Burns. I tried to breathe.

"I'm so glad we could finally arrange this," I said. I hadn't realized good hostess skills would be so important in my new career, but I was thankful for them. I seemed to be finding myself quite frequently in situations where I was the only one with social graces in a situation screaming for them.

It worked, too, because Juan Carlos, whose eyes hadn't left Burns since we'd sat down, finally turned his attentions toward me.

"Hmm," he mostly grunted and appraised me.

Puddin reached to the table and took two sheets of paper. He handed one to me and kept one for himself.

"These are the agreed-upon questions we are willing to openly discuss," he said.

I didn't need to look at them. I'd already memorized them before we arrived. Burns thought the whole exercise was ridiculous, so he ignored them.

"You should know that I was initially against this. It's only recently that I've changed my mind about this so-called investigation." Juan Carlos steepled his fingers under his lips, his elbows perched on the armrests.

"Oh, yeah, not too keen on having your murdering outed by the chickie, eh?" Flynn asked from behind the couch.

Juan Carlos scowled at Flynn. Puddin coughed and crossed his legs. Burns sat completely unmoving, but his gaze shifted from the pretty man to Juan Carlos. Feeling Burns's eyes on him, Juan Carlos returned the stare. He took a large pocket knife from his pants, opened it, and then leaned forward and stabbed an apple in the bowl.

"Tell me, *la investigadora*, do you think my family are murderers?" Juan Carlos asked. His voice was husky and controlled. He sat back with the apple, removed the knife, and began to cut a piece from it.

"I don't think that's the question that matters here. Under the right circumstances, anyone can take a life," I said. I didn't think reminding them of my recent history would be a bad thing for the conversation.

He put the piece of apple in his mouth and chewed while watching me.

Before he could finish chewing, I added, "What I'm charged with figuring out is what the circumstances were that led to Nile Toucci ending up at the Taco-Saki."

"We already told you everything we know. We have no reason to withhold any information," Puddin said.

"Except that's not quite true, is it?" Burns asked loudly, addressing the pretty man in the back.

From Burns's earlier question, I'd thought he didn't know who the man in the back was, but it seemed as though I might have been mistaken, that maybe he was pressing Juan Carlos about the man's presence for a reason. The pretty man stilled his fidgeting.

Juan Carlos put the apple on the coffee table. He reached across to Puddin, took the paper with questions on it, and jabbed the knife into it, sticking it to the coffee table. Sitting back, he took out a handkerchief from his pocket and wiped his hands. Too few men carried those lately, but they were always very handy, I thought.

"What do you *really* want to know?" he asked finally.

I sat up on the couch and moved into my final-question pageant posture—spine straight and stomach in for the best abdomen breath, which helped with articulation and enunciation. I looked squarely at Juan Carlos. "I want to know why I'm here," I said. "I want to know why the Palmeros aren't screaming from the rooftops that they bagged the heir apparent to the Toucci family dynasty, whether they actually did or not."

Both Burns and I caught the increase in fidgeting from the pretty man in the back, but neither of us wanted to derail Juan Carlos's answer.

He finished wiping his hands and threw the handkerchief onto the coffee table, covering the apple, and plucked the knife out of the wood.

"As I understand it, señorita, you are new to our business, yes?" he asked. His pose in the chair was relaxed. He played with the knife, opening and closing it. "You would not have cause to know how difficult business has become over the years. St. Louis is a little fish in a very big pond. Yet it is also the center of the country."

"A hub," I said. I didn't understand yet where he was going, but he looked contemplative. I wasn't sure whether it was because he didn't know how much to tell me or he was making up a lie.

"Exactly. The pass-through point for many activities on their way to other places. The cartels have been at war with one another for many decades. They only grow more violent, more ruthless." He clicked the knife closed one last time and then set it down on the table. "I do not like violence for the sake of it."

I wasn't sure if I believed that, but he said it with a confidence that led me to believe it was something he had spent some time thinking about. I didn't think I wanted to know what circumstances had led to the introspection.

He stood up then, and I wondered if that was the end of the conversation—if I had missed some grand clue somewhere. I remembered Saul saying something similar at our lunch, about the Russians and how disgusted he was by their reliance on violence for the sake of it, and I wondered if the Palmeros and the Touccis were more involved with each other than either had let on.

He didn't move, though. Instead, a wistful look came over him, his eyes softening, a strange look for a consummate killer. "There is an old Spanish proverb," he said. "*Enfrenta al el amor de frente porque la muerte no tiene fuerzas.*"

He didn't say any more but started moving toward the door. I translated it in my head. "Face love head on, because death has no strength."

Before I could ask what that had to do with the whole mess, he spoke. "Come. I have something to show you."

Chapter 27: Who's Watching the Watchers

Whatever had overcome Juan Carlos in his office had passed by the time we made it into the hall. He ushered us toward one of the other closed doors in the narrow passage. The handsy skinny guy stood guard in front of it. He opened the door, and we all moved into the room. Burns glared at him as we passed. I noticed the pretty man hadn't left the office. Maybe he didn't have anything to do with this and happened to be there.

We walked through the door into a familiar sight. Neutron's eyes grew wide as he scanned Palmero tech central. Monitors and computers littered every surface. Lights blinked. The room was quiet except for the whirring of the machines and a light tapping at a keyboard. I strained my neck to find the frantic typist.

I finally spied a black ponytail bobbing up and down while the tapping increased in ferocity. The person growled.

"*Que pasa, hombre?*" Juan Carlos asked loudly as we walked farther into the room.

The person at the keyboard didn't turn to see who had entered.

"Nowhere. I'm nowhere with this *pedazo de mierda*," he said to the room, still not turning. He kept typing.

We stopped behind him. His thick horn-rimmed glasses matched his shiny black hair. They made him look older than he probably was. He had the bushiest eyebrows I thought I'd ever seen and wore a T-shirt with some anime thing I couldn't quite make out and jeans.

A massive TV monitor hung in front of him. Multiple machines covered the surface next to him. He switched from one keyboard to another and typed something before finally looking up at us and scanning our group, dismissing Burns and me with barely a glance. When his eyes fell on Neutron, he finally smiled. "You brought help."

"Do you two know each other?" Burns asked Neutron.

I watched Flynn move closer to the bug-eyed genius. *Possessive*, I thought with an internal smile. Protective, he rested his hand on his gun.

"Nah, man. Relax," the ponytail man said. He raised his hands to make sure we knew he wasn't carrying. "Everyone knows the best hacker in the city works for you. And I was pretty sure it wasn't the big guy over there." He pointed at Flynn. "Man, that takedown of the Supreme dude? Epic!"

Burns had rescued Neutron from a psych ward where he was being evaluated after the genius had sent a lifetime supply of Viagra to the chief justice, purchased with the chief justice's very own credit card, in a misguided attempt to help his wrongly maligned mother.

"Great, a fan girl," Flynn said.

I thought the man might take offense, but his smile widened.

"This is Monarch," Juan Carlos said. He clapped the man on the shoulder.

"As light as a butterfly," Neutron said, pointing at Monarch. He stepped up to shake the man's hand. "You did those Godzilla road signs. That was awesome work."

A bunch of the city roads had recently been shut down when all the digital roadwork signs had been changed to dire warnings of an impending Godzilla attack. Despite the ridiculousness of the threat, the city went into a panic. The press had billed it as a harmless prank.

But it wasn't the first time weird things had happened to the roads recently. Burns hadn't been convinced it was all so harmless and had Neutron looking into whether something else unusual had occurred at the time of the shutdown. The Palmeros' hacker being involved gave credence to his gut feeling.

I noticed Flynn scowling as the two geeks became lost in their own conversation, as though the rest of us didn't exist, much to Flynn's apparent dismay. I turned to Burns to share my amusement at that, but Burns was ignoring the whole thing. Instead, he glared at the large TV monitor.

"That's why you won't turn over surveillance," Burns said and pointed at the screen.

I looked up at the monitor to the squiggly lines that crisscrossed the jumbotron. Occasionally, a figure could be made out on the screen, but the interference kept any distinguishing marks from being recognized. As it played on, it became obvious that the whole thing was pretty much useless.

"The security footage was the first thing we checked when the body was found. I figured that would be the easiest way to clear up this mess with the Touccis or give us a bargaining chip if we needed it." Juan Carlos put his hands on his hips and squinted up at the grainy footage.

"This is how you found it?" Burns asked.

"Sort of. The file has been tampered with," he said and turned to Burns. "When we went to view them, we noticed the surveillance room had been broken into. The system files were open, and this is what we found.

"It's some kind of weird virus that distorts files. It's really kind of clever. If they'd erased the file, we could still probably have recovered it, but this overwrote what was there, making it unreadable," Monarch said.

"So whoever did it isn't stupid," Flynn said.

"At least not about computers," Juan Carlos replied.

His lips thinned into a stiff, straight line. His chest puffed out, and I felt the tension in the room thicken. Whoever did this, Juan Carlos was going to make them regret it.

"We haven't been able to fix it, and I didn't think la investigadora would let it lie for much longer," he said.

I stood taller at that. He was right. Burns and I both would have pushed for it. The timeline of things just didn't add up. This video could help us figure out what had happened.

"I know it doesn't look good, but Monarch assures me your boy wonder here could figure that out. We want to know who's behind this as badly as you do."

That, I believed. I'd never understood the term "looked murderous" until now.

"Who had access to the security room?" Flynn asked, giving Monarch the stink eye.

"Dude, if I'd wanted the file to disappear, trust me—I wouldn't have left this behind," Monarch said.

"Anyone with access to the Taco-Saki would have been able to do this. We don't centrally house the majority of our security footage. Each site holds its own."

"I've tried all the obvious recovery strategies. When the boss man told me he was meeting with you today, I knew it was a sign to turn it over to a higher power." He smiled at Neutron.

Flynn glared at him again.

Neutron leaned over and looked at several of the laptops on the table that were running programs. "May I?" he asked and put down the gun he'd been holding.

Monarch looked at his boss, who nodded then gestured to the keyboard. Neutron's fingers flew across the keyboard. Code flashed up on the screen then down again. I held my breath. It felt like everyone in the room was.

Everyone except Flynn. His eyes sparkled as he watched Neutron. *I wonder if he knows.* I wondered what Burns thought of it. Flynn and Burns went way back, but that could be a sticky situation. I made a mental note to ask later.

"Okay. I can probably recover the file but not here. I need my gear," Neutron said.

"You want us to give you the files?" Juan Carlos asked.

"You want to know who did this? You heard him. He can't do it here," Burns said and held Juan Carlos's gaze.

Neither of them blinked for a minute.

"Fine. You can take a copy under the condition that once it's fixed, we get to see it before the Touccis."

I rolled that around in my head and could see that Burns was doing the same thing. I wasn't sure we had that kind of authority. Fergus would have a small cow when he found out about the arrangement.

But I couldn't see Saul having an issue with it. He wanted to know where his family's loyalties lay and who'd killed his nephew, even if it was someone close.

"No dice," I said.

Burns looked at me, startled. He had probably come to the same conclusion I had.

Juan Carlos leveled his evil stare at me.

"We can't agree to something that might leave the Touccis in a vulnerable position. What I can agree to is that we will show you whoever tampered with the tape, regardless of what affiliations they have."

Juan Carlos relaxed some at that.

"I can also promise that if anyone from your organization is seen having a connection to Nile's situation, I will let you know before I take it to Saul."

"We have the file. I don't have to agree to any of this," Juan Carlos said.

"True," Burns answered.

I appreciated the backup. I wasn't used to negotiating with people who could have me killed with a nod.

"But you won't get to see what's on it without Neutron's help. The bottom line is you have a leak. Someone with access and knowledge of your setup didn't want you or us to see what's on that file. If it were me, plugging that hole would be almost as important as appeasing the Italians."

"Who, I might add, will only be more suspicious that the Palmeros were involved with Nile's murder when they learn you have a way to see who was involved and are refusing to show it to us," I said. Then bit my tongue so that I didn't say anything else.

"Fine. I agree to your terms."

Neutron whipped out a thumb drive from somewhere I didn't want to think too much about, and Monarch copied the files.

IT WAS TWILIGHT BY the time we finished with the Palmeros. We'd brought two cars to the meeting. Burns had client meetings across town. Flynn went with him. Neutron and I climbed into the boat. We were taking the files back to McPhee Security so Neutron could begin to work his magic. We'd picked up DC on the way. They were going to check on the progress Neutron's searches had made in finding Kimi.

"How hard can it be to find one woman?" he asked from the back seat.

"It's a big country. She could be anywhere," Neutron said.

"We have to find her. Now that I'm learning Korean chess, I'm sure her family will love me. There's a lot to do if I'm going to have to move to Korea."

"You're not moving to Korea," I said, looking back at him in the rearview mirror.

He wasn't really serious, was he? Sure, I wanted him happy, but Korea was a long way away.

"A minute ago, you were totally against getting married," I said.

"Since Kimi disappeared, I've done some soul-searching. Do you know what's worse than becoming Korean or even worse than getting married?"

I looked at him through the rearview mirror expectantly.

"Being alone," he said with anguish in his voice.

I maneuvered the boat out to one of the side streets a few blocks from the Palmero headquarters. That time of night, side streets back to Burns's were a better bet for avoiding traffic jams. Even St. Louis had its issues with traffic density.

Suddenly, we were all jerked back and forth with force. Someone had slammed into the back of us.

"What was that?" DC yelled.

A truck was behind us, the bright headlights blinding me in the mirror. The car showed no signs of slowing, but I knew Ray Ray was going to freak over my being in an accident, even if it wasn't my fault. Did mobsters have insurance, and how was I going to exchange information anyway?

I started to slow down and made the customary "I've had an accident" move to pull over to the side of the road to check it out and yell at the person who'd hit us.

"No, you can't stop!" Neutron screamed and grabbed the wheel, swerving back into traffic.

"What do you mean, I 'can't stop'? We have to exchange information. This is a mobster rental," I said.

The car bumped us again, taking off a good chunk of the back bumper.

"Drive, Kat!" he yelled and pulled out his cell phone as I stepped on the gas. "Boss, we've got a problem."

"Is that Burns?" DC asked. "He'd better be sending helicopters to shoot these morons."

I frantically tried to avoid being hit again, swerving in and out of traffic as the truck followed.

Neutron put Burns on speaker.

"Where are you, Kat?"

"Eighth and Madison, I think, heading north."

"Whatever you do, don't stop, I'll pick you up on the security system and send Flynn to intercept."

"I'm coming," Flynn said in the background.

"I don't know how long she can hold them off," Neutron replied. The other side of the road emptied of oncoming cars, and the truck swerved out, trying to pull up alongside us. "Faster, Kat!"

Was that a second car in the rearview mirror?

"It's a boat, not a sports car," I said. "It doesn't go much faster!"

"Flynn's coming, Kat. You just have to hang on," Burns said.

As the car got nearly parallel with ours, the window rolled down, the muzzle of an automatic weapon appeared, and it started shooting at us. Neutron ducked, and I scrunched down, trying to steer, one hand on the wheel, the other on Neutron's cell phone. It had flown into the air when the first shots broke the glass.

"Is that man yelling at you?" I asked.

The man with the gun pointed at us was trying to say something.

"I don't think this is the best atmosphere to have a congenial conversation," DC said.

More shots fired. I screamed, turning my head to try to avoid the flying glass. I tried swerving, but the other car still had a pretty open shot at us. The sound of the bullets spraying into the side of the rental was deafening, like the sound of a plane engine starting. Neutron wailed in pain, and I swerved again, causing the cell phone to go flying. I could hear Burns's faint voice around my feet.

"Is that blood? Is he bleeding? I don't do blood," DC yelled from the back seat.

"You work in a morgue. How can you not do blood?" Neutron replied, trying to put pressure on his leg while avoiding bullets.

"That's dead people. It's totally different," DC said and stuck his head between his knees, I guessed to head off the hyperventilating more than to duck the bullets.

"What's happening?" Burns asked.

Before I could try to find the phone and answer, a large SUV barreled down the other side of the road. A figure that I recognized by the shape as Flynn was half out the window of the passenger side, almost sitting on the window, a large weapon pointed at the car coming toward us. He shot several times, causing the car next to us to slow down and get behind us. As the SUV passed us, whoever was driving swerved right at the car following us and slammed on the brakes to avoid being hit and skidded, causing it to swerve off the road to keep control. Neutron screamed, and I tried to keep the car going.

"Neutron, what's wrong?"

"Pain. I think I've been shot. Flynn's gonna be so pissed."

I could see through the back window that the car following us had come to a stop and quickly reversed to get out of there. The SUV followed. Feeling safer now that we weren't being kamikazed by a two-ton killing machine, I maneuvered our car to the side of the road to try to figure out how badly Neutron was hurt. Before long, both the other vehicles were out of sight.

I flipped on the inside car lights. Neutron was slumped down in a half-fetal position. Blotches of blood seeped through his shirt in multiple places. He sobbed. I tried to put pressure on the wounds. I didn't know where DC was but could hear his voice in the background.

"Kat, Neutron!" The faint sound came from somewhere around my feet. My hands were shaking as I frantically searched for the phone.

"He's been hit. He can't die!" That was all I could think, over and over, that I was going to be responsible for getting him killed.

The next hour of my life was a long blur. Burns talked DC and me through assessing Neutron. DC helped pull him out of the car, onto the ground, and rolled him from side to side, checking for entry and exit wounds. None of the wounds on his upper body looked serious, mostly cuts from the shattered glass—one in his shoulder and a more serious one in the side of his abdomen below the ribs. Blood oozed from his trousers, but I couldn't find a hole. I did as Burns instructed, applying pressure and packing the wounds.

By the time the ambulance arrived, Neutron was unconscious, and DC was hysterical. We knelt over him, holding his hand and trying to convince him, convince us all, that it would be okay.

"You cannot die like this and leave me to tell your boyfriend that he likes you," DC said. "You have to live so I can see the shock on his face when he finally figures out that the two of you are dating."

Neutron didn't respond, but I had to agree with the sentiment. Neutron could not die.

The ambulance came at some point and loaded Neutron and DC, who was in shock or bleeding or something. I didn't know anything anymore.

Burns must have pulled up. I didn't remember seeing him come, but one minute I was talking to him through the phone, then there he was.

"I can't stay long. I need to check on Flynn and get him to the hospital with Neutron. The cops and the press will be here soon." He was standing directly in front of me, his hands on my shoulders as he checked me out. "Vick says you did good."

"Vick?"

"Ambulance driver. He said Neutron's in much better shape than he could be." He swished my bangs out of my face. It was such a gentle motion. He put his cheek next to mine and whispered into my ear, "Everyone's okay. Breathe."

Tears streamed down my cheeks. "An average of one hundred ninety-five thousand people die of potentially preventable hospital medical errors each year."

"Your head's bleeding. We need to get you looked at." He ran his hands through my hair, assessing. "Doesn't look too bad. Some glass. You'll have a wicked scar," he said. "I've called for reinforcements. I'm Neutron's medical proxy, so I need to go to the hospital."

We both heard the ambulance siren and jumped. He kissed the top of my head, then he was gone, as mysteriously as he had come. I headed back to check on the car but didn't make it far.

"Stretch, this is no place for a proper date. I'm starting to think you're a headline junkie." Even in the middle of a major accident scene, Fletcher Reid looked casually in place. "Whoa, Katherine, are you...?" And that was the last thing I remembered before I passed out.

Chapter 28: Follow the Money

I woke up in a strange bed, a massive pounding in my head and wearing a strange T-shirt that smelled familiar, all woodsy and male. Rolling over to escape the sun peering through the window, I saw a note on the nightstand. Next to it were some aspirin and a glass of water.

"Take the pills. I had some errands. I'll be back soon." It wasn't signed, but there was no doubt it was from Burns.

I got up and found my way to a bathroom and took a shower. Afterward, I stared at my clothes. They were covered in blood. Burns had left out a McPhee Security uniform for me. I slipped back into the safety of Burns's T-shirt and put on the McPhee standard-issue cargo pants. I rolled the cuffs and headed into the main space of the loft.

At the click of the front door latch, I jumped.

"Nice shirt," Burns said from behind me.

"I like your space," I said, turning around.

Burns looked especially nice in charcoal-gray pinstriped suit pants. The sleeves of his dark dress shirt were rolled up. Dark hair on his forearms poked out underneath. Burns had great forearms. I wanted to pet them. He eyed me up and down. I could see the approval of my outfit. He moved toward me and took me in his arms.

We seldom did this. Whatever weird relationship—situation-ship—space we were in had kept the normal affection that happened between people connected like we were from flowing. I could feel the heat of him through the embrace. The worry. The need to hang on.

We both thought that after the Russian mess, I was safe. Today was a sharp reminder that wasn't true.

"The majority of car accidents occur less than five miles from home," I said.

I felt his smirk against my hair. He took a deep breath and released me.

"I'm pretty sure this wasn't some random fender bender," he said.

"I'm letting myself believe that Neutron and DC are fine, because otherwise, you wouldn't be here."

"They're okay. DC is more hysterical than injured. Cuts and scrapes from the glass. I left him with Bradley, drinking cocoa and looking at suit magazines."

I smiled at that. The way to DC's heart was through chocolate and fine silk.

"Neutron has a pretty big gash on his leg. Needed stitches. I left Flynn to fuss over him."

My smile widened at that. Burns looked thoughtful.

"Uh-huh," I said. "Fussing's one word for it." His eyes met mine, and I felt relief when I saw the mischief in them. "Do you think they know?"

"Honestly, I have no idea. I don't even know if Neutron's ever had a date in his life, male or female. And Flynn, well, no one would ever describe him as emotionally aware."

"But you're okay with this, right?" I asked. It seemed safe, like I already knew the answer, but if things were going to go the way they looked, I thought it would be healthy for everyone to say it out loud.

"The whole thing makes my head hurt. Flynn's been my best friend since kindergarten. Neutron's like a little brother to me. I don't know who to have the shovel talk with. And that's if we can drag Flynn out of the closet far enough for him to acknowledge things."

"I don't know him that well, but I don't think he's going to get there without a serious amount of help, Burns."

He blew out a big breath and ran his hand through his hair. "Yeah. Me either."

"They are very cute, though," I said and watched the intended wince contort his face. I giggled.

"Watching Flynn dote on him like a panic-stricken schoolgirl with a crush was all I could handle for one day. Let's talk about something easier, like who's trying to kill you this time."

At that, it was my turn to sigh. "You really think it was attempted murder?"

"No, not really," he said. "Neutron said someone was shouting about a thumb drive, and the whole thing had an aura of amateur hour to it."

"It didn't feel that way when people were shooting at me."

He stepped back to me and pulled me into an embrace. "I know. I'd happily give up this adrenaline-fueled side of our relationship."

"I'm not sure that's going to happen anytime soon." I let myself melt into him for one more moment of calm.

BURNS'S LOFT WAS ABOVE the McPhee Security and Ingensys offices. Living so close to his workspace probably made some of his longer nights easier. Between late-night client meetings and being close anytime something went wrong with a security gig, he didn't work a regular nine-to-five, by any stretch.

We walked through the back passages, and he key-carded us through various doors, until he came to a halt as we turned the last corner.

"Greg," Burns said, and the man at the war-room door startled.

Was he listening at the door? I recognized Greg Hardt, Burns's partner in Ingensys. He now seemed to be acting like a stalker and making Burns tense.

Ingensys was on the third floor, where the view was the best for impressing clients. I wondered what had brought him down here, to McPhee Security, the back hallway maze, and into the war room.

"Oh, there you are," Greg said and plastered a smile on his face.

I'd worked the pageant set for years. I knew fake when I saw it.

"I'd thought you'd left," Burns said and eyed him as we walked closer.

"Yes, well..." He paused. "I heard about all the unpleasantness and thought I'd come see how everyone was doing."

A lie. Why was Burns's partner lying to him?

"We're all fine," I said. The pressure from Burns's hand at the small of my back increased. "Minor scrapes."

"Do you have any idea what happened?" he asked, eyes wide, seeming genuinely curious.

"That is the question of the day," Burns said. "And where we were headed." He pointed at the war-room door.

"Oh, right," Greg said. "I'll let you get back to it. So glad everyone's well." And then he practically fled down the hall.

I looked at Burns watching Greg scurry down the hall. I didn't ask about the strangeness of that. We had enough on our plates. I filed it to ask later and pulled Burns's attention back to me by reaching into his pocket for his security card.

He smiled down at me, the contact warming us both. I turned and opened the door.

"Why would Kimi be in Cleveland?" DC asked, a note of hysteria in his voice.

"How should I know? Maybe she wanted to see the Rock-n-Roll Hall of Fame before they kick her out of the country," Neutron replied. He was sitting in front of the extra-large monitors, tapping away. Two stick-skinny legs stuck out the bottoms of his gym shorts and were covered in a fine reddish-brown hair. One was propped on a chair, a thick white bandage around the thigh.

"I'm sorry I almost got you killed," I said.

They both turned toward me.

"You should come with a warning label," DC said. He held his mug of hot chocolate with both hands.

Flynn walked in, carrying an armful of bags and a drink tray full of shakes.

"It's okay, though. Flynn brought White Castle," DC said then jumped from his seat and moved toward Flynn.

"White Castle makes everything better," Neutron said with a smile at Flynn.

"Not only White Castle, I think," I said and nudged his shoulder.

He looked up at me, bafflement in his eyes. This might be a harder love match to make than I had first thought. Why were men always so clueless?

"So which mobster do we expect tried to off you this time?" Flynn asked. He'd handed over the food to DC for distribution and was fluffing the pillow under Neutron's elevated leg.

Burns shook his head and turned toward the screen.

"Hard to say," I said. "I am very popular in certain circles these days."

Flynn rolled his eyes at that.

"None of them, I think. This was an amateur job," Burns said as he watched the security-cam footage of the chase play out across the screen.

"Tell that to Neutron's leg or my beautiful, now-blemished skin," DC said and patted one of his several bandages. The stark white of them stood in brilliant contrast against his dark skin.

"You're really okay?" I asked Neutron.

"He's going to be fine," Flynn said before Neutron could say anything.

"Doc says I should be up and around in no time. In time for our first match for sure. You're going to come, right?"

"To the juggling thing?" DC asked and then looked at Flynn.

"I can't very well let the idiot play by himself now, can I?" Flynn said and fussed with Neutron's pillow again.

Neutron beamed at him.

"Provided no more mobsters try to kill us again, we'll be there," I said.

"If this had been the Palmeros, we wouldn't have seen them coming," Burns said, turning back to the video.

"Same with the Russians, as much as it pains me to say," Flynn said. He was pushing more food toward Neutron.

"No hits on the plates. Stolen. No camera picked up an image for facial rec, but I'm still processing it."

"We can't rule out that this was Toucci related," Burns said and turned toward the board that had all the photos and known information we had collected since first meeting Saul.

"I have made more progress there," Neutron said.

Without being asked, Flynn handed Neutron a different keyboard. A picture showed on the screen.

"Meet Laurence Paulson. Masters in English from Washington University. Stayed after graduation. Worked at Teach for America for a year before joining the staff at Saint Francis of Assisi, teaching her." A school photo of Joni and Niles's adorable daughter appeared next to the picture of Laurence Paulson.

"Wow," DC said.

If Grand's boyfriend, Claude, had had a young nephew, he would have looked exactly like Laurence Paulson, from the combed-over bowl haircut to the bow tie and thick-rimmed glasses.

"What is someone like Joni Toucci doing with the likes of him?" Flynn asked.

Which was the absolute wrong thing that Flynn could have said. Neutron was immediately defensive.

"Oh yeah? And what's so wrong with him?" Neutron asked. He set the keyboard down a tad harder than necessary, crossed his arms, and stared right at Flynn, daring him to answer. "Just because he's a bit"—he waved his hands at the screen—"geeky looking." He sighed, taking the wind out of his own sails. "Doesn't mean he can't have other things to offer." His voice cracked.

"Now, don't go getting all defensive, Baby Einstein," DC said. "You and that guy are not even a bit alike. Everyone knows you're fierce. You could kill a man with your keyboard. Right, Flynn?" DC stared right at the ex-soldier.

Flynn turned bright red but side-eyed Neutron to see if DC's words had appeased the situation.

"Uh, right?" Flynn replied.

I didn't know if the questioning tone was going to do anything for Neutron's insecurity. I appreciated his effort, but those two's issues were not going to get solved today.

"Okay, but we already knew that Laurence and Joni were having an affair," I said.

Neutron picked up the keyboard again, softer now. "Yes, but we didn't know that Laurence here was being blackmailed by none other than..." He tapped the keys, and a third picture appeared.

"Nile Toucci," Burns said.

"Wasn't he a lovely boy scout," DC said.

"Our professor here is married to this woman," Neutron said as a picture of a lovely blond woman came on the screen. "Nile was threatening to tell Laurence's wife."

"I didn't think teachers made enough money to be blackmailed. Even posh-private-school ones," Flynn said.

"Oh, no, Nile wasn't after money. I managed to get into one of his social media accounts and trace that to a hidden email. Nile was leaning on Laurence to spy on Joni and run her down to Saul." A picture of a bunch of men standing in a row came on screen. "Saul is on the board of Saint Francis, and Laurence is the teacher liaison to the board. Nile was after sole custody of Camila."

"I can't imagine Saul supporting that," I said.

"Maybe if Laurence did his job well enough, he'd be persuaded," Burns said. "Whatever the situation, looks like we have two more suspects to run down."

"I'm still trying to figure out Marion's money situation," Neutron said.

"And the Palmeros?" Burns asked.

"That's been a less successful endeavor. I've got the program to fix the surveillance file running, but it's going to take a while, probably a couple of iterations. The harder part has been the Palmero business model." He ran his fingers over the keyboard, and newspaper articles filled the screen.

I moved closer so that I could better see what they were. DC followed me.

"These are all articles about police drug busts," I said.

"Lots of Russian names there," DC said, pointing.

"Right? It seemed weird to me too," Neutron said. "Either someone's selling out the Russians in the drug trade, or the Palmeros could just be better at bribing the police."

"It's not totally surprising. We've learned that the Russians are a bunch of morons," Flynn said.

"Yeah, but this is a new thing. The Russians and the Mexicans are the biggest players in the drug trade here. Up until a couple of years ago, the known Palmero associates were getting busted about as much as the Russians. Now, it's only the Russians. But it's not just that. They're shifting businesses. Divesting."

A bunch of court documents appeared on the screen. Sales documents. Coin laundries, bars, donut shops.

"They're dumping all their cash businesses," Burns said. "Looks like the Palmeros are getting out of the drug trade."

"So how are they making money?"

"That is the magic question," Neutron said.

"Well, we may not get Palmero answers anytime soon, but we do have an opportunity to make some progress on the Touccis tomorrow night," I said.

"Wait until you see my outfit," DC added.

"Outfit?" Neutron asked.

"It's game night!" DC exclaimed. "Tennis, anyone?"

Chapter 29: Too Many Cooks

The next day, I tried to put the whole attempted murder by car chase out of my mind. Game night at the Touccis' would need me bringing my A game if I was going to find out anything more about Nile's killer. Without blowing my cover and directly confronting some of Saul's family, we were starting to run out of leads, and Saul was adamant about not upsetting his family through this.

We had decided to play down the car chase with the Touccis. The cut on my head was mostly covered by my hair and a good makeup job. One would have to look closely to see it. DC's cuts were hard to conceal, but we'd decided to play them off as a botanical misadventure.

I looked down at the pink box I was holding and resisted the urge to bury my emotions in one of the excellent eclairs before I should. The pastries were a weapon with a job to do. I rang the bell.

"Oh, you're here, Ms. Katerine," Georgia, the maid, said and ushered me into the foyer. "We were not expecting you so early." She wore the same gray dress and had her red hair in the same bun she had before. Her gapped front teeth showed when she talked.

"Do you like pastry?" I asked.

Georgia looked at me strangely until I opened the lid on the pink box.

"I thought maybe you and I could have cups of tea or coffee before the festivities, if you aren't too busy. To get to know each other. These pastries are from Van Zants and are to die for." I gave her my best smile, hoping to look nonthreatening and friendly.

She peeked into the box and then back up at me with a beaming smile. "I can spare a few minutes. Come." She led me down the beautiful corridor to the back of the house, through several doors and into a tidy modern kitchen. There were stools at a breakfast counter.

She saw me eyeing them. "Most meals are served in the dining room, but Jackson and Fergus both sneak in here for snacks," she said.

"Fergus?" I asked with a smile, imagining the burly man sneaking around for a cookie.

"Mmm. He hasn't been able to resist my snickerdoodles since he was a tiny tyke. He and Jackson are partners in crime, now, impossible to keep one or the other out of my cookie jar."

"I can't picture the two of them getting one over on you," I said.

"They are very close. I think Jackson reminds Fergus of himself at that age."

I couldn't think of two people more different than gruff wise guy Fergus and budding film geek Jackson.

The surprise must have showed on my face, because she said, "They are both essentially orphans."

My mind leafed through what I knew about the pair. Jackson's dad was in prison on a narcotics charge. His mom wasn't in the picture, although we didn't know why. I didn't know anything of Fergus's family situation, but hearing her say Fergus was an orphan, too, clicked a puzzle piece into place for me. It was no wonder he was so protective of Saul.

Georgia was one of those people with timeless features. I was usually great at figuring out ages, but I would never have guessed she was old enough to have been feeding Fergus snickerdoodles since he was young.

"So, you've been with the family a long time, then?" I asked.

She studied me for a moment before answering. I knew I was being assessed. Finally, confidence came over her face. "*Si.* I was hired by Mrs. Toucci to help nurse Andrew. God bless his soul." Georgia made the sign of the cross, her eyes clouding.

Andrew was Saul's son who had died young. I remembered the cherub face of a small boy in Saul's arms in a black-and-white photo in one of Neutron's files.

"I'm sorry. That must have been horrible for you."

"For all of us. No one more than Saul and Fergus." Georgia turned to the sink to fill the kettle.

I stayed quiet. The air felt heavy with the untold story.

"You'd never know it now, but Fergus was a runt when he was a child. Neglectful parents. The boy rarely had regular meals. Until he met Andrew. Andrew had always been a bright child, glowing with joy. The two of them were as thick as thieves from the moment they met."

I tried to imagine a younger Fergus, full of boyish mischief. Every now and then, I caught a glimpse of it, but for the most part, Fergus seemed tense and wary these days.

Georgia turned from the sink and put the kettle on the stove. "It wasn't Saul or Fergus's fault, what happened to Andrew, but you couldn't tell either one of them that. Saul had been driving the boat that day. They were hit by another boat. Mechanical malfunction. It pinned Andrew under. Fergus tried to save him, but he was so small, only six and half Andrew's size at the time."

I couldn't imagine it. The grief and the loss.

"Saul lost a son that day, but he also gained one. Not that Fergus was a replacement for Andrew. But a thing like that, it bonds people," she said. She took the water off the stove and turned to the cupboard to get out mugs and plates.

"I can only imagine. Poor Fergus. I can see why he would never want to disappoint Saul."

She turned back to me, her hands full of china and a big grin on her face. "He said you were a smart one." I wasn't sure whether she meant Saul or Fergus. "You should know that I know you and Fergus aren't dating."

That was the last thing I had expected her to say. She had been exceedingly nice to me because I was Fergus's girlfriend. Or so I thought. Did the rest of the family know?

"Oh," I said. The shock must have been on my face.

"No worries, deary. No one else knows, but Fergus and I do not have any secrets. That terrible day, Fergus became mine as much as Saul's. The Touccis were understandably devastated, and here was this heartbroken little boy. I could not resist. I can still not resist. My Fergus, he is a good man. Too good, I think sometimes."

She poured the tea and put the pastries on plates while I contemplated what to do with that information. She was confiding in me about Fergus for a reason. I had tried not to suspect him. I believed him when he said if he had killed Nile, he would never have handled it that way. No body left, he'd said. Also, I couldn't imagine Fergus ever intentionally betraying Saul. Especially knowing what I knew now. But he was definitely keeping things from me and trying to prevent me from telling Saul things he thought would hurt him.

"I'm not sure Fergus wants me to succeed in finding Nile's killer," I said and watched her reaction as I blew on my tea.

"The thing you must understand is that ever since that horrible day, Fergus has decided that it is his job to keep Saul from ever feeling pain again. Especially regarding the family. Even if it is at his own expense."

For being on the social circuit as long as I had been, I would've thought I'd be better at innuendo, but it was always one of my weaker skills. What was she trying to tell me, and how could I get her to say it outright?

"I don't want to hurt Saul," I said. And that was true.

"No, I do not think you do. In fact, I think you will be very good for my Fergus," she said.

Before I could ask what she meant by that, we heard voices outside.

"Now, the crowd is starting to gather. If you go out that door and turn right up the back hallway, you will find the door that leads to the games outside."

I thanked her for the tea and headed out in the direction she had sent me.

"Fergus, we cannot have all these people here," came a heavily accented voice in the corridor. "Especially not that nosy woman and her friends."

I peered around the corner. Fergus was standing very close to a man I recognized from Charlie Guido's as the cook, Enrique.

"Leave that to me. It will be okay," Fergus said.

Someone opened the door then, and the men jumped apart. I took that as my cue.

"There you are, Fergus. It's so easy to get lost here," I said, coming up to them.

The cook uttered something to Fergus in Italian and pushed around me, fleeing down the hall.

"He has a lot of cooking to do. We're expecting a good turnout," Fergus said. "You look great. Very sporty." He looked me up and down.

I'd worn my white-and-green-striped Tory Burch tennis skirt with a matching green polo shirt.

"Thank you." I curtsied, playing it cool, and let him take my arm to lead me outside.

Chapter 30: Tennis, Anyone?

With as beautiful as the front of the house was, I should have expected the back to be equally breathtaking, but I was caught off guard by how gorgeous the back grounds were. The house must have sat on several acres, because no neighbors were visible. Instead, the backyard appeared to be an endless expanse. A veranda stretched out across most of the back of the house. Elegant brown-and-cream furniture dotted the space, which was covered, the roof making the perfect second-story deck. The railing that enveloped the deck was an intricate black wrought iron. I imagined the view from there was breathtaking.

The soft whites and vivid greens of the sunken Italian garden glistened under the sun. The sound of the fountain bubbling in the background was soothing. Graveled paths jutted about the garden in all directions, starting at a lime walk of pleached lindens. Meticulously manicured box hedges angled to create private sitting nooks that were punctuated by blooms of color.

Fergus walked us down the crunchy gravel path toward the tennis courts in the back. I could hear the volley of the ball before I could see the court from around the potted lemon trees.

"Oh, you're here!" DC said, enveloping me in an embrace before I'd even noticed he was there.

Fergus kept moving toward the courts.

"Does this outfit make me look like an Oreo?" DC asked. He stood back and displayed himself. He was dressed in a white tennis shirt, white shorts, long white socks that stopped just under his knee, and white tennis shoes. "Because Elise said this would look great on me, but I don't know." He had a racket in his hand and hoisted it over his shoulder in a *Tennis Monthly* cover pose. "Why couldn't we play golf? I could channel my inner Tiger then."

"Do you know how to play golf?" I asked.

"I'm an excellent study, especially when I look debonair."

"I think you look quite handsome, and the two of us are striking together. No one would think of trying to murder us when we look this good."

He smiled at that.

"How did your lunch with Elise go?" I asked.

DC had met Saul's granddaughter at the botanical gardens. They were supposed to do a tour then talk pot politization. Really, he was going to try to probe about why we'd caught her dangling from a Palmero dumpster—subtly. I was holding my breath because DC and subtle were not often said in the same sentence.

"We had a lovely day, but that girl is for sure hiding something. Anytime I asked about her friends or life outside of plants, she got all nervous and changed the subject."

"There's a lot of that going around," I said, eyeing Fergus as we neared the court.

"Also," he said quietly, lightly touching my arm to get me to stop. "Elise is not exactly heartsick over Nile's death."

"I can't believe you brought him here!"

Francesca's voice was loud, but I couldn't see her anywhere yet. On the court was little Camila, looking adorable in a tiny tennis outfit. A man I didn't recognize because he had his back to us was crouched down next to her, demonstrating how to do a forehand hit.

Finally, I spied an umbrella behind them. It towered over one of the box hedges. Through a gap in the hedge, I could see Francesca.

"I would have thought you'd want to get to know the man who will be spending time with your granddaughter," Joni answered, emotionless. Without another word, she stormed away from Francesca, moving toward the court.

DC and I watched as the man stood and kissed Joni lightly on the lips. Then I realized I had seen the man before. He was Laurence, Joni's adulterous lover.

"That's ballsy, even for tennis," DC said.

"Mm-hm. Think they'd mind if we asked them about Nile blackmailing him?" I asked.

DC grinned.

"Jackson, put that camera down, and join one of the games," Francesca said.

Jackson stood across the court, filming the whole scene. I wondered if that bit would make it into the documentary. Jackson didn't put the camera down but, with impressive talent, proceeded to hit balls from the ball shooter while he filmed.

Fergus emerged from behind one of the hedges then. "There you are. Come on, doll. The best action's this way."

DC eyed him, and I shrugged. We followed him through the hedge, into another courtyard. People we didn't know had crowded in, making it difficult to see what they were watching. Finally, we broke through the crowd, onto the edge of a large bocce area that held multiple professional-looking courts. They were all raised and framed, a mix of stone and crushed oyster filling them. Players flanked the ends of each court. Spectators huddled around. An official-looking person held a tape and a clipboard.

"Oh, bowling. This seems more my speed, Fergie. How do we play?" DC asked, ignoring Fergus's scowl.

"This is not bowling."

"I'm good at bowling. Kat and I used to play in a league," DC replied.

That was not true. I played in a league with smarmy Marshal from the morgue as a trade-off for his help with the Russians the previous time, and DC used the kiddie ball shooter and bumpers to knock some pins down.

"Ah, Mr. Clayborn!" Saul bellowed from the far end. "I think you would make a marvelous addition to our team."

DC moved down to the court where Saul was. Marcus and Lucia were there too. I wondered where Marion was. When I peered around, the crowd looked like a mix of an Italian supper club and a teamsters meeting. Men in sharp button-downs and fedoras mingled on the courts with beer-drinking muscle types. Everyone was intent on the game.

"I'd better make sure he stays out of trouble," Fergus said. "There's a food-and-drinks tent right behind that hedge, if you want something." He pointed at a white tent that stuck up over the top of the back hedge toward the house.

I entered the tent and took in the beautiful display of food and drink. That was not how game night went at my house. Okay, we didn't exactly have game night, but if we did, I imagined it would involve a Scrabble board and a plate of canapes, not a fully catered event that would make any bride jealous. Regardless of what was going on with Fergus and the cook, that man was brilliant in the kitchen.

When I went to peruse the dessert table, I saw Jackson. He was filming with one hand and stuffing a cannoli into his mouth with the other. He was remarkably dexterous with that camera glued to his face.

Happening upon him was good fortune. I needed to find a way to get a look at Jackson's film library. Who knew what footage he had that he didn't even realize meant something. Or maybe he did, and that was part of the reason so many Touccis became visibly tense anytime Jackson and his camera showed up.

"Those look good," I said.

He swung his camera around toward me while shoving the last of the cannoli into his face.

"So good," he mumbled with his mouth full.

"What else do you recommend?" I asked.

Since it was my first opportunity alone with Jackson, I was hoping I could get him talking. He tensed a bit. I could only imagine that when someone grew up a Toucci, they learned early on to be leery of strangers inquiring about sugary goodness.

"I hear from Georgia that you're quite the snickerdoodle aficionado."

His shoulders visibly relaxed at the mention of the maid, and he took his camera from his face for the first time and looked over the dessert table, searching. He finally spied what he was looking for and pointed over to some shortbread-like balls. "Those there are sleepers. They look all plain and innocent, but they are very dangerous."

"I bet since you're a film person, you notice a lot of things other people don't," I said and took one of the suggested treats. He was right. "Oh my God, so good." The shortbread on the outside hid the most delicious rich toffee filling on the inside, and the whole buttery thing melted in my mouth.

He sighed and with a scowl put the camera back to his face. "Most people don't like to be noticed," he said. "You have to be sneaky to get all the important stuff."

Ah-ha. "I'd love to see what you have of your documentary," I said.

"Aren't you supposed to be on the tennis court?" someone asked from behind me.

I turned to see Marion, Saul's sister, staring at us intensely.

The boy sighed again. "They never let me film anything good. Grandmother and Aunt Joni are arguing about that man who came with her. So they said I should take a break." He nicked another cookie from the table.

"Nonetheless, it is game night, not snack night," Marion said. "Why don't you go find Fergus on the bocce courts. I'll cover with your grandmother."

At that suggestion, Jackson beamed. He grabbed two of the shortbread balls and ran from the tent toward the bocce court.

Marion took a big drink from her wine as she watched him leave. "I try not to take sides, but I can't for the life of me understand how that shrew of a woman thought bringing her gigolo lover to her mother-in-law's was even remotely appropriate." At that moment, she must have realized who she was speaking to. "Forgive me. I'm sure our little family drama isn't exactly riveting conversation."

"It's all right. My own family has me wanting to pull my hair out sometimes too. I can only imagine how difficult Nile's death has been on everyone. Were you close?"

"When you work with family, for better or worse, you live in each other's pockets." She took another drink and eyed me over the top of the glass.

I tried to look casual and reached for another treat. "I don't have any siblings, but I can imagine keeping secrets when you live and work together would be nearly impossible."

She looked closely at me then. I thought her eyes drifted to the cut on my head.

"Yes, well, as Nile's death proves, we work in a dangerous business, don't we?"

Was that a threat?

"There you are," DC said, running into the tent. "Look at me." He turned around.

Marion and I both burst out laughing at the sight of him.

"I look like a bad football referee," he said. Two equidistant black stripes ran from the top of his shoulders all the way down his body, ending at his butt.

"What happened?" I asked, trying not to laugh again.

"Elise showed up, and we were talking about some of the new strains she and I are developing, and some of the players wanted to try them, so we went up to this study that opened onto the upstairs deck. You would think people would put a damn wet-paint sign on something if they're going to go and leave it all wet and painty," he said.

Marion snickered. "I'm sorry. Fergus probably didn't think to have the crew put a sign up, not expecting anyone would be up that way tonight."

"He was having kittens the whole time about us being in there, and now I know why. Damn thing has pinchers. I feel like that railing was trying to poke a hole right through me, and I can't even rub it 'cause I'd smear paint everywhere," DC said.

We left the tent and found our way to a guest bath to get DC cleaned up as best as we could. Elise found DC a sweater to cover most of his back. We watched a few more games of bocce and left shortly after. I hadn't been able to get any more Touccis alone the rest of the night. Marcus kept Saul monopolized. Francesca stuck close to Jackson while throwing glares at Joni. Joni stayed with her lover and played with Camila. Lucia and Marion kept eyeing me, and every time I got close to being able to speak to one of them, there was Fergus, poking his big nose into our conversation and dessert into my mouth.

I was barely out of the Toucci driveway, headed for his place to debrief, when my cell phone rang. Without even looking at the caller ID, I could have guessed who it was. The auction viewing was the next day, after all.

"Hello, Simon."

"Katherine, I heard about your recent trouble," he said.

"No one you know, I hope?"

"Now, why would I want you to be anything but at your best for tomorrow's festivities?" he asked. "I trust you are well?"

"Yes, just bumps and scrapes."

"Good. See you tomorrow, then."

The phone went dead.

I knew Simon would not be at the auction viewing in person. I shuddered, knowing that meant he would be watching instead.

Chapter 31: Country Club Collectors

"What in the world are you wearing?" Mom asked.

Grand had emerged from the bathroom in all black—black pants, black shirt, black shoes, and topping it all, a short black wig.

Maybell snorted and sniffed her, trying to suss out what was going on.

"Jeffery and I discussed it and decided we needed to fit in. I'm going as a ninja."

"Jeffery?" I shuddered a little at the thought of Dr. Jaffe and Grand teaming up to scheme but was thankful we had both managed to get the day off. I was milking some sick days from my reported car accident, and Dr. Jaffe had put in for a seminar day.

"Yes, while you were cavorting with mobsters over Jenga, I visited Elizabeth for our regular bridge game, and he came by. We decided if we left it up to you and the GI hunk, we'd lose the locker for sure. There's a lot riding on this."

I hadn't needed that reminder. We had a real chance to gain some information on how Claude and possibly Dad were involved with the mob. I was more concerned with keeping us all alive, though. From the first call from Simon, I'd been wondering if it was some elaborate ruse to get payback for Chentinko's death. We still didn't know what the car chase was all about, and Marion's threat from the previous night echoed in my mind.

"This can't possibly be what our future is down to," Mom said. She left the room to feed Maybell.

Maybell wobbled after her, giving Grand one last leery look before turning to the kitchen.

"A ninja?" I asked. "Did I miss something on the flyer about it being a costume party instead of an auction viewing?"

"You saw your honey's breakdown of the players. These are professionals. They all have an angle. Like the Consignment Couple or Loose for the Goose. If we're going to win, we need something too."

"So you're Granny Ninja?" I smiled. It seemed improbable that it would work, but she was clearly invested. The wig was a nice touch.

"I'll have you know that in Asian cultures, elders are admired for their patience and skills." She walked to the closet, I assumed to get a matching bag. Instead, when she turned around, she was holding a giant samurai sword. My face must have looked horror stricken, because she said, "You and the hottie won't let me carry a gun. I need to look menacing."

The sword did look menacing, but I didn't have the heart to tell her that she looked more like something from one of those new-age toddler shows than a badass from a kung fu movie—more adorable than threatening. She leveled her best disappointed-grandmother scowl at me in an attempt to look hostile. While I did feel like I should go make sure I had all my homework done, I didn't think I was frightened for the reasons she wanted.

"Where did you get that thing, anyway?" I asked.

Grand was fond of sneaking in and borrowing things from our old house. The crime-scene tape was to keep other people out, she had told me. She made frequent "shopping runs," as she called them. Usually, Claude took her. Sometimes, they Ubered, which was odd to think about, an Uber driver waiting curbside for an old couple to commit grand theft. But I didn't remember our having any kind of sword collection.

"Jeffery nicked it from his uncle. Terradyne Defense has a mini museum of historic weapons."

"Huh," I said. I didn't want to contemplate what having a stolen sword that was who-knew-how-old would do for our karma.

"Try not to poke an eye out," I said with a smile.

"Got it covered." She pulled out a weird-looking belt and tied it around her waist then sheathed the sword. Because of her height, the sword almost touched the ground, but it was a functional solution.

"Is that what you're wearing?" she asked.

I'd gone for casual summer wear because I thought we weren't trying to call attention to ourselves.

"You can't wear that," she said before I replied. "It wouldn't kill you to look like you're trying to snag Mr. Tall-Dark-and-Sexy. If I didn't know better, I'd think you were trying to keep me from getting my own watermelon squished-faced fruit baby."

I opened my mouth then closed it again without saying anything.

"Oh, don't look at me like that. I've seen how you go all gaga eyed and stupid whenever he's around. You're almost as bad as those two nitwits of his."

"Flynn and Neutron?" I asked, happy for a subject change.

"Even a blind man could see the sparks flying between that clueless pair of dopes."

I giggled. "Unfortunately, I'm not sure they'll ever let it happen."

Grand was fairly progressive for her generation. She'd grown very close to Neutron since her kidnapping, and the star-crossed not-yet-lovebirds had grown less subtle over the months we'd known them.

"Morons. Life's short. My story's a lesson for them in that. For all of you," she said, glaring intently at me. "And it's a different world now from the one I was raised in."

The antique German cuckoo clock she'd pilfered from our old house chimed the hour. "Damn, we're going to be late. You need to get fancier." She shoved me into the bedroom.

"Surely this isn't all about me and Burns," I said.

"I won't spoil the surprise of your cover, but you need to wear something showier. Expensive."

I wasn't sure I wanted to know what she and Jeffery had cooked up, but when in Rome.

"And hurry up. We want to get a good spot to watch everything," she said.

I changed into one of my museum suits, a lovely Brunello Cucinelli in a cream linen blend with a single-button blazer and a black pinstriped camisole underneath. I wore it whenever I was meeting with high-end buyers. With how much I was dressing up lately, I'd have to start doing shopping runs to the old house, where I stored my off-season wardrobe.

Grand handed me some of her finer-looking jewelry on the way out of the apartment.

Before I'd left McPhee Security the previous night after the Toucci-game-night debrief, Steven and Ray Ray, my chess-playing parking saviors, had shown up.

"I knew you'd be trouble," Ray Ray said with his usual snark, although it seemed to have a bit less bite to it.

"It's not her fault she has powerful enemies," Steven said.

"Not surprising, the way she treats her wheels. It's a tragedy," Ray Ray said.

I had expected they'd give me my wagon back. It had been in the shop long enough that it should be running in top condition. Instead, they handed me the keys to a sports car.

"The only way someone's going to get to you in this is if they plant a bomb," Steven said. "You do know how to check for bombs?"

I didn't want to think about someone targeting me with explosives. Flynn had taken the keys from him and given him a "We've got it covered, kid" brush-off.

"Like you had it covered last time?" Ray Ray asked. "Do you know what kind of heat Steven and I got because of that fiasco?"

I was impressed he knew the word *fiasco* in proper context. Book smarts didn't seem to be his strong suit. But I would never have taken him for a chess pro either. It went to show that one couldn't judge by appearance. I, of all people, knew that.

Flynn looked appropriately chastised. I hadn't asked how they knew where to find me and the shot-up pimpmobile Escalade or how they even knew there was a shot-up SUV. The result was what mattered, and this result was a newish-looking Camaro with tinted windows I guessed were bulletproof and an engine that would let me outrun any more trouble I found myself in.

"Nice wheels," Grand said. "At least I don't need an elevator to get into this one."

We agreed we'd meet the McPhee team and Dr. Jaffe at the milkshake place near the storage locker half an hour before the viewing to get geared up and ready. Neutron had already confirmed he could get into the footage of the security cameras covering the unit and even the city-traffic cam that covered the turn into the parking lot.

Since we knew where the place was, the drive was quick. Despite not loving the boat getting shot up with us inside it, I did relish being able to pull into a parking spot with ease in the sports car. A McPhee Security van was already there.

"Oh goodness," I heard as we stepped out of the Camaro.

I turned to the voice to see a vision of *Country Club Quarterly* staring at me. Dr. Jaffe wore branded plaid knee shorts, an Orlebar Brown polo, and Gucci loafers. A cardigan was tied around his shoulders. His hair was full of the right products to give the tousled-rich-boy look, and his dark Cartier sunglasses hid what everyone would assume to be a bored gaze brimming with conceit, his nose slightly tilted into the air.

I knew that look. I'd grown up with it and gone to school with it. At one point, I'd been engaged to it. I'd been brought up to appreciate refinement, but Jeffery's outfit was not that. It was old money worn well, the sole purpose to announce its presence. I'd known the Montgomerys were loaded, but Jeffery never put on airs, never flaunted it at the hospital or in the morgue. Despite his prickly disposition, he seemed rather determined to succeed in spite of his family's connections, not because of them. Maybe that was why we felt a kinship, no matter how much we got on each other's nerves, since I was living the same dream.

"This is a fine machine, Kat," he said. He ran his hand along the dark-purple hood. "I didn't know you had access to something like this. It will complement our cover story perfectly."

"Cover story?" I asked.

"You're the Country Club Collectors," Grand said and handed me one of her Yves Saint Laurent handbags.

I suddenly understood why I was in a Brunello Cucinelli to go to a two-bit auction of a mobster's loot.

Chapter 32: The Sneak Peek

The McPhee team approached.

"I told you to stay put, and I'd get the chickie geared up, you idiot," Flynn said.

"I need to know it's done right," Neutron replied. He hobbled closer to us. He was off his crutches but still limping. It would be another couple of days before the stitches in his leg came out. A messenger bag hung around him, freeing his hands to hold on to things for support.

"Oh, for Christ's sake. You're gonna pull your stitches, and then I'll have to hold your hand and listen to you whine for another hour while they restitch you. It's some mics and a camera, not a nuclear installation. I'm pretty sure I can figure it out," Flynn said.

With unexpected tenderness, he took the bag from around Neutron's neck, his fingers brushing the side of it. Neutron blushed, but Flynn was already turned to us, focused on his task.

Grand rolled her eyes. I smirked at Burns. Flynn handed one mic set to Burns and then turned toward Grand and Dr. Jaffee.

"Careful, you lug. I bruise easily," Grand said.

Much to her dismay, since she'd been snatched by the Russians, everyone was extra cautious around her. The whole situation had us reliving memories I was sure none of us wanted to revisit. Even Dr. Jaffe, who was unreasonably thrilled by the auction, was on alert about the Russians.

Burns microphoned me and plugged in my earpiece. He pinned an expensive-looking brooch to my suit. "This is a pin camera. None of the surveillance cams can see into the locker. We'll need you to get as close as you can for us to get a good look." He brushed a lock of my hair behind my ear. Since the attack, he had been more open, more attentive. While I hated that it had taken an attack for him to open up to me, I couldn't help but revel in the result. Maybe fresh starts were overrated.

"That's what I'm talking about," Grand said. I didn't know if she was excited about the James Bond spy gear or Burns and his PDA.

"No heroics today," he said, looking into my eyes. "For any of you." He looked toward Grand.

"You do your job, and we'll do ours, sonny. Okay, people. Enough catering to the hormones. It's showtime."

"Shall we?" Jeffery asked and led us to the Camaro.

I revved the engine a bit as we pulled into the parking lot of the storage area. The place was packed, so finding a spot was difficult. Embracing our cover for the day, I created my own parking spot, and we all got out of the car as if the place had been reserved specifically for us. A few pedestrians moved out of the way and eyed the car.

The locker facility had been done up for the event. Balloons were everywhere. A few food trucks were on the lot. A DJ played music near them. I could hear the patter of the auctioneer over the intercom.

The storage-place owner had decided to hold the viewing on an auction day, figuring, rightly so, based on the crowd, that he'd pull in some buyers not part of the local crowd he usually catered to.

"Check, check" came the familiar voice of Neutron in my ear.

"Tell me you're not going to be yammering the whole day," Jeffery answered, appearing to talk to the air or himself.

"We'll keep it light, but stay focused," Burns said in our ears.

Jeffery tucked his hands into his pockets and surveyed the place without taking off his shades.

"Quaint," he said and motioned us toward the registration table sitting in front of the entrance. I turned in a full circle to give the McPhee team a good view of the layout.

"Can I help you?" a man at the table asked.

"Where is the manager?" I replied.

"He should be expecting us," Jeffery said tersely, as though scolding a waiter who'd brought the wrong food.

He looked at us then down at his clipboard then back at us. Jeffery turned away in a show of disdain. Grand clutched at her sword.

"Oh! It's you. You're here," an unfamiliar-looking man said, jumping up from his place behind the table and rushing over to us. "I was starting to think you might not come. We've told everyone all about you." He pointed at a group of thirtysomething nerdy-looking men milling about behind the table. "Everyone, this is the famous Theodora Waters," he said.

The group looked genuinely thrilled and surrounded Grand.

"Katherine, must we do this now?" Jeffery asked. He tilted his head to display his impatience as a way to rescue us from the crowd.

"Who are you?" I asked, stepping between the man and Grand.

"Oh, I'm Drew. Glenn's in the hospital. It's very sad."

The group behind him nodded in agreement and muttered among themselves.

"What happened to him?" Grand asked.

Drew hesitated.

"He was attacked," one of the men shouted from the back.

"Yes, I'm afraid it's true. Someone tried to break into your unit. Well, the unit we all think of as yours. But Glenn stopped them."

"Neutron's checking on police and hospital records now," Burns said in my ear. "Stay focused."

"Katherine, please," Jeffery said insistently.

"I'm sorry about Glenn, but we are here for a purpose," I said.

"Certainly. Yes, of course."

"If you round up some pens and a flyer, I'll sign autographs before I leave," Grand said to him.

The group lit up with enthusiasm at that.

Drew handed us a paddle. I'd been to several art auctions in the Northeast for the museum. None of those had come with auction paddles in the shape of bank vaults with old-school machine-gun graphics across them.

"The viewing is down aisle three and to your left. They have a few more lockers to finish auctioning before they open yours, if you'd care to participate." He looked hopefully between Grand and me, holding another an auction paddle.

"I suppose there's no harm in looking," Jeffery said, snatching the vault paddle from the manager's hand. "Since we're here anyway." He sniffed and, without looking at me and my frowning face, walked past us toward the aisle Drew had indicated.

"Uh, guys?" Neutron asked.

"Roll with it," Grand said to me and followed him.

I nodded toward Drew in thanks and followed too.

The storage facility was a maze of gray concrete structures and bright-orange metal doors of various sizes. Each row had a sign pointing in the directions of various numbered spaces. Claude's locker was apparently in a special VIP section that came with extra security and air conditioning. That wasn't where we were headed, though.

"Do you really think this is a good idea?" I asked once I'd caught up to Jeffery and Grand.

"We wanted to scope out the competition ahead of time. I bet they're doing the same, so this is the place to be," Grand said.

"What better way to get a look at everyone than watching how they approach their bidding?" Jeffery added.

"It's not a bad plan, especially with this latest revelation," Burns said.

"Watching," I said. "Not bidding."

"Yes, of course," Jeffery replied.

But I knew when I was being dismissed.

"Come on," he said and looped his arm through mine. "I want to make an entrance."

"Never get a second chance to make a first impression," Grand said. She straightened her ninja wig and checked her sword.

We followed the sounds to the crowd and arrived at the back of a large pack. Jeffery stopped and stood still. He seemed to be waiting for the appropriate opening. I watched Grand move around the side of the group.

"And *sold*!" The auctioneer's voice reverberated through the crowd as he struck his gavel on the makeshift mobile lectern. "To the Consignment Couple for four hundred twenty-five dollars."

A murmur ran through the crowd. I wished I had Jeffery's sunglasses so that I could scope out the crowd more discreetly. I caught a glimpse of the couple I recognized from Burns's photos as the Consignment Couple. She was looking pleased, while her partner appeared to be pouting. If I remembered from their background, their MO was that one of them would pretend not to want a locker, and the other one would swoop in at the last minute and outbid everyone.

The crowd was a mixed bag of middle-class couples looking for something to do on a Saturday, a group of older women hoping to catch some good antiques, and several men in suits with phones glued to their ears. I wondered if they were Simon's people.

"If you could excuse us, we're coming through," Jeffery said, an air of authority in his voice I was used to from the autopsy room. He began to move forward, making the crowd part. The plan worked, and I was able to get almost everyone in the crowd on the camera for Neutron to analyze later.

"Welcome, there, little lady," the auctioneer said as we approached. He winked at me.

Ew.

"Really?" Jeffery said to him and took off his sunglasses.

Then the auctioneer winked at Jeffery, and Neutron giggled in the earpiece.

I couldn't see Grand any longer, but I imagined she was lurking about, doing her ninja routine.

"And now for today's main event. I'll have to ask anyone not holding a paddle with a vault on it to please exit to the main parking lot. Those of you with Al Capone paddles, please follow me."

The crowd began to thin out, giving us our first solid look at all the competition. I recognized Larry, "Loose the Goose." He had a Russian handler practically attached to him. The Consignment Couple had their Capone paddle, as expected. We still hadn't been able to figure out who was funding them.

I looked past them, straight into the face of Puddin. I gasped. Jeffery took my hand to steady me.

"What in the devil's name are the Palmeros doing here?" Burns asked.

Puddin saw me and quickly moved out of sight.

Then Neutron gasped. "And the Triads. All we need now is some Dixie Mafia, and we can hold a whole mob UN."

I moved my gaze in the direction my brooch pointed. There, next to Grand, hovering in the shadows, were several simply dressed Asian men wearing dark looks as they watched the crowd.

Jeffery pushed us up to the front so that we would be some of the first to see whatever was in Simon's locker. The auctioneer's assistant moved the mobile lectern into place.

"All right, my bidding beauties, this may be different from our usual fare but just as exhilarating. We cut the lock." He gestured to a burly man holding bolt cutters. "We open the locker." He pointed at the door. "And the clock starts ticking. Everyone with a paddle will have five minutes at the front of the locker to take it all in and pre-pare for bidding."

He motioned to the man with cutters. Tension filled the air. The lock fell to the ground with a loud thud, and the roar of the wheels on the garage door track had everyone craning their necks to get a view.

"Holy crap!" Neutron yelled into our ears.

Chaos erupted as we all stared into an empty locker.

Chapter 33: Garden Party and Private School

Burns was done. He was done with crazy Russians and misdirecting Italian mobsters. He was done with cryptic Mexican cartels and weirdly helpful Chinese syndicates.

I watched as he strapped a backup weapon to his ankle. I had seen this side of him once before, at the final showdown with Chentinko, the Russians, and Dr. Hawthorne when Grand had been kidnapped.

Burns was in soldier mode. When I was ogling him in one of his sexy suits or when he was teasing me about my crazy family, it was easy to forget what lay at his core. But this was a sharp reminder that Burns was first, last, and always a soldier.

And his snap to attention had Flynn at ready alert, which had everyone else on alert. The building was in lockdown, security tightened. Weapons were carried and handy. No one was allowed in or out without Burns or Flynn okaying it.

As soon as the door had gone up on the empty locker, the storage facility became a war zone. I couldn't see who had fired first. A Palmero crew, several I recognized from our meeting, seemed to materialize out of nowhere. Puddin was giving commands in an intense exchange with who I assumed were Simon's people. With Puddin's help, Jeffery and I had made it to cover and out of the line of fire. Oddly, the Chinese Triads had made sure Grand was safe, delivering her to us with a small bow and pointing at a way out. Burns and team were already in the parking lot by the time we made it back to the Camaro.

Then we saw it. On the windshield of the Camaro was a large note. "Stay away!"

Burns took the keys from me and pushed Grand, Jeffery, and me into the SUV. Flynn took charge of the Camaro. I sighed with relief. I did not want to have to tell Ray Ray I had lost another car to a shoot-out.

Once we were all safe inside McPhee Security, Burns had announced a change of direction.

"You really think this is the way to go about this?" I asked.

"I'm through worrying about Saul's delicate sensibilities. We tried it his way, and it almost got you killed. His family is threatening you. Now it's my turn."

"We don't know that Marion was threatening me. It could have been the Russians that put that note on the car," I said.

None of us had seen it happen because all eyes were on the storage locker, not the entryway. The only cameras for that area were the ones we were wearing at the time.

"Why would the Russians put a note on your car, waving you off a locker they wanted you to get into and are pissed as hell because you didn't and that it's empty?"

He had a point. But if the Russians didn't want me to stay away, who did? And from what?

"We need to start knocking suspects off that list," he said, eyeing the suspect board.

"You're not going without me," I said.

He raised an eyebrow.

"I'm trying to do my job. I don't know what you want from me."

"What I want is for you to not let yourself for one minute forget who these people are. I was wrong to be so complacent. Saul may come off all grandfatherly nice, but he's a killer, Kat. His organization is responsible for the deaths of a lot of people, and none of the

players here would think twice about you or Grand being expend-
able."

The minute we had cleared the storage unit parking lot, my
phone started ringing. I sent it to voice mail. I knew it was Simon,
and I didn't know what to say to him. It rang repeatedly for more
than an hour. Then Burns decided we were moving Grand into
McPhee Security permanently, and he would send someone to make
sure my mom was safe.

"I just want you to remember these are bad people. Despite what
you think of Saul, no one with decent morals is in the mob, let alone
running it. These are bad people."

He must have seen the look of horror come over me at those
words, because he slouched in on himself and ran a hand over the
back of his neck, lowering his gaze.

"Bad people like me. Like my dad?" I asked.

He softened his tone. "You know that's not what I meant. Jesus,
Kat."

"It's not what you meant, but it is. At some point, we both have
to come to terms with the fact that I'm not who we thought I was.
That instead of a trust-fund baby with a silver Gucci spoon, I'm Al
Capone's niece, and my dad's probably the mob's favorite numbers
man." That was the first time I'd said it out loud. We were both determined to see Nile's investigation to the end, but I didn't think either
of us doubted much what Saul was going to tell us about my dad.

He sighed and dropped his hands then stepped closer and gently
stroked my shoulders and arms with the backs of his fingers. I tin-
gled.

"I know exactly who you are," he said. "And so do you." He kissed
my forehead. "Okay. You can come. But you stick close to me, and
for once, do what you're told."

I laughed. "Agreed. What terrible Toucci are we taking on first?"

He looked at the board. "The bodacious botanist, I think."

I smiled and looked at the picture of Elise in her floral dress, trying to imagine her being menacing.

"You'll want DC for that. He's developed quite the rapport with her," I said.

He nodded. "Then we should hit Joni's lover. See what he has to say for himself and go from there."

IF WE WEREN'T THERE for unpleasant business, I would have loved being at the botanical gardens. They were a St. Louis treasure for a reason—gorgeous, lush, and fragrant. The perfect weather was only adding to the appeal.

But feeling the metal of Burns's gun on his hip as he pressed me forward over the Japanese garden bridge, I was starkly reminded that we were there for something unpleasant. Neutron was friends with the man at the security desk and had Elise's location for us in no time. Burns thought it might be easier to get Elise talking if Flynn and his many weapons of destruction stayed in the car. Plus, that way, he'd have easier eyes on the parking lot and a getaway if Simon decided to make trouble.

We spied Elise's red hair flittering near the gazebo and the bridges. She had her back to us, so we were able to get fairly near without her realizing we were approaching. Up close, I could see earbuds in her ears. She wore another of her signature flower dresses, but it was mostly covered by a smock. Her feet were in Crocs, and she was bent over a tub of little plantings.

"Elise," DC said loudly, not wanting to frighten her. When that didn't work, he softly placed a hand on her shoulder.

Elise turned with a start, and seeing DC, she looked happy, a bright smile on her face. She took out her earbuds.

"DC, so nice to see you. But I wasn't expecting you. Did we have a date?"

Then she saw who was with him, and I tensed.

"This isn't a social call," DC said.

Her already-pale face went ashen.

"Oh God. You know," she said. She sat down the bench and tried to calm her breathing. "This cannot be happening. We've tried so hard to keep it quiet."

"That you killed Nile?" I asked.

"What? No! I swear we didn't. You have to believe me." She looked pleadingly at DC.

"We want to," DC said. "Anyone this good with flowers can't be all bad, but you have to help us out here."

"It wasn't Uncle Nile's body being dropped that I cared about," she said with a sniffle. "If anyone looked further back on the tape, they would have seen. They would have found out."

"That you're involved with Dante Palmero," Burns said.

"Yes." A blush reddened her cheeks.

I looked up at Burns, surprised. He hadn't told me he had figured that out.

He caught my eye and said, "The pretty-boy twink at the meeting. I couldn't figure out why he would care about any of this. From all accounts, he has nothing to do with the Palmero business. But I had Neutron pull phone records."

"We didn't use our own phones," she said.

"No, but once Neutron tracked the burner phones to one of you, the other was easy to locate. You two are quite the conversationalists," he said, turning back to Elise.

"So, you're the one who tampered with the file?" I asked. "To cover your affair?"

"Like I said, I didn't care who killed Cousin Nile. If I had known, I would have sent them flowers. I know that sounds horrible, but he was an awful human being," she said.

"Surely in this day and age, your dating a Palmero wouldn't be the end of the world," I said.

"You don't understand. I think Uncle Saul would have been furious about our relationship, not because of the risk to the family business but because he was adamant about my not having any involvement in things. But that wasn't the main problem," she said.

"It was the blackmail," Burns said.

"Yes. At first, it was just about my and Dante's affair. But then things changed."

"What do you mean?" I asked.

"Grandpa announced that he would be making a decision on succession soon, and everyone seemed to lose their minds. Nile and Cousin Marcus were especially becoming more aggressive. Nile increased his payment demands."

"But you couldn't meet them, so he wanted you to use your influence with Saul," Burns said.

"Yes. But I'd already made it known that I support Lucia."

"But Nile wasn't going to take no for an answer, so that's when you killed him?" I asked.

"What? No! I told Nile I couldn't do it, that Grandpa Saul wouldn't believe my change of heart. So he upped the ante. He was threatening to go to Grandpa Saul and tell him a lie—not that I was having an affair with Dante but that I was selling out the family, giving the Palmeros family secrets. He wanted to impress him. Wanted me to help him. And if I didn't, he said he'd give Grandpa pictures and documents that proved I was a rat."

"You told Dante," Burns said.

"Yes. He convinced Nile to meet with us that night at the Taco-Saki, and he showed us the pictures and the files. They were fakes but good ones. We agreed to his terms."

I ran the timeline through my head. It didn't make sense that no one had found Nile's body at the Taco-Saki until dawn, if he had been killed that early. Plus, there was nowhere high at the restaurant that Nile could have fallen from. So someone had taken his body back there after killing him.

"What made you go dumpster diving, then?" DC asked.

"I thought I felt someone watching me that day," she said. "That was the first chance I'd had since it happened to do it. Nile had thrown the pictures into the dumpster. When Grandpa said he was investigating the Palmeros, I knew it was only a matter of time before someone went searching. We couldn't take a chance."

"Dante was the one who tampered with the file?"

"Yes, he has this friend who knows things about computers, and he connected him to someone he bought the virus off of right after he heard Nile was found dead there. We knew the security footage would be the first thing checked."

"Well, I admire your cleverness," DC said. "You didn't happen to take a sneak peek of who offed your uncle before doing the dirty deed, did you?"

"We didn't have time. We knew Juan Carlos's people would be back soon."

"I have a distinct impression that Juan Carlos already knows you were the ones who messed with the file," I said. Knowing that Elise and Dante were involved made our meeting with him make more sense. He'd told a story about love being the downfall.

"Yes. He and Dante are quite close. When I learned that Grandpa would be investigating things, Dante went to him and told him everything."

"How did he react?" Burns asked.

"He was furious at first. Said we were lucky we hadn't started a war. I don't know much about their business, but something big is happening, and Nile's death was awful timing."

"What do you mean?" I asked.

"I'm positive the Palmeros didn't murder Uncle Nile accidentally or on purpose. But Juan Carlos is worried about this, and Juan Carlos never worries."

WE WEREN'T GOING TO get any more out of Elise Toucci. She was emotionally spent, and I didn't think she knew any more than she had told us. While talking to her had solved part of the puzzle, it had only added more questions. That the head of a ruthless drug cartel was worried had me concerned. I thought about the storage locker and Simon's crew shooting at Puddin. *Are the Russians behind all this, and if so, why target Nile?*

Maybe we would get more from the next stop on the list of Nile's blackmail victims—Joni's lover, Laurence Paulson.

The drive from the botanical garden to St. Francis of Assisi, Camila's private preschool, wasn't too long but long enough for us to come up with a cover story.

"No one would believe Kat and I are rich parents," DC said.

"Or me and the skirt," Flynn said with a smirk.

"I think society is infinitely more open-minded about who can breed these days," I said with a smirk.

"Fine. Kat and I will pose as a couple investigating schools for our nonexistent child," Burns said.

"You do want children, though, right?" DC asked.

Burns and I both glared at him.

"Have you been talking to my grandmother?" I asked.

"Maybe. But I'm not going to be married all by myself. If I have to do this wedded-bliss thing, I want company in my misery. Besides, Grand keeps talking about watermelons and fruit salads and squishy babies, and the whole thing makes me really hungry."

"I think it's great practice," Flynn said and laughed.

"Oh yeah, practice, right. How's juggling practice going?" Burns asked.

Flynn turned red, and Burns and I were both happy to let that conversation drop when we turned into the parking lot of St. Francis.

We convinced the receptionist that we were prospective parents and that we had an appointment for a tour of the school with a friend of a friend, Laurence Paulson. She didn't think twice about our story, gave us both name tags, and directed us to his office.

"With security like that, we would never send our kid here," Burns said.

I kept walking. That would be in the box to sort out after we dealt with our multi-mob melodrama.

Laurence Paulson wasn't there when we arrived. We let ourselves into his office. It looked like I'd imagined all school administration offices—messy desk, knickknacks, and teamwork posters. He did have a picture of him and a woman—not Joni, so I assumed his wife—on his back credenza.

"I'm sorry. Did we have an appointment?" Laurence Paulson asked as he stepped into his office.

We were sitting in the chairs across from his desk and didn't get up when he came in. I twisted my body toward the door and was about to introduce us when he cut me off.

"It's you," he said.

He must have recognized me from game night. I wondered what Joni had told him.

He came into the room and around to his desk. He didn't sit but stood at the corner and stared at us for a minute. "What do you want?" he asked finally.

"We want to know if Nile Toucci's blackmail of you was enough for you to finally kill him," Burns said. There was really no reason to beat around the bush, and Burns kept his tone matter-of-fact.

Laurence Paulson was even less impressive in person than he was on Neutron's computer screen. Between Joni and Francesca's argument on the tennis court, DC's paint disaster, and Marion's veiled threats, I hadn't had a chance to size him up at family game night. He was shorter than I had guessed and had a comb-over. He definitely gave off an academic vibe in his tweed suit jacket sitting over a slightly rumpled striped button-down that pulled slightly at the buttons, drawing attention to his small, round belly. His eyes and hands both looked soft.

"Why should I tell you anything?" he asked. "I could call security and have you thrown out." He reached for the phone.

Burns started to get up. "That's fine. We'll let Saul Toucci and his goons know you're at the top of the list of suspects for killing his nephew."

The man paled.

"Oh, fine." He slammed the phone back down. "I didn't kill the bastard, but I'm not sad someone did." That seemed to be a common refrain from people who knew Nile, but it was odd to see it come out of such a timid-looking face. "Leslie and I married to appease our families, who thought it was time for us both to settle down. We weren't passionately in love, but we were happy. Cordial."

"Until you met Joni Toucci," Burns said.

"The minute Joni and I were introduced, I knew I had made a mistake marrying Leslie. The best days of my life were when I fell in love with Joni." He looked far away, as if caught in his own reminiscence. "And the worst," he said, bringing his attention back to us.

"Nile," I said.

"I knew who I was getting involved with. The Touccis. I'm not an idiot, but I never expected what happened. Joni says Nile wasn't always like how he ended up. At least, until they had kids. You can't stay out all night, partying, when you have a small human to wake up to in the morning. Heck, even getting to go out becomes a small event that involves way more coordination than you'd like. Babysitter schedules around naptimes and feeding schedules. Not that you ever feel like going out. You're always so exhausted. But it's worth it, ya know. You've made this whole little person that's this perfect mix of the two of you."

Paulson peered up at us wistfully. I could feel Burns looking at me out of the corner of his eye.

"Joni's pregnant," I said.

Paulson nodded. "We couldn't let Nile ruin everything."

"Did Joni know about the blackmail?" Burns asked.

"Yes. By that point, we didn't keep secrets. Joni and I were sorting things out. She was preparing to file for divorce from him even before we met, but Nile was threatening to take Camila. To use the Toucci name to take her away. I was preparing to tell Leslie everything. I thought if I were free, I could help make a case to get Camila from him and end this madness."

"Until he started threatening your career," Burns said.

"Yes. I think he figured out I was stringing him along until my and Joni's divorces were final. So he upped the ante. Started claiming he had proof I'd been inappropriate with students. Even the hint of that kind of allegation would sink my career."

I hadn't known about that. Looking over at Burns, I didn't think he had understood the full extent either.

"But we didn't kill him, and I can prove it."

"That would be most helpful, Mr. Paulson," I said.

"Professor. It's Professor Paulson still, for now, anyway, and neither Joni nor I could have killed Nile that night. We have an airtight alibi."

"Okay, Professor. What would that be?" Burns asked.

"We were at the hospital. Joni had a scare with the baby. We were there well into the early-morning hours."

That explained why he'd told us about her pregnancy.

"Do you or Joni have any ideas about who might have killed Nile?" Burns asked.

"I suppose when you deal with a family like that, it should be expected. But I guess I thought, it's family, ya know. A bunch of back-stabbing, conniving weasels, the whole lot of them, but that cousin's the worst."

"Cousin?" I asked.

"The *Jersey Shore* wannabe." *Marcus.* "I think even Nile was afraid of him, and that's saying something. I'd be careful around that bunch, if I were you. They find out you're making waves..." He made a slashing motion across his throat. "Wouldn't be surprised if you find a horse's head in your bed. Can't wait to get my Joni-pie and Camila away from there."

"Thank you for time, Professor," I said.

We walked back down the hall toward the exit in silence. The professor had given us a lot to think about, but more importantly, we could officially cross two more suspects off the list. And move another one higher.

Before we were out the doors, Burns's phone rang. "Neutron, everything okay?" he asked.

"I've got it, boss. I know who was on the tape and dumped Nile Toucci's body."

Chapter 34: Juggling Suspects

"Did he say anything else?" DC asked on the ride back to McPhee Security.

"No, we told him we'd be right there," I said.

"Did he say anything about Kimi?"

The last we had heard, they had tracked her to Cleveland, but then she'd gone to ground. No credit card usage, her cell phone hadn't been turned on, and she wasn't contacting anyone in St. Louis that they both knew. Burns had some connections up there, and they were looking for her. I wasn't sure what they were going to do once they found her. If I were her and thought burly men were following me, I'd run, but Burns seemed to have some sort of plan.

"No, but we can ask him when we get there," I said.

"How hard can it be to find one woman in Cleveland?" DC asked.

"She is a small woman," I said.

"If people don't want to be found, there are a million ways to stay hidden," Flynn said.

DC smiled at him. "Ain't that the truth. Lots of ways to hide in the closet."

I choked on the water I was drinking. Flynn ignored the comment entirely and turned into the McPhee garage.

Neutron had told us to meet him in the basement. He was working on something. Flynn key-carded us through the security doors, and we took the elevator down to the basement. I had never been in that part of the building before. It looked much like the rest of the McPhee space, with its dark woods and sleek metal accents. We heard a commotion coming from behind one of the doors.

"Oh, for Christ's sake," Flynn said as he opened the door.

Instead of cubicles and office workers, we were met with a large open space and what looked like a workout group all clad in gym shorts, T-shirts, and tennis shoes.

The first thing I noticed was all the clubs in the air.

DC did, too, apparently, because he said, "Holy Ringling Brothers and Barnum and Bailey. It's like a clown practice convention." He said it quietly, so as not to break the jugglers' concentration.

"And steal" came a voice from the back of the room.

At that, all the jugglers lunged at those next to them. I couldn't see what happened through the crowd, but we heard a cry, and then the legs of one of the jugglers flailed on the floor.

"Ray Ray, we talked about this. You can't punch people directly. You have to use your clubs on their clubs."

I finally recognized the voice as Neutron's, but I couldn't see him in the crowd of jugglers yet. Ray Ray's Afro stuck up over the top of the crowd, so I followed it to the two of them.

I looked around at the faces of the other jugglers and realized I recognized even more of them besides Ray Ray. Crimson's red ponytail was bouncing as she worked to keep all three clubs moving. Next to her, Steven was only passing two clubs between his hands while he simultaneously made moon eyes at Crimson. I was pretty sure she would have slugged him with a club if she had seen him, but she was a focused juggling machine.

"You made it!" DC exclaimed and ran over to Ray Ray.

"What the hell is this?" Flynn asked.

"Neutron's helping me out," DC said.

Flynn raised an eyebrow and gave him a scowl. "How exactly is turning our gym space into a clown romper room helping you?"

"I need to learn Korean chess. The chess kids need more extracurriculars besides chess for their college apps. Neutron said you needed more people for your league."

"We're gonna be badass," Crimson said and deftly flipped a club into the air with more skill than I would have expected.

"See? It's a win-win," DC said.

"Neutron, you said you had something for us," Burns said. I could tell he was amused by the whole thing.

"Right, boss. It's in the lab." He gave the chess kids some instructions then led us into the adjacent lab. The room was cold and held racks and racks of large computers. Several work stations and a big screen were set up at the back of the room.

"Monarch and I had to reconfigure the program several times before we could get a decent look at the footage. The whole file was corrupted, so it was slow going to even get the right part of the footage isolated."

Neutron pushed Play on the file. I tried to think back through what I remembered of the layout of the Taco-Saki. The angle of the camera wasn't the best. We could only see part of the seat where I knew Nile would end up and part of the parking lot.

After a minute, a dark SUV drove up to the Taco-Saki patio. The side door opened, blocking our view of what was on the other side of it. For several minutes, nothing happened where we could see it. The door shook every now and then. Finally, the door closed. We watched as a figure in black struggled to move a body into the patio space. Nile wasn't a large man, but this person seemed evenly sized with him. That ruled out Marcus, who would have had no trouble throwing Nile around. I breathed a sigh of relief as I realized that Fergus was off the list as well. If he did have something to do with the killing, it wasn't in framing the Palmeros for it.

The person was having trouble lifting Nile into the chair. I felt everyone in the room tense, and I winced as the body dropped partly to the ground before the person pushed him up into the chair.

Their back was to the camera the whole time they adjusted Nile in the seat. They placed his hands on the table as if he were about to have a meal. His head kept tipping back. They adjusted it, but it wouldn't stay in place. Finally, they tilted Nile's head to his chin.

They put their hands on their hips as they surveyed the scene they had created then gave a nod. Finally, the body dumper turned around, and we all stared into the face of Marion Walker.

"I'd say I'm surprised, but I'm not really. How do you want to play this?" Burns asked me.

Maybe Marion had gotten sick of Nile's blackmail. *But then what? She somehow managed to impale him with something and push him off a building?* It didn't seem likely. Maybe she was protecting one of her kids. Framing the Palmeros would have played into Marcus's hands, but Marcus had had a meeting with Saul that night, and Saul didn't think he looked disheveled. And I couldn't imagine Lucia being involved in any of it. *Plus, why send someone so unprofessional after us?* If Marcus were involved, he would have used professionals.

And none of Marion's involvement explained why Fergus was so monumentally freaked out every time I got close to learning something. Maybe he knew Marion had killed Nile and thought that would be too much for Saul, but that didn't feel right.

"I don't think she's the whole answer here," I said. "If we go to Saul now, we may never find out what's really going on. Do you feel like a little antiquing?"

"Neutron, where is Marion's store?" Burns asked.

The familiar clicking of the keyboard sounded, then three pictures popped up. The first was of a row of saltbox buildings. A sign for Toucci's Treasures adorned the middle of one of the redbrick buildings. The second was of a giant warehouse-like building. A white sign with a black silhouette of St. Louis, arch and all, proclaimed St. Louis Antique Mall. The final picture was of a building I thought I recognized but couldn't think of from where. The building did not have a sign.

"Neutron, where is that last building?" I asked.

"It's not open yet, but she applied for permits a bit ago. And you'll love this—it's on Cherokee Street."

"What is Marion Toucci doing opening a store in Palmero territory?" Burns asked.

Neutron pulled up a map that showed that the Palmero headquarters were only a block from Marion's soon-to-be new store. "She's at the store in Soulard, boss."

Since they'd taken over security for the Touccis, Burns had eyes and trackers on all the family members. I was certain he'd neglected to share that detail with Fergus.

We drove to St. Louis's oldest neighborhood in amiable silence. As we came closer to our destination, I picked up the faint smell of hops. Soulard was nestled between the Anheuser-Busch brewery and a ginormous old-world outdoor market. Kitschy shops and restaurants filled the space between the two.

Burns found street parking a little down from Marion's store, and we walked a few tree-lined blocks. The storefront had picture windows with vignettes flanking either side of the door. One depicted a lady's sitting room of old, complete with a baroque desk and a Louis XVI settee in a lovely teal. The other side I pegged to be an Italian Renaissance–era dining scene, although without a closer look, it was hard to place the era.

The doorbell chimed when we opened the door. The space inside was orderly for an antiques shop. Similar to the displays, collections were grouped by function. Prices were visible but discreet. The treasures were all high-end. I wandered over to the paintings on the wall. Between several paintings of landscapes and Madonnas, one beautiful piece caught my eye. As an art history major, I was never able to resist a look at the classics when I could. The colors and fashions were divine.

I felt Marion's presence but did not move. She stood next to me as I admired the painting.

"Is this an actual Sabatino?" I asked.

"You know your art," she said.

"Art history major."

"That's right. I think I remember hearing something from Fergus about a Boston museum."

I filed that away. I wasn't sure why Fergus would have that information, other than I assumed Saul had been thorough in checking me out. *Still, why would it have come up in conversation with Marion?* I furrowed my brow at her.

"Fergus used it as pretense for getting us to like you so that you could weasel your way into family secrets," she said.

"Does everyone know?" I asked.

Burns came to my side. Marion looked at him then back at me.

"Let's just say that if you know Fergus the way we do, you would know it was an impractical plan for deceit." I wondered about that, but before I could ask, she said, "I knew you would figure it out eventually. You seemed like a smart cookie."

When we had tracked her down at her antiques shop, I thought we had the element of surprise, but it didn't seem as though we had tracked her so much as she was waiting for us.

"Is that why you sent those men after Kat?" Burns asked.

"Oh my, you do know things, then, don't you? Come. If we're going to discuss unpleasantness, there should be tea."

She led us to a back room, where a Meissen tea set sat on a table between two Chippendale couches. Burns and I took one of the couches. Marion poured the tea, handed it to us, and sat on the other couch.

"Why don't you tell me what you think you know, and I will fill in the gaps," she said.

"You seem awfully cavalier about this for someone who tried to have me killed."

"My idiot son. Had I known, I would have stopped it. He was trying to protect me from what was on the files you had recovered from the Palmeros."

"We know you were the one who dumped your nephew's body at the Taco-Saki. An effort to make his death look like the Palmeros were responsible," Burns said.

"Nile was a pinheaded twit, hardly useful alive. I thought we could at least make use of him in death."

"And with Nile dead, a war with the Palmeros could only be better for Marcus," I said.

"Do you have siblings, Katherine?"

I replied that I didn't.

"I love my brothers unconditionally, but their offspring?" She shook her head and took a sip of her tea.

"We know someone was giving you money. Nile, we suspect. What I don't understand is why. Any of the inventory in here would be enough to settle your financial troubles. The Sabatino alone would do that," I said.

"It wasn't for the money," Burns interjected.

"No. But what Nile knew is moot now. The truth of the matter is no one killed my nephew. It was an unfortunate forklift accident."

"Forklift?" Burns asked.

Burns and I both knew that wasn't true. *Why is Marion trying to convince us it is?*

"Yes. I had set a meeting with him to finally end his blackmail. I was ready to go to Saul with the whole thing. I figured by this point, I had as much on Nile as Nile had on me. While Saul wouldn't appreciate my deceptions, he would understand. Eventually. Especially if I served up his nephew as the mole in his organization. Saul does not take kindly to family disloyalty. I was determined to see Nile learn that lesson the hard way."

"But something went wrong?" I asked.

"The meeting never happened. We had set it for quite a while after the family dinner wrapped up to keep away anyone who might have suspicions. When I arrived, I found Nile dead in the warehouse. He was wearing coveralls, and the forklift engine was still running."

"Why not just tell Saul that?" Burns asked.

"My children had no idea that Nile was blackmailing me. Finding a dead man, especially one that I know, is a traumatic experience. It did look like quite the fortunate accident. I didn't want any suspicions, so I called Marcus to have him help me figure out whether I should call the police, Fergus, or Saul. And I was terribly worried about Francesca. She was and is devastated. Children are everything. We would do anything for them," she said, sadness in her voice and tears in her eyes.

"Marcus had other plans, though," Burns said.

"It's difficult for a boy who grows up without a father. Always trying to prove themselves. To matter. He so desperately wants them to notice him. He thought it would be better for everyone if we all had someone besides the idiotic Nile to blame for his own death. And I certainly wasn't against bringing strife to the Palmeros."

Is that anger in her voice? Why is she mad at the Palmeros? Equally important, she seemed sincere. She honestly believed that Nile had died in a forklift accident.

"But Marcus had a meeting with Saul that night," I said.

"Yes, right after dinner, and it lasted for a long time. Saul had agreed to hear him out one last time about moving into the drug trade. I phoned in the middle of it, and he convinced me not to tell Saul. So I stripped Nile out of anything that could identify that he had been at my warehouse and dumped him at the Taco-Saki.

I didn't think about the cameras. Everything is so high-tech these days."

"Can we see where you found him?" I asked.

"Of course, but I don't know how that will help any of this."

We drove to the warehouse district down by the waterfront. The warehouse was a sea of boxes. There was no place high enough Nile could have fallen from.

"This doesn't make any sense," I said, looking around. *There is no way this is where Nile was killed.*

Chapter 35: Movie Night

My medical leave was up the next day, and I went to work in a daze. I was surrounded by McPhee security the whole way. They escorted me into the building, checked my locker, and checked both the office space and the autopsy area.

I headed to the coffee bar. Since we had done the morgue makeover, I didn't bother with coffee at home. This was the place to be. My coworkers Meg and Henri waved at me from a table nearby.

"Can I just say that I'm glad you have the friends you do. Can we keep them?" DC asked, meeting me at the coffee bar. He waved to the McPhee guys.

I looked through the glass window of the coffee bar area toward the office of our mutual boss. "Dr. Mitchell didn't even blink when I told him I'd have a security detail with me today."

The doctor had replaced Dr. Hawthorne after his death and the mess with the prostitute serial killings. He had given both DC and me a wide berth since he arrived. I thought he was mostly glad we weren't going to sue the city but equally had his hands full with straightening out Dr. Hawthorne's issues. Apparently, blackmailing the Russian mafia hadn't been his only shortcoming.

I finished making my espresso and turned my attention to DC. "What are you wearing?"

He was dressed in a long Korean-looking coat. There was a vest and shirt under, and he wore trousers that puffed at the leg.

"This is a hanbok, traditional Korean dress. I figured I needed to practice wearing it."

"Still no word on Kimi?" I asked.

"No, but her hearing is next week. Do you think she will come for it so that I can marry her?"

"You're really ready to get married?"

"Why are you so against marriage?" he asked.

"Asks the guy who was willing to have me fake having PTMD to get out of his own," I said. I took a sip of my coffee and sighed. "The only two people I know who have had lasting relationships all have someone in prison. Look at the mayor and his wife. Thirty-two years of wedded bliss, only to find out your wife's running a prostitute ring and covering for a serial killer. Dad's in the slammer. Grand's boyfriend."

"Grand was lucky in love the first time. Plus, all those people you named... Sure, their people might be psycho, but they're all in times of crisis, and you know what they aren't? Alone."

I left DC and got on with my day, followed by my entourage. Filing notes on the case of a man who'd died in a freak fishing accident while sitting across from my best friend decked out in Korean ceremonial garb should have been the weirdest part of my day, but it wasn't. Not even close.

I wasn't going directly back to the security tower. I had a meeting with Fletcher Reid. Okay, a date. Taking my situationship's security detail on an un-date with my definitely-not-boyfriend was only slightly awkward.

If I hadn't told Burns that I was seeing Fletcher that night, it wasn't because I was keeping things from him. I figured his people would or had done that. It wasn't exactly a secret that I was getting information from Fletcher to help with the Toucci investigation. Fletcher had as big of a stake in the outcome as Burns did. Gillian had been his best friend.

Besides, Burns had called Fletcher to the car wreck. I only followed with a nice thank-you for his services in taking care of me when I passed out. This was merely a friendly get-together while we exchanged information on mobsters we both knew.

Creve Coeur Park was not as big as Forest Park, but the bluffs and the lake it overlooked made it more beautiful in some ways.

Usually, McPhee security did a decent job of remaining inconspicuous, but in a crowd so large, I could tell they didn't feel comfortable. I was flanked on both sides, one slightly walking in front of me to the left and one slightly waking behind me to the right. We followed the crowd. I passed a sign that listed the movie, but I didn't have time to read it as I was nudged to keep moving.

Fletcher was easy to pick out, his floppy hair sticking up above the crowd easily.

"Stretch, if I'd known we were double dating, I would have bought more popcorn," Fletcher said when we reached him. He was eyeing my security detail. His facial expression kept moving between amused and concerned at a rapid pace.

I took a handful of popcorn and smiled at him.

"Popcorn's that way, guys. Why don't you give us a few minutes? I promise not to let her get kidnapped while you fuel up."

The men looked at him, looked at me, and looked at the crowd then without a word headed to the concession stand.

I settled down on the blanket. Fletcher handed me a soda and stretched out his large body, his head near my lap and his feet hanging off the end. I caught sight of a file folder next to him.

"Usually, Burns's overbearing nature grates on my nerves, but I can't say that I mind right now." He smiled his big, lazy grin, but the corners of his eyes were tight with worry.

"We don't really talk about it, but I can tell he's concerned. It was bad after the thing with the car, but there was another note at the storage-locker fiasco, and he has everyone on lockdown now. We've moved Grand into the tower."

"I am glad to see you looking better than the last time I saw you." He ran his hand over the healing cut on my forehead, inspecting. Satisfied, he gently let it run through my hair before returning it to the popcorn bucket. "I heard about the locker. A regular who's who of St. Louis organized crime."

"All for nothing," I said.

He raised an eyebrow at me.

"The locker was empty. But Burns doesn't think it's the Russians trying to kill me this time. The car thing seems to be some amount of Toucci idiocy, but that doesn't explain someone setting me up to take the fall for the locker."

"What do you think?" he asked, taking a handful of the popcorn.

"I don't think it's a coincidence that the Palmeros were at the auction of a locker that only a handful of people supposedly knew was a stash for the Russians. Or that the Chinese Syndicate showed up and made sure Grand got to safety."

"Maybe they heard about it and couldn't resist the opportunity to put pressure on the Russians. Too good to pass up," he said.

"That doesn't explain the Triads helping Grand, doesn't explain who stole whatever was in that locker, and doesn't get me any closer to who's trying to kill me or who killed Nile Toucci."

"You lead a complicated life," he said, laughing at my summary. "Maybe the Chinese just didn't want to see a cute little old lady shot to death in front of them." His tone had turned serious. He had a real soft spot for Grand.

"Maybe. She was dressed like a ninja, and she said they bonded over her samurai sword, even though it was Japanese."

"Of course she did," he said, the lightness returning to his voice. He wiped the popcorn grease off his hands and picked up the file. "I'm not sure if this will help or make things more confusing." He handed me the file.

Inside were two things. One was a set of financial records—purchases of trucks.

"The Palmeros were getting into the trucking business," I said. "Isn't that Toucci territory?"

"Not necessarily. Shipping is a big world. The Touccis don't appear to have lost any contracts over the course of time the Palmeros have been gearing up. Also, they're buying up space at ports." He flipped the page in the file for me. Palmero rental contracts had been placed in all the major US port cities. "Our guys are going national."

I tried to square that with what I knew about the Palmeros getting out of the drug trade. None of it made sense.

"This was more intriguing," he said and flipped to the last page in the file. It was an archive photo and an article. A quick scan of the article told me that there had been a large art and antiques auction. No one I knew was mentioned by name in the article. The picture, however, was a different story.

"You're lucky my intern is a true-crime groupie. This didn't get picked up in the search because neither of their names is mentioned in the article directly. But the intern knew I was gathering everything we had on the Touccis and the Palmeros and made sure I saw this. He seems to think it's scandalous."

Marion Walker stood in an opulent hotel ballroom. She was dressed in a high-priced Oscar de la Renta gown. Her hand was reaching for the arm of a distinguished-looking gentleman in a refined suit. I didn't recognize him. Her expression was warm, almost pleading, if I had to give it a name. The pose looked intimate. The camera had clearly caught something it wasn't meant to.

I read the caption under the photo. "Marion Toucci Walker rubs shoulders with Alejandro Palmero at Auction Gala." I looked back at the photo. The man's expression was intense. Familiar. The date on the photo was eight years ago.

"I've hit all my sources, but none of them know anything about what was going on in that photo or what happened in the story next," Fletcher said.

I looked at the photo again. There was definitely a story there.

The opening of the movie began to roll while I ate more popcorn and contemplated things. "What's the movie?" I asked.

"*The Godfather*," he said with a laugh.

THE MCPHEE SECURITY team took me back to the tower after the movie. They at least seemed content to have eaten some snacks and watched a good film while babysitting me.

Burns, on the other hand, was anything but content. He snarled and stomped around without saying two words to me. I didn't know whether I should address it—if either of us was ready for me to address it—or if it'd be better to let his temper over my seeing a movie with Fletcher run its course.

"I'm going to go see Neutron," I said and left him stewing.

Luckily, inside the tower, I was security free. I'd been there long enough to know my way around and carded myself through the hallways and into Neutron's lair.

He was standing with clubs in hand and juggling them with more ease than the first time I had watched him do it.

"Hi. You're getting good at that," I said. "Your leg doesn't seem to be bothering you as much either."

He put the clubs down and rubbed his thigh a little. "The stitches itch more than anything now," he said. "But I'm glad you think I'm getting better. Our first match is next week."

"That's quick," I said.

"Yeah. It takes years for someone to be good enough for a real juggling competition, but combat juggling's meant to be picked up fast."

"How's Flynn coming along?" I asked with a smirk.

Neutron rolled his eyes and sighed. "Flynn's never going to be what people would call agile, but he does have some good moves."

"I'd imagine all that tactical army training would pay off. But it's good to spend time together?" I asked.

He became quiet then, playing with his clubs. "That was why I proposed this to start with. I thought he would like it if we could do something together that played to his strengths. He said he was open to our joining a team."

"I think you two have a different definition of organized sports."

He laughed. "Can any of us really see me on a football field?" he asked, his face contorting to a snarl.

"Can I ask you a personal question?" I would have to be careful with my phrasing. It didn't seem like either of them was talking openly about what was going on.

"Have you dated someone like Flynn before?"

I wouldn't have thought it possible, but Neutron's eyes became even bigger. "Dated? Flynn?" His voice squeaked. "Boss and Flynn aren't really a lot alike. Are you interested in dating Flynn?"

Clearly, I had more work cut out for me than I realized. *How is that what he took away from that question?*

"I thought you were dating the boss," Neutron said quickly, his eyes intense as he waited for my answer. "And that reporter that drives Bossman so insane."

"Don't worry," I said, nudging him. "I'm not trying to home in on your territory."

He relaxed and sat back in his chair. "I don't mind your dating the boss. I think you've been good for him."

The "but no dating Flynn" portion of that sentence went unstated. Evidently, we were not going to talk about their situation, at least if I wasn't going to be more direct. I was curious as to his last statement.

"How so?" I asked.

"Well, he at least gets out some now. For a while, after Gillian, all he did was work. All the time. Plus, he seems lighter with you around, even with all the new mobsters in our lives." He smiled at me, and I realized I wanted to talk about Burns and my situationship about as much as Neutron wanted to talk about Flynn.

"What are you working on?" I asked and pointed at the computer screens, where some kind of recognition software was running.

"Oh! This is a new crawler program I put together. It's going through all the footage I could scrounge of the storage locker for the last six months. There's no telling how long it's been empty, so I started from when you said Grand had last visited with her boyfriend. The program screens the footage I could get against all vehicles I entered in this second file. If it matches something, it isolates the footage for me to review. I'm starting with the latest and working backward."

"That's brilliant," I said.

"Yeah, slow work, but we'll know if any of the families have been anywhere near that locker lately."

"Do you have time to look up something else for me?" I asked.

"Sure. I'd love to help."

I handed him the picture of Marion Walker and Alejandro Palmero.

"Wow," he said. "I didn't see that coming."

Neither had I.

"Can you get into the records of this auction? I want to know everything either of them purchased that night."

"I should cross-check against every other auction she's been to. Auction records are pretty easy to get. Most of the time, the auction house is very encouraging of sharing who made major purchases of what and for how much."

He dug into the searches with an energy I'd become accustomed to. Neutron liked being good at his job and never hid it. A few minutes later, he printed something and walked to the printer to pick it up.

"Marion Walker didn't purchase anything that night, as far as I can tell. She could have hidden the purchase in an anonymous buy, but it doesn't seem like her style. Alejandro Palmero, however, did make a purchase. A large one, at that." He handed me the printout.

It was a bill of sale from the auction house to Alejandro Palmero. The only item on the purchase agreement was a painting—a Sabatino.

I sat frozen, trying to roll it all around in my mind. *Does this have anything to do with Nile, or is it just a coincidence? And what does it mean anyway?*

"Oh my God," Neutron said.

I turned to look at him, thinking maybe he'd found something else between Marion and the Palmero head. Instead, I came face-to-face with my car.

"That's my station wagon," I said. The footage showed my beater Escort pulling up in front of the storage locker. *How on earth did my car end up at that locker?*

We both sat there dumbfounded, watching the footage on repeat until Burns showed up. "What do you got?" Burns asked.

Neutron must have texted him while I was busy being shocked.

"I did not steal the contents of a Russian mafia locker!" I shouted.

But I did. Or at least my car did. We watched as a familiar face drove up close to the fence in sight of the camera. Two people ziplined from a tether on the roof of the storage locker past the fence. The guards didn't even look up. They unhooked from the line in front of the car. One of them was holding what looked to be books.

"I know that ponytail," I said. "And that Afro."

"Is that some kind of saw?" Burns asked.

Neutron made the camera zoom in on the equipment the group was carrying. He then switched to one of the other keyboards, and pictures of tools came on the screen. "Yup, top-of-the-line cordless metal saw, available only at the home store nearest the chess club."

We all kept watching as Ray Ray, Steven, and Crimson got into my car and sped off.

"I think we need to go play some chess," Burns said.

Chapter 36: Check

"That old lady's gone crazy," Flynn said.

The McPhee team was readying to storm the castle—or at least the chess club. Weapons were out, and the SUVs were being packed. Flynn had just come out from the security offices.

"Grand?" I asked.

Between the latest issue with the Russians and remembering the last time, when Grand had been kidnapped because of them, the whole McPhee team was on hyperalert when it came to her. I hoped she was just feeling a bit stir-crazy under all the scrutiny, but it seemed like there was more going on.

"I'll go talk to her," I said and headed back in.

"Do you know who you're talking to, sonny?"

I could hear Grand yelling before I even got through the door. When I went into the war room, Grand had Neutron and two of the McPhee guards at sword-point.

"I'm a ninja warrior princess, and I'm not afraid to slice your bugged-eyed, scrawny butt," Grand said. "Besides, if I laid you up, you'd have more time to work our farm." She smiled at him then, but it wasn't her usually warm Grand smile. Her whole face seemed scrunched and tense.

"Neutron," I said.

All their attention turned to me.

"Go help Flynn get the SUV packed."

Grand lowered her sword, Neutron nodded at her, and he and the other two left the room.

"You can't go."

Burns and a guard appeared in the doorway then but didn't attempt to enter the room or the conversation.

"It's a bunch of chess kids. What are they going to do? Check me to death?" she asked.

"They might. We don't know what we're dealing with here, but we definitely know *who* they are involved with, one way or another."

"Exactly. All the more reason for me and my ninja prowess to come. This is my life, Katherine, and I'm not ceding it to no damn Russian psychos. I have to come with you and see for myself."

"Surely you understand that after the last time, none of us can take that kind of risk," Burns said.

She bowed her head but didn't respond. I thought we had gotten through to her and turned to leave.

Until she yelled, "Katherine Marie Waters, you will not take one more step out that door without me!"

Grand never used my middle name. Ever. It was a mom trick that she knew infuriated me. I stopped and turned back to her.

"I may be an old bird, but I'm pretty sure I can outsmart this pitiful lot." She pointed at her guard still standing by the door. "Either you can know where I am because you drove me, or you can keep a watch on the skies for my ninja entrance, but one way or another, I am going."

"Grand…" I didn't really know what to say next.

She walked up to me then and patted my face. "You're sweet to try, but you can't keep me safe from this. Waters women stick together. Besides, I'm better at chess than all of you put together. Now, let's roll," she said and strolled right past us.

I looked at Burns, who was looking at me. *What could I say?* She'd said almost word for word what I had told him not too much earlier in the day.

He opened the door, and we followed her out.

NEUTRON HAD CONFIRMED as best as he could that Ray Ray and the rest of the chess kids were at the club. No other mobsters appeared to be there. Maybe Grand was right. We'd talk to the kids and be in and out. *How dangerous could it really be?*

We waited for Neutron to take out the electronic locks on the place so that we could move through the building unencumbered and went inside. I figured they'd be in the same place we found them the first time, and I was right.

"So, who wants to tell my why my car was the getaway vehicle for your game of mobster felony larceny?" I asked.

They all turned to me.

"Uh-oh," Crimson said.

But Ray Ray just smiled. "I told him you'd figure it out."

"Where're the books you took?" Burns asked.

No one answered or moved.

Flynn cocked the trigger on one of his guns. I thought it was more for effect, but it worked.

"I am not getting shot over this," Steven said finally and moved out of the crowd to the back of the room.

Ray Ray began texting like mad on his phone. I assumed we would have company soon.

"You know what kind of people these are? What they do for a living?" Burns asked.

Ray Ray nodded. "Until this, he's never asked me to do anything."

"That's not a good reason to start doing the tango with the Italian mob, sonny. They're like that song 'Hotel California,' about being able to check out but not leave," Grand said.

"Look, do we appear to you to be a group brimming with opportunities? He's been good to us," Ray Ray said. "My being here, most of us being here, is because of him. I'm headed to Mizzou on scholarship, thanks to him."

"Saul's a generous guy. That doesn't mean you climb into bed with the mafia," Burns said.

Ray Ray's eyes widened and shifted from me to Burns. So did mine. Because I knew we weren't talking about Saul.

"Props for the dope ninja moves," Grand said to Crimson.

"Thanks." Crimson's ponytail stood a little taller. "We knew if we were going to succeed where others had failed, we'd need a different approach. The Russians are big and clunky. That's why they could never get past the ground detail without making a scene."

Steven came out of the back, holding the books.

"Why on earth would anyone store something so valuable here?" Flynn asked.

"Who'd think to look for them here?" Ray Ray asked. "He thought this was the safest place. One of us is always here. And it had security." At that, he looked sharply at Neutron. "You can ask him yourself, though."

"Hello, doll" came from behind me, and I turned around.

"You have to get better fake boyfriends," Grand said.

"Hello, Fergus. I've been expecting you."

Two men I recognized from Saul's manor stood behind him, holding weapons. Fergus was surprisingly unarmed. Although I didn't doubt that he could change that in an instant.

"I believe you have something of mine," Fergus said.

Steven walked past us and over to Fergus. He was carrying three large accounting ledger books. They looked old school and worn. He hesitated, though, and didn't hand him the books immediately.

"Except they aren't really yours, are they?" I asked.

"Possession is nine-tenths of the law," Fergus said and smiled widely.

I could feel the tension in the other chess kids behind me. They began to shift nervously. I needed to figure out a way to get a look at those books. *Is that why the Italians hid them? To keep Burns and me from seeing them?* Maybe they held the mystery to the nuclear launch codes from Grand's incarca-scrapbook. Or the secret of why Gillian Mathers had known Burns was accidentally mixed up with the mob somehow.

"I only want to look at them for a moment," I said. "Look, you clearly have your secrets and, apparently, many of mine. I think I'm entitled to understand what and who is at play in my life. If I were your girlfriend, you'd think that was only right."

He looked thoughtful.

"That access is not his to offer," Juan Carlos said loudly as he and his entourage strolled into the hall.

His group pointed their guns at Burns and his team. Fergus's men pointed guns at all of us.

"The highest ranked Mexican chess player was Gilberto Geurro, although he never got very high," I said, looking at all the guns.

Juan Carlos frowned at me. Fergus's eyes twinkled. I thought he was getting used to me in our time in a fake relationship.

"How did Palmero ledgers end up in a Russian storage locker, stolen by the Italian... family?" Burns asked.

"That is not my story to tell," Juan Carlos said. "I'm only here to complete a transaction."

"You're working together," I said, looking from Juan Carlos to Fergus. "Because you have a common enemy."

"Enemy is such a strong word," someone with a Russian accent said.

I looked past the Mexicans in their plaid shirts and blue jeans and the Italians in their fine suits to a group of men entering the hall in camos and T-shirts.

The man who'd spoken was average in build and wore a well-tailored suit. I looked down to his Russian calf shoes, which I recognized, then up again to his face. He had a large scar on his left cheek. *Simon.*

"Hello, Katherine. I wish we were meeting under more pleasant circumstances."

"You're welcome to join us for a friendly game," Grand said from the back.

"Everyone knows my homeland is best at chess." He smirked. "And as I believe this is checkmate, I will be taking those books now." He put out his hand to Steven.

Steven looked at Simon then at Fergus, whose face was blank, then at Burns and me. Simon stood waiting patiently. The hall was as silent as I imagined a big chess competition would be as everyone awaited the final moves in play.

Chapter 37: The Hubbub

But Steven didn't move.

Instead, a loud whistle sounded from the back, and Neutron screamed, "Peterson formation!"

We had all startled at the whistle, but for several moments, no one moved.

"Now!" Neutron yelled.

Then suddenly, the hall was rushed with chess kids moving through a very confused crowd. Steven eyed them, ducked around the books to give himself time to get away from both Simon and Fergus, then threw the books into the air.

"The books!" Simon called out.

The surprise attack let the chess kids take out some of the various mobsters. Crimson grabbed the guns of two of the men standing next to her, and they flew into the air. Ray Ray took down one of the Russians, and those guns similarly went up. Before long, half the hall was disarmed, and the kids were juggling books and guns across the room. The body of one of the Russians dropped to the ground.

I was thankful no one was shooting yet, but it would only be a matter of time. I needed to get Grand to safety. When I looked for her, though, two of the chess kids already had her tucked away in the back of the room, barricaded behind overturned chess tables. That was probably the best anyone could to do. The next task was getting to those books. I didn't really see a scenario in which I walked out of there with them, but I could at least get an understanding of what was inside them.

I made my way to the back of the room, where Neutron was whistling and calling plays.

"Neutron, I need those books, and I need time to look at them," I said.

He nodded at me and whistled some more.

The mobsters were desperately trying to get their guns back. The kids were moving quickly enough that they were able to avoid being good targets while simultaneously keeping the guns and the books in the air. Every time one of the men got close to one the jugglers, they were rapped on the head with a gun or a book. Ray Ray seemed particularly proficient with his hits. Even Flynn was using some of the moves, although he was more attuned to the combat portion of the routine than the juggling.

Before long, I was being handed the first ledger book. I jumped over a table for safety and opened the book.

No one could be the daughter of an accountant and not pick up a few tricks of the trade. I let my eyes drift over the columns, trying to understand the layout. From the handwriting, I could tell that more than one person had been updating the entries. The column headings were in a very neat print—tidy, tight letters written in an easy-to-understand shorthand. The row entries were messier. Some entries were printed, and some were in muddled cursive that was difficult to decipher.

From the headings, I was quickly able to determine that it was some sort of shipping log. One column was for tag numbers. Some of the entries looked like license plates, some like something else. Another listed the number being shipped. Columns for Start and Finished catalogued the pickup and drop-off point of each shipment. The ledger was organized chronologically and looked to be more of an accounting of the money and numbers movement than it was concerned with the movement of the shipping fleet. Every entry had a column for the amount of money collected and who the responsible payer was. Sometimes there were notes about refunds or favors collected. The most curious column was Yes/No—Papers.

"Neutron, switch!" I yelled and tossed him the book.

Quickly, the next book was thrown into my lap. It was set up completely differently. There were tabs that separated the pages. On the top of each page was a vehicle number with a description. The current tag number was listed underneath, but it was clear those changed, as there were multiple entries and extra space to add more. The ledger looked more like a schedule of where certain trucks were supposed to be when, what their capacity was, and their current location. Some of the numbers didn't make sense in comparison to the description of the vehicle. For instance, a large shipping truck was listed as only having a capacity of twenty-five. Routes with drivers were listed in the back of the book.

"Switch!" I yelled, sending the second book back into the juggling fray.

I jumped when I heard the first gunshots. A high-pitched scream echoed through the large hall as more bullets started flying.

The last book wasn't a ledger at all. It was a tracker with names, titles, schedules, and personal details about certain entries. There were also more detailed descriptions of routes that could be tied to those names, where patrol units would be, and who was manning border crossings when.

I flipped back to the beginning to look closer at the names and titles. Many were immigration officials. The border details were schedules of guards.

The Palmeros were moving people. The books were trafficking ledgers. And it looked like they had recently taken over a large international piece of the trade.

I looked up at the scene in the hall. The Italians, the Mexicans, and the McPhee team had finally decided to work together to drive the Russians from the hall. In no way did I think this would be the end of things with Simon, but at least the room was full of friendlier fire, I supposed.

"You have to give that to me now," Fergus said. He was looking down at me.

The ledger was still open in my lap. "St. Louis is a hub," I said. "Juan Carlos said to me that they couldn't compete with the drug cartels but that St. Louis had other advantages. A shipping hub."

Fergus didn't answer me. He stood, appraising.

"Are the Russians gone?" I asked.

"Yes. They have been adequately dealt with and removed from the premises."

"I want to see Juan Carlos."

The Mexicans were gathering in the front of the room. Several men, both Mexican and Italian, stood guard at the door. The chess kids were righting some of the tables. I watched as they helped Grand up.

I found Juan Carlos at the front, talking on his cell phone. When I approached, he ended his call.

"Elise said that Dante came to you and told you everything. You knew when you gave us the file who had messed with it and why," I said.

"Yes, but in the lovebirds' haste to cover their tracks, they erased the key piece that we needed in our trade with Mr. Fergus."

"Proof that it was Marcus selling out Saul," Burns said.

"That sounds like a family matter, Señorita Inspector." With that, Juan Carlos took the book from my hands and handed them to Monarch.

"It's been a pleasure doing business with you," he said to Fergus.

Then he turned to me and Burns. "We thank you for your assistance in resolving this issue."

Looking at all of us, he said in his commanding voice, "My people will be in touch." Then he and his people turned and left.

"Are you going to start talking now?" I asked Fergus, mustering my best death glare.

"We had an arrangement. Nothing that you needed to be concerned with," he said.

"I think it's everything I need to be concerned with, if it leads back to you killing Nile Toucci."

"I didn't kill him."

"Does Saul know?" I asked.

"I told you I didn't kill him."

"No, does Saul know you made a deal with the Palmeros?"

"A while ago, I would have said no. Now, I'm not sure." He didn't say any more.

I didn't think he was going to tell me or Burns one thing more than we hadn't already figured out. The only way I was going to get the rest of the story was through Fergus's main weak spot.

"I think it's time for a sitrep with our employer," I said.

<hr>

WE ARRIVED AT THE TOUCCI estate in a caravan. Fergus, who was leading, punched a code into the gate, and we followed him through.

Saul was waiting in his study when we arrived. "Katherine, I understand you have news," he said as we all filed in.

Chapter 38: Retirement Accounts

Saul's study was quintessentially him, oozing with old-world charm and warmth. The walls were covered in an indigo wallpaper veneered with giant fan leaves in a darker blue. A white coffered ceiling with gold inlays brightened the space. The furniture was dark, old, and rustic, including Saul's large desk. Breathtaking scenes of Italy's coast adorned the walls in their ornate gold frames. Leather couches that looked as soft as butter and the perfect spot to read a book or have a drink flanked the space in front of Saul's desk, which was spectacular. Late Renaissance, if I had to guess.

Fergus wouldn't look up.

"I suspect we found what you already knew," I said.

Fergus did look up at that, peering at me then at Saul.

"That my nephews are not men who live up to the Toucci standard? Yes."

"You already knew," Fergus said. A statement, not a question. Fergus had come to the same conclusion I had. Saul Toucci was not a man to ask questions he didn't already know the answers to.

"Fergus, my son, I love you for wanting to protect me. There is no one whose loyalty I depend on or respect more than yours. And I am sorry for putting you through all this. Alejandro was insistent that this was the only way."

"The day Nile was discovered wasn't the first time you and Alejandro Palmero met," Burns said.

"Very good, Mr. McPhee. It was not. Alejandro and I had been in negotiations since he discovered his grandson and my granddaughter planned to elope."

"You knew they were seeing each other," I said.

"Yes, and Elise is correct that I would not have been happy about her becoming involved with the heir to a drug cartel."

"But the Palmeros are getting out of the business," Burns said. "Or you saw an opportunity that they could."

"I think this conversation requires more to drink than we currently have."

Fergus shook himself out of his stupor and followed toward the bar.

"No, no, my friend. I've got this. You sit. Try to relax, Fergus. I hate to see you so pensive."

Saul poured drinks, remembering perfectly from when we were at dinner what all of us drank. I helped to hand them out. He turned back to us and cleared his throat, a gesture to signify he was about to make a speech or give a performance, but I could tell it was the emotion he was trying to lock away. He took one last drink then began.

"About six months ago, Alejandro arranged for a secret meeting between us. Of course, I was suspicious, but he said it was in the mutual interest of our families to talk. He implored me to keep our meeting to myself. Naturally, that only fueled my suspicion, but when he offered me Juan Carlos as collateral, I knew he was serious. If it was a trick, I couldn't see how, so I agreed to meet him."

"That's why you hired those other guys," Fergus said.

"Yes, I didn't want to take any chances of anyone in the family finding out. *You* were not supposed to find out."

Hurt shone in Fergus's eyes.

"It's not that I didn't trust you. I didn't want to put you in harm's way, and I knew the fewer people who knew, the better. This is a delicate matter. So I arranged for you to be elsewhere, set up the security as best I could with the out-of-town hired crew, and went to meet Alejandro. I should have known you would find out. You are excellent at your job."

Fergus perked up a bit at the praise.

"And that's when you learned that Elise was in love with Dante Palmero," I said.

He smiled. I was sure he was uncertain about how much of the story we knew. So was I.

"Yes. I was surprised, but I tried to be understanding. My Marie is forever reminding me that love and youth alike can be impetuous. With family, you can always add, but subtraction?" He shook his head. His gaze was far off. "And you can't always choose who you love," he said, looking directly at Fergus.

Saul took another drink and composed his thoughts. "While interesting, and I appreciated that our concerns ran along similar lines, our grandchildren's devotions were not the real reason he wanted to see me. Not entirely anyway."

"He wanted to do business," Burns said.

"Surely you didn't trust him, regardless of Elise," Fergus added.

"He was quite persuasive, my friend. He presented me with an opportunity I couldn't refuse. A way of ensuring Elise and Dante's happiness while dealing with what had become our common enemy."

"The Russians," I said. The puzzle picture wasn't all clear yet, but I was beginning to understand how some of the pieces fit together.

"Yes. Like me, Alejandro had been doing some soul-searching. Reflection. I suppose it's what we old men do. I don't think it had become apparent yet, but he'd made some recent business decisions."

"To get out of the drug business," Burns said. That answered that piece of the puzzle.

"I don't regret my choice of profession. When my father brought us here, we had nothing. Spit on for our Italian heritage. He had trouble finding work, barely able to keep us fed. I promised myself and him that my family would never know that kind of want. And I'm thankful they never have. But it is a different world now. Between the increased pressure from the government and the ruthlessness of the competition, I feel my family is more at risk. There are safer ways we can make money."

"And the drug business that the Palmeros are in is twice as brutal," Burns said.

"Precisely. The cartels running the drug trade these days have no values, no honor. We need only look to our Katherine's recent troubles to know that."

"Chentinko," I said with a shudder, remembering my previous tormentor.

Burns brushed his hand on mine.

Saul nodded. "We agreed that the state of affairs with the Russians was becoming untenable. But that wouldn't have been enough for either of us to get involved directly. Together, we could have put more subtle pressure on things here to drive the Russians back out of the city."

He set his drink down on the bar cart and headed back to his desk, where he unlocked and opened a desk drawer and pulled out a large envelope. "It was when he showed me this that I knew the Russians needed to be dealt with."

He walked over and handed the envelope to me. I took out a set of large surveillance photos, like those I'd seen Neutron produce. The first photo was of three men sitting at a table at a restaurant. It was a side angle, so it was hard to make out anyone's faces. Two men were on one side of the table and one on the other. The next photo was a blown-up front-view closeup of the two men sitting together. On the left was a man in a white shirt, muscles bulging, gold chains hanging from his neck—a smiling Marcus Walker. Next to him sat a very alive and very animated Nile Toucci.

I handed the photos to Burns, who looked at them and handed them to Fergus, then I saw the next photo in the stack and gasped. Across from Marcus and Nile sat Claude Pedersky, bow tie and all. Grand's Claude was working with the Touccis.

"No!"

Was it all a setup? Did Saul want revenge on Grand, on us for something with his nephews?

I took a breath and tried to calm myself. Burns took the photo. I felt his whole body go tense. If he were feeling a portion as vulnerable as I suddenly was, he would be halfway to panic. He felt for his weapon.

Realizing our alarm, Saul held his hands out in a gesture meant to calm, but I wasn't sure it did. "Please, Katherine, I assure you that you are amongst friends here."

"This whole thing was a setup. You've been using me to get to Grand, to get to the Russians."

"Not exactly," he said. "There is more to tell. If you look at the last photo, I believe you will see something familiar."

I turned to the last photo in the stack. The picture was a close-up of the ledger books—the Palmero ledger books. *How does all this fit?*

Chapter 39: Candid Camera

"Wait. If the ledger books ended up in a storage locker that the Russians entrusted Claude with, that would mean your nephews were the ones to give him the books. At this meeting," I said, holding the picture back up to Saul.

"The question is, then, how and why did they get the books from the Palmeros?" Burns asked.

Saul blew out a breath. "Let me tell you a story."

And he did. We were enraptured as Saul told us about another boy and girl who had fallen in love a lifetime ago. They'd met by the river and become enamored to the sway of the currents. She brought books from the library, adventure for him and art for her. Their families had both been immigrants, and they took turns teaching each other English from the words on the pages.

But neither of their families approved. They were from different worlds. When their families found out, they separated them. He was sent off to war and she to school. By the time they both returned to the city, they were married to other people.

In a perfect world, that would have been the end of it. They would each have let go of their first loves and moved on to build happy families. They both had children and spouses. But they were like magnets. Soon, she was pregnant with his child.

But he was a man of responsibilities and commitment. By the time the child was born, his empire in the city was already coming into focus. His marriage dissolving, especially in scandal, would have called his authority into question. He had already made powerful enemies. It would put them all in danger. And her family would never forgive her. She could lose both of her children. He wasn't willing to let that happen. They agreed it would be for the best to cut all ties.

And they did. For twenty-nine years, they watched each other from a distance. He watched his son grow to a man, hoping that, one day, maybe he could change things but knowing that was a selfish choice.

Before we could ask any questions, the door to the study burst open. "You cannot go in there, señors," Georgia, the maid, yelled, but there was no stopping the steamroll of Touccis entering the room.

Marion, Marcus, and Lucia all entered, Francesca right behind them.

"It's all right, Georgia," Saul called.

"It's not what you think," Marcus said.

"Oh, no?" Fergus asked, standing. "Do you want to tell him why you sold the family out to the Russians, then?"

Marcus didn't say anything for a moment, ducking his head. When he lifted it back, he looked between Saul and his mother and said, "I was angry with them."

We stood there in silence, waiting for someone to make the next move.

Then it clicked.

"Wait, 'them,'" I said and turned to Marion. "You said 'them.' 'He wants *them* to notice him.'"

Marion didn't say anything. I didn't either. It wasn't my secret to tell.

But Burns asked. He looked at Marcus. "How did you find out?"

Marcus looked at his mother with angry eyes. "From Nile." He almost spit the name at her. "My own mother couldn't tell me who my father was. I had to hear it from that two-bit rat fink."

Francesca gasped.

"I'm sorry, auntie, but Nile was not a good person. He was using it against Mother, that I'm Alejandro Palmero's son."

"We only wanted to protect you," Marion said.

"Because he didn't want me. I saw the letters."

"Marcus, that's not true. He wanted you desperately. But surely you can see how unsafe it would be," Saul said.

"You thought if we took over that space, he'd want you or at least have to deal with you," Lucia said, having put some of her own puzzle pieces together.

"But Nile blackmailing your mother was never part of the plan," Burns said.

I looked at Saul. *How much of this did he know? What is he waiting to hear?*

Saul's eyes never left Fergus.

"It's why you killed him," I said and turned to Fergus. I didn't think that was true, but Fergus knew what had happened. I thought if I pressed him, he would spill, divulging who in the room had.

Everyone turned to him.

Francesca approached him. "Well, did you do it? Did you kill my baby?"

I waited for his rebuke, for the denial. Instead, I heard a faint "yes."

"Fergus!" Saul barked at the same time Francesca slapped him.

"Stop! You can't do this." The tall, gangly Jackson ran into the room, camera gripped tightly against his stomach.

"You shouldn't interfere in things that don't involve you," Fergus said. "I did it. The little weasel was on my last nerve, with the things he did to this family, and he needed to be taken care of. Now, everyone, get out, and let Saul deal with me!"

No one moved except Saul. He came around the desk and stepped up to Fergus. "My sweet son. Did you think I would care? Did you think I would not still love you?"

"Don't you dare be nice to this buffoon. This two-bit orphan. He is not Andrew!" Francesca yelled.

"No, he is not." Saul put his hand under Fergus's chin and lifted it. "But Andrew would be very proud of you."

"He killed my baby! How can you say that?" Francesca screamed.

"No. No, he didn't," Jackson said barely audibly.

"No, Jackson," Fergus said gruffly and got up.

"He didn't kill Nile, because I did."

The room gasped collectively. Francesca let out a wail.

"What do you mean?" Lucia asked. She knelt by her cousin, taking his hands in hers.

Tears ran down Jackson's face. "He and Cousin Marcus had been fighting about his real father and Aunt Marion."

"You wanted to help Marcus?" Lucia asked.

"Not exactly. I was filming." He held up his camera. "I heard Uncle Nile come back into the house. He had rushed out after the family dinner but came back yelling for Uncle Marcus. Uncle Marcus was in the middle of a meeting with Grandpa Saul, but he came out when Nile started yelling. I followed them to the back balcony off the study."

Fresh paint, new iron railing, I thought.

"They argued," Lucia said. "About Uncle Marcus's real dad?"

Jackson nodded. "When Uncle Marcus went back into the house, Uncle Nile spotted me. He tried to get my camera away. To destroy what I'd seen. He pushed me back against the railing, but it must have been loose. I saw he was going to lunge for the camera, and I was quick enough to move out of the way." Jackson broke down in full sobs then.

"And the railing broke. Nile went flying over the edge," I said.

Lucia took the sobbing Jackson into her arms.

"Oh, my poor baby," Francesca said. "It was just an accident."

"You'll hate me now!" he said.

"You didn't want that for him," I said to Fergus.

"I know what it's like to feel responsible for the death of someone you love," Fergus replied. "I couldn't change that, but I could at least make sure he didn't have to deal with the rest of the family knowing too."

"Fergus, we never blamed you for Andrew's death. Never," Saul said.

I didn't know if they had ever talked about it before, but I was certain that no matter what Saul said, Fergus would not believe that.

"So you wanted to make it look like a forklift accident," I said.

"You moved the body to the warehouse, where you knew Marion would find it. But you didn't expect Marcus to hatch his plan to get back at his father," Burns said.

Marcus ducked his head.

"How much did you know when you hired me?" I asked, turning to Saul.

"Enough. I didn't know for sure how Nile died, but Fergus would never hide something sinister from me. That could only have meant it was some sort of accident. One that played on his past, I expected."

"And the Palmeros had a problem. They didn't know who in their organization had given Marcus the ledgers," Burns said.

"Yes. I convinced Alejandro that a direct confrontation with his son would not get him what he wanted. Neither would confronting you and Grand."

"Because his books were in Grand's storage locker. Well, her boyfriend's anyway."

"Yes. I will say, Marcus, you knew exactly how to cause your father the most headaches."

"Nile and I figured there were as many disgruntled Palmeros over his decision to leave the drug trade as there were Touccis over your refusal to take up the slack. I rented the space across from their headquarters in Mom's name. It was only a matter of watching and waiting before we found the right people to persuade."

"Juan Carlos needed time to figure out where his leaks were. How far into the organization it went. And you wanted to figure out how much we knew," Burns said.

"Yes. What we did not count on was Fergus and his heart," Saul replied.

Fergus blushed but stayed quiet.

I rolled it all around in my head, trying to put it all together.

"You're cheating on me," I said. "You're sleeping with Enrique, the cook!"

Epilogue

"What if I took you out somewhere," Burns said.

We moved to sit on my porch to people-watch. That had become a post-mobster wrap-up habit for us. Maybell trailed behind us on her leash.

"Like on a date?" I asked.

"I hear that's how it's done." His face tensed. "Flynn's out on a date tonight." He handed me a wine cooler and took a beer for himself.

I perked up at the news.

"With a woman from accounting," he added, opening his beer and sitting.

"Oh no. Poor Neutron."

"Yeah. The kid's trying to act like everything's fine, but he's buried himself in the computer lab for a gaming marathon with Monarch."

"That's rough." I sat down on the stoop.

Maybell plopped on the step below us.

"It's not like Flynn hasn't had... partners before. We've never really talked about it, but I always knew, from the time I walked in on him kissing Jimmy Norris when we were fourteen. He looked at me, and I could tell he was scared to death about what I'd say. He'd just beaten the shit out of these three guys two grades up who were giving me a hard time. What the hell was I going to say? I shrugged at him. Said, 'Whatever,' and that was it. It's not like we talk much about my love life either." He eyed me then and smiled.

I didn't want to imagine what Burns and Flynn's conversation about me would be like.

He shifted and put his beer on the steps. "Especially once they legalized gay marriage, I always kind of figured we'd both just know when we were supposed to show up at some courthouse with rings to act as the other's best man."

"You realize you might actually have to say words with this," I said.

"Yeah, the dumbass is going to screw this all up then give me hell for months while he gets his head out of his ass. Never mind the havoc having a disgruntled computer genius in the ranks does."

"Hey, they won their first combat juggling match. Maybe there's hope for them still. Monarch, eh. I'm not sure how I feel about that. Neutron getting cozy with the mob."

"At least we know why the highway has been mysteriously shutting down under fear of Godzilla attack now," Burns said.

Monarch was testing his ability to control shipping in and out of the city because of trafficking.

"Besides, apparently I'm already in bed with the mob."

We each took a drink, and I petted Maybell for comfort. I couldn't stop thinking about everything we had learned in the last twenty-four hours. Saul had kept his end of the bargain and provided us three key pieces of information.

The first was classified Pentagon papers on an operation named Covana that dealt with the Afghani arms trade. The lead officer on the operation had been none other than Lieutenant Commander Gregory Hardt, Burns's partner. Burns had a traitor in his midst.

"We were both suspicious of him. That's why you ordered the security upgrade," I said.

"I didn't want to be right. All we can do is sit on it right now. Watch him. Let Neutron dig."

He hadn't said, but I could tell he was relieved to have found the connection Gillian had tried to point him to. We both expected there to be a Russian in the middle of things.

"Still no further word from Simon?" he asked.

Maybell snorted at the name. I thought Grand had been training her.

"I know you're tracking my calls. So you already know I haven't."

After the chess club mess, Simon had mysteriously disappeared. Not that we were letting our guard down. It was a coin toss for who was more eager to see Simon taken down.

The second piece of information Saul had provided had been less appreciated. They were documents proving a connection between Simon and Dr. Hawthorne, my former boss and the man responsible for killing Gillian Mathers. It might have played into his hands for other reasons to get rid of her, but Dr. Hawthorne had been paid to kill Gillian. The Russian money had come from somewhere else. Neutron hadn't tracked it down yet.

"At least Fergus found some happiness out of all of this," I said, looking for a subject change. DC and Kimi weren't the only ones who had been caught in the latest immigration crackdown. Fergus had made a deal with Juan Carlos. That was what had caused the gap in the timeline with Nile's death. Apparently, the Palmeros had quite the operation in forged papers recently, and he promised he would get the Palmero ledgers back if they would get Enrique papers to stay in the country.

Fergus hadn't counted on Saul hiring me when he made the deal. He figured he could hit two birds with one stone, so to speak, and get proof for Saul that his nephew was a rat while getting Enrique papers. Nile had been holding Enrique over Fergus's head, threatening to tell Saul, which was why Fergus had been playing him up to Saul before Nile was killed. Fergus was between a rock and a hard place. Either he lied to Saul about Nile, or he disappointed him with choices. Enrique and Fergus had been together for almost fifteen years, and he'd kept it from Saul all that time.

"They planning a wedding now that Fergus knows Saul won't reject him?" Burns asked.

"I think so. I was hoping their story would soften up Flynn some."

"I don't think family rejection is what has Flynn all in knots."

"No. That's probably more a commitment issue, although I always took Flynn for the marrying kind."

"Speaking of commitment issues, how's DC doing?" Burns asked.

That was a whole other mess. Burns's guy had found Kimi in Cleveland, at the home of her new husband. She was in an arranged marriage by her parents to a respectable banker twice her age but legal and willing.

"If she'd only waited, I think he would have come around," I said.

"Or waited for us to finish this case. Can you believe the Palmeros sent DC papers for Kimi as a thank-you to you? Think he would have taken them?"

"We'll never know now. We'll have to schedule our date around my DC consoling time."

"That bad, huh?"

"You have no idea. He spent the whole time at the spa crying to the masseuse about his woes."

The Palmeros weren't the only ones handing out thank-you gifts. Francesca, of all people, had been so overcome with gratitude that we had helped solve her son's death and taken care of her nephew that she sent all the Waters women and DC to the day spa, all expenses paid. Burns and I had used his connections to get Jackson into a therapy group for kids who had accidentally caused a death, so my skin had a cozy glow for more than one reason, and for the first time in ages, my hair did not look like a bad frizz explosion.

Maybell got up and started moving down the steps, having spied Grand and Mom coming up, their arms full of craft-store bags.

"Where in the world are we going to put all that?" I asked.

"Now that we have the missile-launch-code information, I need to update your father's scrapbook," Grand said.

The last piece of information Saul had given us was sheets from a different ledger book. The entries matched the missing missile-launch codes, which proved not to be launch codes at all but rather stock-transaction numbers. Neutron hadn't figured out the money flow yet, but at least it was something. The money had been equally tied to art transactions and other things. It was as likely my dad had no idea he was actually laundering money for the mob as it was that he was their main numbers guy.

"You're out on the porch," Mom said.

Everyone had noticed how stuck Burns and I had been before the Toucci case. I was thankful they hadn't said anything about it—until now.

"We're thinking about where to go on a date," Burns said.

"I hear you can ask a certain reporter if you need tips," Grand said with a smirk.

"Maybe he can take you out," Burns said. "I hear he's got a thing for you, and his dance card has suddenly been freed up."

"It has?" I asked with a coy look.

Before Burns even said anything, I had already told Fletcher I couldn't see him anymore. I told him when I gave him the info Saul had provided us on Gillian. I thought he understood. My head and, if I was being honest, my heart were somewhere else at the moment.

"Yup," he said, getting up and taking the bags from Grand. "Ask Flynn. I always got low marks in school for being bad at sharing."

"Well, come on, sonny," Grand said. "We've got a game to watch and a scrapbook to work on before we can get started on Clarke's case."

About the Author

The owner of a boutique chocolate factory in Atlanta, MJ O'Neill loves to write lighthearted, romantic mysteries with a sweet twist. She has a degree in business communications from North Carolina State University. Through creative endeavors in her IT career, she has written everything from technical manuals to corporate blogs, and as a certified project manager, MJ is sure everyone's life needs a project plan!

MJ has recently survived transplanting from the Midwest, where she was raised, and is now soaking up the Southern hospitality of Atlanta, Georgia. When she's not spinning a sweet yarn or creating delicious confections, she spends time with her husband, Brian, their kids, who range in age from 24 to 7, a hyperactive cocker spaniel named Divo (after the band), a princess tabby cat named Twilight (before the book stole her name), and a collection of stray fish. The whole gang can be found tooling around the back roads of the South in their RV, where MJ uses the downtime to hatch her next sweet plot.

Read more at www.mjoneillauthor.com.

About the Publisher

Dear Reader,

We hope you enjoyed this book. Please consider leaving a review on your favorite book site.

Visit https://RedAdeptPublishing.com to see our entire catalogue.

Check out our app for short stories, articles, and interviews. You'll also be notified of future releases and special sales.